The Hidden Lady

Amanda Moncrefe

The Hidden Lady

Copyright © 2016 Amanda Moncrefe

Published by Amanda Moncrefe

ISBN-13: 978-0-9972143-5-2

Dedication

This book is dedicated to every woman who has found her internal
Lady, and had the courage to let her reign.

Quote

"Time will bring to light whatever is hidden; it will cover up and conceal what is now shining in splendor."

-Horace

Table of Contents

Acknowledgements

This series has been a pleasure to create! I hope you've enjoyed reading it just as much as I've enjoyed spinning and weaving each *Lady's* struggles and triumphs into the storyline. There are so many people to thank, but first and foremost, I must thank my family for being the supportive structure that triggered the start of it all, the creation of Jaymes and Asha's story.

Thank you Classandra Green and Jawanna Cook, the Mocha Girls Read true heroines. If the walls at Cooper's Hawk Winery could talk, oh the stories they would tell!

Once again, thank you to my Superhero, who has been the muse for many of these amazing stories!

And finally, thank you to Ms. Vera Williams, the woman who taught me that anything is possible, if you just believe in yourself.

Prologue

Chicago, Illinois
East Garfield Park Neighborhood
Summer 1986

Nathaniel Alastair Kerr, age 14

"Come on, Darrick! You're taking too long! It's starting to get
dark out here, man. We need to hurry up and get back to the crib," Nate
Kerr urgently pleaded to his younger ten-year old brother. When Darrick
finally walked into the late evening air, Nate's frustrated glance caused
Darrick to just roll his eyes in irritation. They'd just left the corner
convenience store off Madison Avenue on Chicago's west side, after
having gotten off the Chicago Transit Authority (CTA) green line train.

The young boys had taken the elevated 'L' train downtown earlier
that morning to catch glimpses of their favorite football team, the
Chicago Bears, and were now on their way home. The city was
celebrating the team's latest Super Bowl win, and everyone was ecstatic.
The Chicago mayor, along with his elected city councilmen, or *aldermen,*
had elected to throw a congratulatory parade later that summer in honor
of the win, since people were still celebrating months after the event.
Everyone, both young and old, were caught up in DA BEARS fever, and
Nate and his younger brother Darrick were certainly no exception.

Their mother worked as a bus driver for the CTA, and hadn't
arrived home yet from working the overnight shift before they'd left
home earlier that morning. Since she sometimes pulled a double shift,
Nate didn't want to wait on her. Instead, he decided to leave her a note
letting her know where they'd be. After throwing a couple of sandwiches
and water bottles into his backpack, he hauled his brother out of their
second story, two-flat Homan avenue apartment before sunrise, heading
downtown to the parade.

Upon arriving downtown, and clothed in blue, orange, and white Chicago football paraphernalia, the two young boys ran along with the rest of the crowd from Randolph Street to Grand Avenue, waving at the convertibles transporting their favorite players: Walter Payton, Jim McMahon, and William 'The Refrigerator' Perry. It was one of the most exhilarating moments of Nate's life, up until that point. He'd been swimming in awe and excitement, along with the rest of the hundreds of fans that had shown up for the event.

At one point during the parade, Darrick left Nate's side to use one of the porta potties strolled along the parade route located on one of the side streets. When he returned, Nate noticed that his brother looked a little funny.

"What's wrong with you, Darrick?" He'd asked. "You look weird. Are you getting sick?"

Darrick just shook his head, his eyes wide in shock. "I just saw something I don't think I should've seen." He then shrugged his thin boyish shoulders. "I guess the parade brings out everyone."

When Nate looked questionably at his brother, Darrick just shook his head and told him not to worry about it.

After the parade, the boys began their journey back home. Darrick asked to stop at the store to get a quick snack, since the sandwiches they'd eaten earlier had long been consumed. Nate agreed, thinking he'd much rather face his mother on a full stomach. They'd gotten so swept up in all the excitement, that they'd lost track of the time, not realizing they'd been gone for the majority of the day. Nate hadn't intended to be out so late, knowing that their mother would worry.

Glancing quickly through the plastic shopping bags they both sported, he noticed Darrick had filled them with Twinkies, Fanta Grape sodas, and Flaming Hot Cheetos, three out of the five basic food groups. Nate ripped open the bag of Cheetos and began to nervously munch away while they walked toward their building. The only thing they were missing was Velveeta nacho cheese sauce and some sour cream in order to make the ideal meal for a 14-year old inner city youth; but unfortunately the corner store didn't supply that kind of commodity.

Now, they were less than a block away from their home, and Nate was getting anxious. He knew his mother would be pissed. She didn't like for them to be in the streets when it got dark.

She'd always said it was too dangerous for young boys on the west side of Chicago to be out by themselves after the sun went down.

Munching on his Cheetos, Nate began to think of excuses he could possibly give to his mother as to why he and his brother were getting home so late.

Hmm, Darrick threw up blood and we had to make a stop at Stroger Hospital to check it out? Naw...his mother would follow-up with a call to the hospital and bust them both.

Walter Payton was giving away free, signed footballs, and the line to get one took over 5 hours? Believable story, but since they weren't walking in with a football under their arm, she'd shoot that excuse down too.

The green line train got derailed, and they needed to wait until another train was dispatched to ride home? Another believable story, but knowing their mother, she'd call to check that story out as well.

Nate sighed as he continued to nervously chew, resigning in the fact that he would just have to tell her the truth and deal with the fallout of whatever punishment he knew Belinda Kerr, sometimes referred to by her sons as the *Wrath of Belinda Khan* when she got angry, would administer.

Suddenly, a loud screech of tires sounded nearby. Nate looked over his shoulder and saw a black Ford Crown Victoria racing toward them at a chillingly fast pace. His eyes widened as he realized that he and his brother were in open range for a potential drive-by shooting, something that occurred all too often in his neighborhood.

Terror, ice cold and blood curdling, ran through Nate's blood. He dropped the grocery bags, grabbed Darrick's hand and began running toward their apartment building, praying that whoever was behind the wheel wasn't targeting them in their murder attempt.

When gunshots began to fire, Nate knew he and his brother had only seconds before the cruiser was close enough to make them out as targets. Nate pulled on his brother's arm, dragging him as fast as he could until they finally reached the steps of the steel entrance doors of his building. Still holding onto his brother with one quivering hand, he jammed his other inside his jean pocket, pulled out his keys, and began to fumble with the lock to hurriedly unlock the door.

Shots fired again, and Nate felt the hand holding his brother's jerk in response. His heart stopped. Painfully, he closed his eyes, listening to the car speed off into the distance. Screams sounded all around him while tears pricked his lids, dripping down onto his lean, chiseled cheeks.

NO!

NO!

NO!

NO!

"Darrick?" Nate whispered, his eyes were still closed for fear they would validate what his heart already knew to be true. "Darrick, man. Are you ok?"

Silence greeted him where he stood, still holding his little brother's hand. But now, the weight of his brother's hold was heavier, pulling down toward the ground, as if Darrick wasn't able to support himself anymore. Nate slowly opened his eyes and looked down, sheer horror clawing painfully across his chest.

The streets had claimed yet another young, innocent victim. This time that victim went by the name of Darrick Latrell Kerr.

^^^

Three weeks later...

"The arrangements are already done. You leave Tuesday." Belinda Kerr announced as she looked at her eldest son.

Nate clenched his fists in frustration. He didn't want to leave Chicago. Chicago was his home. He also didn't want to admit that the idea of starting somewhere new completely scared the crap out of him.

"Ma, I don't want to start high school in another city. All my friends are going to Marshall next year. I won't know *anybody* in Ohio."

Belinda looked unmoving at her son. "That's the whole point. You won't know *anyone* who could get you into trouble in Cincinnati.

Those friends you've got at Marshall High school are going nowhere fast, and I won't have my remaining son taken by these streets, especially when he has an opportunity to get out of here."

She stood and moved over to her son, wrapping her strong arms around him. She kissed him gently on his still frowning forehead and gave him a small squeeze before stepping back to look at him with a pleading look on her face.

"I love you, baby boy. Your brother loved you too. Darrick would want you to take advantage of the opportunity being given to you. I need you to get out of this area, to get away from all this crime and senseless death. Go out in the world and make something of yourself. Promise me that you will be better than your circumstance. If not for me, do it for your brother. I want you to grow up and become someone he would be proud of, and leaving this city is the only way you'll be able to do that."

Mustering up his inner strength, Nate straightened his lanky shoulders and stood up a little taller at his mother's words. He wiped the tears that had drifted down his cheeks and nodded his head in her direction.

"I promise, Ma. I promise to be someone Darrick would be proud of, if it's the last thing I do."

Chapter One

How many times do you have to put yourself through this, you idiot? Paige Clarke asked herself for what seemed like the thousandth time that day. She'd been warring back and forth with herself in her small apartment bedroom for the past few hours. Stalking back to her closet, she grabbed another handful of blouses, and then tossed them precariously inside her open suitcase.

Because you never learn, that's why! You don't believe fat meat is greasy until it's sliding off the plate, as Granny used to say.

She scoffed as she walked over to her dresser to grab the rest of her toiletries. Her grandmother would have a cow if she saw her today. Bending over backwards yet again for ANOTHER man who didn't give a rat's ass about her. She thought she'd learned the first time this had happened. But NO! She had to fall for yet another selfish prick that refused to give himself to her the way she felt she deserved. She paused as emotional anguish ripped through her heart.

But I thought Nate was different....

She shook her head to ward off the pain.

Well fuck this shit.

Paige shook her head in frustration as she threw her toiletries in her bag. Apparently he was just like the rest of the assholes of the world. In fact, Paige thought he deserved the title of the Houston Area Asshole of the Year for 2015.

Smiling at her own sense of dry humor, instead of balling her eyes out like she wanted to, she threw the rest of her clothes inside the suitcase, and then closed the lid with a resounding click. She then turned to stare at her reflection in the overhang mirror above her dresser.

Her mocha cream complexion appeared dull and lifeless under the florescent lighting of her bedroom. Her naturally wavy, wild brown hair, now streaked with honey gold highlights from the sun, fell limply against her cheeks. Her slightly fuller lower lip poked out rebelliously across her face, in line with the rigid set of her curved jawline. The golden irises of her eyes stared dejectedly back at her. Paige watched as a lone tear managed to escape to run its course down her cheek.

Angrily, she wiped the tear away. *No more tears, dammit. Not another damn one.*

She reached over to pull her itinerary from her purse, double-checking her flight time. The redeye flight she'd booked was scheduled to leave in a few hours. Biting her lip, she figured she still had time to run by Escapades and leave a note for Nate to let him know she was leaving, and wouldn't be back. Not ever. Apprehension coursed through her at the possibility of seeing him again, but she quickly shrugged it off.

He'll be too busy playing super hot, mysterious club owner to notice me anyway, she reasoned. Hopefully he wouldn't be paying any attention if she were to sneak inside his office, leave her written resignation, and get the hell out of there before being seen by anyone. Her anger toward him couldn't dispel the fact that she still didn't want him to worry about her.

She didn't want him to worry, but she didn't want him to think she'd continue tolerating his bullshit any longer either.

Now what kind of fucked up bullshit thinking is that?

She shook her head in disgust. It may be a little late for a New Year's resolution, since it was now closer to Valentine's Day, however it was never too late to do something positive for herself.

She threw her flight information back inside her purse before throwing it over her shoulder. She then picked up her suitcase and walked out into the hallway, taking stock of her four-room, pre-furnished dwelling right outside of Cypress that she'd called home for the past 5 years.

Her thoughts drifted back to the day she'd first arrived in Houston. She'd been excited to finally break free out of the confinements of her hometown of Detroit, Michigan. She was especially thrilled to escape the city's pitying stares. Her departure was a step in the right direction, she thought. It proved that she was still fully capable of standing on her own two feet, and that she was immune to Ware Osborn's neglectful and cheating ways.

When she and Ware first began dating in high school, she could readily admit that she'd been completely swept off her feet by his devastating good looks and authoritative demeanor. His easy charm and attentive behavior towards her had been both flattering and exhilarating.

When Ware won a football scholarship to attend Michigan State, Paige had been devastated, fearing in his new life that he'd eventually forget about her. However Ware had made assurances that they would stay together, and that one day he would come back and marry her. She'd been so proud of Ware's achievements, considering herself the luckiest of women in having snagged the star athlete. She willingly agreed to wait for him, content to stay behind until he finished his degree. After that, they could be together.

She filled her time by caring for her ailing grandmother, instead of going to college and becoming a physical therapist like she'd always dreamed. She'd been ok with the sacrifice, especially since her grandmother's massive stroke mandated that someone be available to care for her 24/7. Her younger sister Rachelle had still been in grade school at the time, and since their mother had died when Paige was only 7 years old, the responsibility to care for their Granny fell to her.

She lovingly nursed the woman who'd raised her and her sister, until Granny finally transitioned to Heaven a couple of years later due to a large blood clot in her brain. Later, when Ware had been drafted as a wide receiver for the Detroit Lions, Paige thought for sure that he'd honor the commitment they'd made to each other, since both of their obligations had now been fulfilled.

I was an idiot then, and I'm an idiot now, she thought as she stomped out of her apartment, slamming the door behind her. She moved with long, angry strides toward her car that was parked in the tenant's garage. Reaching her Volkswagen Jetta, she threw her suitcase and purse into the trunk as she felt the familiar remnants of humiliation wash again through her system.

Not only had Ware not married her, but he'd also flaunted his new fiancé all over ESPN. He'd proudly announced his plans to marry a woman that he'd met and had been dating throughout his college career.

The entire time he'd also been dating her.

Devastated, Paige packed her bags and left Detroit, determined to make a new life for herself. Rachelle had begged her not to leave, but Paige just couldn't stay. She refused to remain in the same neighborhood where people who knew both her and Ware would continue to give her looks of sympathy. She needed to go somewhere new, somewhere fresh, where she could plant some new roots. She'd decided that Houston seemed like a good place to go, because it was the furthest distance she could think of from Detroit. She'd decided to come to Cypress to plant her new foundation.

And fell in love with another selfish asshole that couldn't commit to her.

Paige jumped into the driver's seat with a huff. Pulling out a pen and a piece of paper, she jotted down a few words for Nate, and then threw the paper on the passenger seat. She then pulled out her cell and made a quick call to the closest girlfriend she'd made since arriving in Cypress.

"Hey Gena, it's Paige."

"Hey girl! How've you been? I noticed you looked a little under the weather the other day. Are you feeling all right?" Gena Rodriguez already commented on Paige's unique quietness the night before. Paige hadn't felt much like talking, which was a rarity for her, and Gena had definitely noticed. When she asked if there had been anything wrong, Paige had blamed her reserved demeanor on a passing flu bug. She couldn't bring herself to explain about the humiliation she'd felt from a conversation she'd had the day prior with the club's other bartender. It was still too painful and embarrassing.

It was the reason she'd finally decided to leave.

"Look, I'm just calling you to let you know that I...I have to leave. I mean, I'm leaving to go back home. To Detroit. It's a change I've intended to make for a while now, and I feel the time is right for me to move on. I really hate telling you like this, and I know it's not giving you

16

any sort of prior notice, but I think it's for the best. Besides, I hate long, drawn-out goodbyes."

Gena went completely silent on the other end, and Paige assumed she was digesting her words. Finally, Gena let out a long sigh. "I'm sorry you need to leave, honey. Was there something that happened to make you decide that now is the time?"

"No, nothing happened. I just think it's time for me to make a fresh start, you know?" Paige lied. She then took a deep breath. "I know this is a lot to ask, but could you not tell Nate just yet? I'll let him know that I won't be back, but the news would probably be best if it's coming from me."

"Of course, honey." Gena paused for a brief moment. "I'll miss you, Goldilocks. Take care of yourself."

Hearing her friend mimic the nickname Nate had given to her, caused a painful tug inside her chest. She would miss her friend dearly. "You too, Gena. Goodbye."

With that, Paige closed her cell phone and turned off her ringer. Putting her car into drive, she took off for Nate's business and her former place of employment: *Escapades* nightclub.

If she were lucky, she'd be able to sneak in, leave her resignation, and sneak out without Nate ever knowing that she was there.

^^^

Pulling up into the crowded parking lot, Paige's hopes at remaining inconspicuous rose as she observed the long line of patrons standing outside of the club waiting to get in. As in typical fashion, Tony Ulrich, the security guard and night manager, was standing outside inspecting ids to make sure everyone admitted was of legal age.

Tony was a guard that Nate had hired a few years back. He stood at an intimidating 6 foot 6 inches tall, and loomed over most of the customers and wait staff. Sporting a baldhead, a wide muscled frame, gaged ears, and a long, scraggly-looking beard, he was the epitome of a muscled WWF pro wrestler. Nate seemed satisfied with the man's credentials, but Tony had always crept Paige out. She couldn't pinpoint exactly why, but she always made sure she was never standing too close or alone for any point in time whenever he was working with her.

Looking over the crowd of people, Paige chewed on her bottom lip. She wasn't scheduled to work this evening, but with the amount of patrons trying to get in, she wouldn't put it past Nate to try and contact her to work some hours and help out with the crowd. She intended to be on her way to the airport long before that call took place.

Grabbing her note from the passenger seat and stuffing it into her jean pocket, she slid out of her car. Walking around the far side of the building toward the locked back entrance, she glanced over her shoulder, double-checking to make sure Tony hadn't detected her. Verifying that he hadn't noticed her presence at all, she used the passcode Nate had given her months ago after he'd renovated the upper VIP area, and entered the alphanumeric code on the pad next to the door. Pulling on the handle after hearing the resounding click, she walked into the darkened hallway of the club.

The loud, pounding bass of Prince's *Erotic City* echoed through the air as Paige quickly walked over to Nate's office. It was Old School music night, Paige's favorite night to work. She often found herself bopping her head to music she could relate to while she served drinks, rather than listening to the new rap with its weak lyrics being produced nowadays.

Narrowing her eyes, she scanned the smoke-filled room looking for Nate. She finally spotted him speaking with Isobel, the other bartender working alongside Gena near the bar. She watched as Isobel placed her hand gently on Nate's biceps as she spoke with him, causing Paige's nostrils to flare as her heart filled with gut wrenching jealousy. Bristling with anger, she tried to ignore her stammering pulse. *He was never officially yours, Paige, remember?*

Instead of focusing on what she was losing, she decided to take a moment to bask in the sexiness of Nate's appearance one final time. Her eyes scanned his body from head to toe, causing her to sigh with longing. The man had never worn anything except a custom-made suit the entire time she'd known him. Not that she was complaining. The most attractive, titillating thing in the world to her was a man who not only looked good in a suit, but was so comfortable in his stylish dress that he walked like he had gold-plated testicles, daring anyone to test his virility.

Nate Kerr moved like his balls were made of pure titanium.

The swaggered glide in his walk was the sexiest thing Paige had ever seen. His slightly bowed legs screamed out to her lust with every swaggered stroll he made. The closely trimmed goatee he sported made his lips appear succulent and tasty, and the diamond studded earring he displayed in his left ear put her in the mind of a sultry r &b singer. Just watching him made her panties moist. She'd rubbed one out many nights thinking about how good it would feel to have those powerful legs trapping her between his powerful thighs, holding her, dominating her...

She shook her head. No time for idle thoughts right now. She needed to get in and get out without being seen. Quickly, she cast one longing look in Nate's direction, and then scurried toward his open office door.

She frowned slightly as she ran inside. Nate usually kept his office door locked, and she briefly wondered why it was open now, however time didn't permit her to ponder for long. Looking around his office, she could see that he still kept his administrative quarters just like he kept his business: neat and functional. She'd heard tales of Nate at one point in time being an extremely messy and cluttered guy, putting the typical bachelor stereotype to the test. She wondered what events had occurred to make him want to clean up his act...

Not wanting to delay the reason for her visit any longer, she took the letter from her jean pocket and quickly read through its contents once more:

Dear Nate,

Please consider this my letter of resignation, although I'm sure I won't be missed. It's taken me quite a while to realize that once again, I was just a means to an end for you, a way to pass the time. Why I believed I even had a chance with you, I'll never know. I realize now that I could never compete with the real love in your life, and that's this club. Or is it really something else? I guess it really doesn't matter anymore, and I'm tired of guessing. I hope you and she, whatever or whoever it is, will be very happy. In the meantime, I've decided to finally put myself first for a change, and I can't do that here. I'm leaving to go back home to Detroit.

Who knows--maybe over time, I'll eventually be able to compete for a place in your heart.

Paige.

She nervously bit her lip as she continued to mull over her words. She wanted to add that the real reason why she couldn't stay, besides that *bitch,* was because she always seemed to lose herself and her willpower whenever he came around. He had too much control over her, even if he chose not to act on it.

And the vulnerability he caused within her heightened her insecurity, and scared her to death.

So before she lost her nerve, she folded the letter in a trifold, and then placed it on the keyboard of his computer, where he'd be sure to see it.

Glancing back over toward the bar to make sure Nate's attention was still preoccupied, Paige quickly left his office, scurried down the dark hallway, and out of the backdoor. She sprinted back to her car, not caring at this point if Tony caught sight of her. Hopping into the driver's seat, she put the car in drive, pulled out of the parking lot, and headed toward the airport.

Operation Reinventing Paige was now underway.

Chapter Two

Nate walked into *Escapades* the next morning and surveyed the damage that was done from last night's excursions. His eyes did their typical audit of the dance floor and bar area, making note of any possible infractions that warranted his immediate attention.

Seeing none, he made his way over to the bar to greet Gena, his bartender and personal confidant over the years.

"Hey Rodriquez. Good Morning."

Gena looked up from the notepad she'd been studying, apparently doing an inventory count from last night's activities. A look he couldn't quite name passed over her face, before she smiled at him in greeting. "Hey, morning Nate. I was just running the numbers for you. I should have your reports ready in a few."

Nate nodded his head as he took a seat on one of the barstools. "Sounds good. Where's Tony?" He looked around. "And do you know what the lowdown is from last night? Tyson called me and told me there'd been some drama, but when I called Tony, he said he'd handled it. He told me he'd meet me here this morning to fill me in."

Gena shrugged her shoulders. "I'm not sure. You know I had to leave Isobel here by herself to handle the bar because Ricardo got sick. I left shortly after you did. She didn't mention anything to me." Nate nodded his head, remembering Gena's voicemail reminder that she had to leave because her son had gotten ill later that evening.

His part time bartender normally only assisted during the week so that Gena could spend more time with her son, but instead had to pitch in for the remainder of last night's shift. He could see how the rush of a Saturday night party in full swing could have flustered the newer girl.

Hearing the front door open, Nate turned to watch as his head of security walked in. Nodding his head in greeting, Tony strolled over to the bar and took a seat alongside Nate.

"Nate. I wasn't expecting you here until this afternoon."

Annoyance skated through Nate as he frowned at his employee. "What are you talking about? You told me to meet you *this morning* so you could let me know what happened after I left. I got a call from Tyson telling me that there were a couple of guys trying to manhandle some women here, and that I should be aware. I left *you* in charge, thinking that you could handle things, so don't make me question my decision."

He sat up straighter in his chair as he pinpointed Tony with a disapproving glare. "When I called you, you told me that you would look into it and would let me know the details this morning. Well, I'm here and this is the morning. What happened?"

Nate narrowed his eyes as he studied Tony's body language. He hated not knowing what was going on inside his club, and he hated bullshit excuses even more. He'd been trying to take his friend Delphi Allen's advice and not spend his entire waking moment patrolling the grounds of his establishment. However it got harder to stay away when bullshit like what he was hearing now was being tossed around. He wanted to trust that things could run smooth without his direct supervision.

He wanted to free up some of his time so he could give more attention to Paige, like he'd promised her.

Tensing, he waited for Tony's explanation. He glanced over at Gena to see that she'd now moved from behind the bar over to one of the large mounted television sets near the back staircase, in an obvious attempt to give them some privacy.

"Well," Tony started, shifting in his seat so he could fully face Nate. "A couple of new guys came in tossing a lot of money around. They approached Isobel and bought out the bar. Girls were flocking to them like ants to sugar. Some of the regulars took offense that the females were showing all of their attention to the newer guys, so they tried to start some trouble. I'm like, if an idiot wants to make it rain like Jay Z up in here, that's on them. I'll never waste my money on a woman like that."

He shrugged. "In any case, I ended up tossing the troublemakers out, but they snuck back in through the back entrance. Someone left the door unlocked back there. Your friend Levi was upstairs in VIP with that Killian guy, saw that the troublemakers were back, came down to tell me what was going on, and I went and tossed them out again. No harm, no foul."

Nate narrowed his eyes even further. "*Levi* sought you out? Why would he do that, instead of telling one of the other crewmembers? You and he never got along." Nate asked suspiciously. Something didn't sound right. Especially about his back entrance door being open. That door was always locked. Always.

Tony casually leaned back in his seat, seemingly unaffected by Nate's obvious irritation. "Levi's always got his panties in a wad around me. He thinks I tried to muscle in on one of his women one night, before he married that Terri girl. Truth of the matter is that girl wanted me and he couldn't handle it." He shrugged. "I guess he called because he can now finally acknowledge that I could handle it."

Nate shook his head. He didn't have time for dick swinging theories. "And that's all that happened?"

Tony nodded his head. "Yea, that's it. Tyson must have been up there with them and called you, but I already had it covered."

Nate nodded his head once. "Ok, thanks for the heads up. In the future, make sure you put extra security near that back entrance. I don't like the fact someone was able to get in back there."

"Will do. Anything else you need? I wanted to run downtown this morning to take care of a few things, but I'll be back by this evening's shift."

"No, I'm good. I'll see you later tonight." Nate then grabbed the extended hand Tony offered, before watching him stand up and stroll back out of the club.

Unease set within Nate as he watched the man leave. *Something wasn't right.*

"Hey Rodriguez, I'm going to my office for a bit. Holler at me if you need anything." Nate called to Gena as he started to make his way toward the back of the club.

"Sure thing. I'll also call Isobel and ask if she could pitch in tonight as well. Seems like last night might be a good precedent for the weekend."

"Good idea. Maybe I'll give Paige a call to see if she wants some extra hours as well." *If she answers her phone.* He'd been trying to contact her all evening, but his calls were going straight to voicemail.

"Umm..." Gena started, but Nate didn't wait for her to finish. Instead, he unlocked the door to his office and turned on the light. His eyes then scanned the interior of the room.

Something wasn't right. His uneasiness intensified as he spotted a piece of paper sticking out from his keyboard. A piece of paper he knew for certain hadn't been there before.

Who the hell had been in here?

His mind raced through the course of events he'd witnessed over the past 24 hours. He knew he'd left his office open for a short period of time last night to speak with Gena about the upcoming liquor shipment being delivered next week. He then told Isobel to tighten up on her drink measurements, because he'd been getting complaints from some of the patrons that the drinks were too watered down. He'd been standing not too far from the office door to make sure no one entered.

Or so he thought.

After his talk with Gena, he'd ask her to lock his office before heading home for the night. The only two people in the world he trusted to take care of things at the club were Gena and Paige, and he knew Gena had immediately done as he'd requested. And Paige hadn't been here last night.

Somebody was fucking with him. Again.

Tossing his keys back in forth in his hands, he walked over to his desk and sat down in front of his security viewing station. He then tossed the keys aside before switching on the camera security feeds.

Tony had mentioned that the backdoor had been left open last night. That door, along with his office door, was usually always locked.

I think I'll see for myself if that's true, he thought. The unease he'd been feeling for the past few months increased as he pondered on what he might discover. Picking up the piece of paper left on his keyboard, he

24

moved it absently to the side before entering the surveillance codes to narrow down his search on the feeds. He focused his attention primarily on the camera by the back door and on one of the cameras in the dance hall facing his office. He watched as the tapes sped through hours of monotonous footage before he suddenly hit the pause button.

What the hell was Paige doing here last night? He thought incredulously. He didn't even know she was here. Why didn't anyone tell him? And why hadn't she spoken to him?

He watched as she entered the codes he'd given her to open the back door of the club. *Well, that answers that question about the open door*, he thought sarcastically. Frowning, he studied Paige's body language as she walked down the hallway toward his open office.

"What's wrong, baby girl?" He murmured rhetorically. His frown deepened as he noticed the slump in her shoulders and the way her head hung low, like she was unhappy with something.

Or someone.

He shifted uneasily in his chair as he zoomed in to the camera pointing toward his office. He watched as Paige stood for long a moment, staring toward the dance floor. Had she been looking at him speaking with Isobel? Surely she knew he had no interest in that flighty woman. Isobel was great at making drinks, well sometimes, but not so well with holding any sort of intellectual conversation.

Paige then moved inside his office, and then reappeared a short time later, sneaking back down the hallway to rush out of the backdoor.

Confused, he looked around his office again, finally acknowledging the piece of paper he'd earlier tossed aside.

With a sickening feeling in the pit of his stomach, he grabbed the note and read through its contents.

And reread it.

And reread it again.

She left me, he thought miserably.

My baby left me.

"NATE! Where the hell are you, man?" A loud, boisterous voice disrupted his pitying thoughts. Taking a deep breath, he pushed down his feelings of despair, placing the note inside his desk to study later. He then stood and walked to the door to see who had walked into the club.

Plastering a fake smile on his face, he nodded his head in greeting at friends he'd known for years.

"Hey Killian, Lucas, and Lafayette. What's going on Holley? You dyed your hair brown I see. Looks good on you. What are you guys doing here?"

Chapter Three

Killian Devine laughed as he watched Nate close and lock his office door behind him.

"That's not Holley, man. It's her twin sister Harmony. Harmony Rune, meet our good friend, Nate Kerr."

Nate frowned as he walked over to extend his hand to the woman Killian had just introduced.

"Twin sister?" Nate asked, surprise evident in his voice as he raised his eyebrows high on his forehead. "I didn't know Holley had any other siblings, outside of what's already buried in the ground, and good riddance to that piece of shit." He was referring to Holley's deceased brother Jeffrey, who Holley had killed during her adolescence, after years of sexual abuse.

This time it was Harmony's turn to smile. "Holley didn't know either. Our reunion was bittersweet. But yes, I'm her sister. Right now she's at Asha's house catching up with her friends. I decided to come along with Killian and the Blackburn twins. There's a conversation we all need to have that I believe is long overdue."

Nate frowned as he nodded to a set of tables near the bar. "Well, in that case, have a seat. Is there anything I can get you guys? I know its early, but there's orange and cranberry juice in the back."

Lucas Blackburn shook his head. "No, we're fine." They all sat down, and Nate waited expectantly as four sets of eyes stared back at him with serious expressions.

Well shit, Nate thought as he studied their intense faces. *This day just keeps getting better and better.*

"There's something that's been going on for quite a while," Killian started, breaking the tense silence. "We still don't have all of the pieces sorted out yet, but we figured at this stage of the investigation that you needed to be brought into the loop."

Confused, Nate stared back at Killian. "What investigation?" He then quickly looked around the room and noticed that Gena had disappeared. *Where did she go?*

"There's been some illegal activity going on in the Houston area. We have reason to believe that it's trickled down here to Cypress as well." Lafayette stated matter of factly.

"What sort of illegal activity?" Nate asked, restlessness now beginning to grow within him. He hated subterfuge. *State what you mean and mean what you say*, his mother had always told him. He wished someone would just spit it out.

Harmony chimed in. "We have reason to believe that an underground organization known as The Hunter Group (HG), has been stealing and selling young girls and babies into the black market for a profit. They've been under investigation for years, but we've never been able to target exactly who is involved, and where their exchange locations have been set. Each time we've gotten close, they've managed to elude us. Now, we think they've come full circle, and are trying to set up shop again. This time, we plan on getting ahead of them."

Nate tilted his head as he studied the young woman. "And who exactly are you? How do you know so much about what's going on?"

"I've been working with the FBI for many years, Nate. We've run into barrier upon barrier in trying to dismantle this group, but they've always managed to evade us. Please understand, this is not just some local organization. HG has several hubs that they manage throughout the entire world. We've been able to identify two out of three major auction sites here within our own borders, one of which is located right here in Texas. In fact..." She paused. "We have reason to believe that they've actually targeted your club as one of its exchange locations."

Nate jerked at that bit of news. "That's ridiculous. I don't run anything illegal here. And my staff knows I won't tolerate that type of behavior either."

"Nevertheless, we think it's still occurring, bro," Killian advised. "We're telling you because we want you to be on the lookout for anything suspicious. Anything out of the ordinary, just let us know. The smallest clues could lead to the biggest cover-ups, believe me."

"I thought a lot of questions were resolved when that officer who'd kidnapped Holley died. That Stevens character." Nate countered, still trying to reconcile the facts being brought before him. He'd heard about the dirty cop that had kidnapped Killian's fiancé, Holley, in a botched attempt to sell her. The cop had planned to sell her, along with Asha Allen, Killian's sister and famed contemporary singing artist, to the black market.

The plan had been interrupted when Killian, along with Asha's husband Delphi, Nate's former Natchez State University (NSU) roommate, had discovered the women's holding location. They'd saved both women, but ended up killing the cop, along with his accomplice, Tanya Lewis.

"Danny Stevens was just the tip of the iceberg. We believe there are much bigger fish at stake this time." Lucas stated.

Nate sat back in his chair as he digested what his friends were telling him. Somebody was using his business as a cover-up for some illegal shit. Somebody was taking advantage of his niceness while screwing him over, without the courtesy of providing Vaseline.

Somebody was fucking with him.

He looked around his establishment, a feeling of betrayal etching throughout his system. He'd spent his entire life trying to do what's right. Doing what was expected of him. He'd devoted every waking hour to building something his mother and brother would be proud of. He'd believed that in fulfilling the dreams his loved ones had always wanted for him, that he too would get what he'd always desired: to live his life in peace. To raise a family. To grow old with the love of his life by his side.

Now, those dreams were turning into nightmares. Somebody was using his club to sell women. And the love of his life had disappeared.

Fuck.

He thought back over the last few months of uneasiness, taking stock of the various abnormalities he'd noticed during that time. Since they were being so generous with information sharing, he guessed he could be forthcoming as well.

"Guys, I believe you need to follow me." He nodded toward his office. "I've been noticing some things that have been amiss over the past several months, but I couldn't quite put my finger on it. Now, if what you're telling me is true, then those abnormalities are starting to reveal themselves." He led the group back to his office, unlocked the door, and ushered them inside before closing the door soundly behind them.

"I've been noticing some strange things on my security feeds, but I could never place what the issue was, or why I was seeing what I was noticing. A few months ago, several minutes of taped surveillance began to disappear from my recordings. I could never pinpoint when they were erased, who was doing it, or what I was looking for, but I knew that something was going on." Sitting down once again at his desk, Nate programmed the code to pull up several months of missed time that he'd been tracking.

He then pointed at the monitor. "See, on this day, 41 minutes of time was erased." He zoomed through the feed. "And here, about 96 minutes of time disappeared." He continued to scroll through his search. "Here, there's at least 83 minutes missing from this date."

Lafayette furrowed his brow as he studied the feeds. "Do you mind if I take a closer look?" Lafayette was the group's technology guru. Anything dealing with gadgets and electronics, and he was all over it like a moth to a flame.

Nate pushed the keyboard over to him. "Go at it, my friend. I've been studying these tapes for weeks, and couldn't come up with any recognizable pattern. Hope you have better luck." Standing up from his desk to give Lafayette room to sit down, he glanced at the drawer he'd thrown Paige's note into, suddenly remembering the surveillance he'd spotted of her earlier. Quickly, he opened the drawer and pulled out the note.

Harmony raised an eyebrow as she caught his movements. "What's that?" She asked, referring to the note he had clutched in his hands.

"A resignation letter from one of my employees," he replied casually.

"Anything we should be concerned about?" Lucas asked.

30

He shook his head. "I don't think you have to be concerned with her." On the contrary, he was probably the only one with his heart ripped apart right about now. His hand trembled slightly as he held the letter, the earlier pain he managed to push down quickly rising again back up to the forefront.

She left me. Why?

As Lafayette continued to search through his camera feeds, Nate ran through her words that he had now memorized inside his head. A thousand questions pelted his brain as he tried to rationalize her departure.

What did she mean by saying she was just a way to pass the time? What the hell was that supposed to mean? What the hell was she talking about? Didn't she know how much she meant to him? Couldn't she see that? Everything he'd built, he'd built with her and his family in mind. Every hour he'd spent building up this club, it was all done so that he could later bask in its successes, with the hope of freeing more of his time so that he could be with her. To have a better life. For them. For her.

He blew out a frustrated breath and watched the search activity in front of him. He'd heard everything his friends had told him about *Escapades*. However at this moment, he figured he had one of two options: He could stay here and beat his head against the wall to try and figure out who was trying to sabotage his club, or he could jump on a plane, go after his heart, and shake some sense into that luscious golden temptress.

Since he'd been chasing and resolving issues for his side chic *Escapades* for long enough, as she had so blatantly put it, he guessed it was time to devote his attention to his first love. His only love. His heart.

And her name was Paige.

He needed to catch a flight.

"Hey guys. I understand everything you're telling me. But right now, something has come up." He walked over to the door and yelled out. "Rodriguez! Can you come to the office? I need to see you."

Everyone frowned when they heard his exclamation. Lafayette closed down the search feeds and locked the screens, ensuring the details he'd been reviewing remained a secret. They then watched as the shapely blonde with her large brown eyes appeared in his doorway.

"What's up, Nate? You called?" Gena asked. Her eyes swept over the people in the room, lingering a little longer on Lucas, before swinging back to meet Nate's gaze.

"Yes I did. Something's come up, and I need to head out of town for a while. I know you could manage running operations without me, but that's a lot to ask of you, especially when Ricardo has been sick. We're going to have to close the club until I get back. Just for a few days."

Lucas frowned as he turned around to face him. "What has suddenly come up that's so urgent within the past 15 minutes?"

"I need to catch a flight to Detroit."

Killian narrowed his eyes in thought. "I think it might be a good idea if you headed out of town, but I don't think you should close the club. I think it would be good to see how the place operates without your direct supervision."

Nate raised his eyebrow at the innuendo. After a moment of consideration, he nodded his head in agreement. It would be good to see how the place functioned in his absence. It could also be a good way to flush out what was being hidden in the dark.

"You don't need to close things down, Nate. I could do it. I'm sure I can handle things, and Ricardo is doing much better. How long are we talking about?" Gena asked.

Nate pursed his lips as he thought about her question. "Honestly, I'm not sure. Could be a couple of days, could be a week. I can let you know once I get there." He'll know for certain once he's had a chance to talk some sense into Paige.

"If you don't mind, I'd love to help out." Harmony volunteered. Nate raised a questioning eye in her direction. "I use to bartend and waitress while I was in college. I'm sure it's just like riding a bike."

Killian clasped his hands together. "Great idea! Then it's settled. Nate, we'll see you when you get back."

32

Chapter Four

Paige tried to take a steadying breath as she knocked on her grandmother's door for the umpteenth time. She impatiently tapped her foot on the elevated porch as she waited for a response.

"RACHELLE!" She hollered, ignoring the questioning looks of passersby from the sidewalk below. She knew trying to reach her sister by cellphone to answer the door wouldn't do any good. Rachelle didn't own one, and she hardly ever answered the house phone. She'd often stated that Granny's house phone was good for emergencies; however if she needed to speak with someone, she'd just go to their house and pay them a personal visit. She'd argued that the human touch was often underrated in today's society.

Her cynical, younger sister was undoubtedly a seventy-year old woman, trapped in the body of a twenty year old.

Rachelle had also decided to stay in the house after Granny passed, which had been fine just with Paige. Their grandmother would have wanted family to reside in the huge two-story duplex anyway. Since Rachelle was still attending junior college, it had seemed the logical choice to make.

Now, as Paige stood outside the door hammering away at the frame with her fist, she wondered if it actually had been a good idea to leave her sister alone for so long. The anticipation she'd felt before arriving was quickly turning into anxiousness as she thought about the past twenty-four hours.

After arriving in Detroit late last night, Paige decided to crash at a cheap motel close to the airport. Since her visit would be a surprise to her sister, she didn't want to give off any false alarms by arriving on her doorstep at four in the morning, carrying a suitcase, and looking like she'd just been through a shredding machine.

Even though she felt like it.

She decided instead to get a good night's sleep, along with a good hot brunch at Duly's Place, before heading over to the North End. Her grandmother's house was located in Highland Heights, a suburb of Detroit.

Trying to shake off her waves of guilt, Paige once again knocked against the screen door. She hadn't spoken with her sister in over four months. How would Rachelle take the news that she wanted to come back home?

"I just chose the lesser of two evils, that's all," she muttered to herself as she practiced her excuse. She could have either stayed in Texas, where the pain of being around Nate while he continued to ignore her would have ultimately killed her, or she could come back here to Detroit, where hopefully the memories of what happened between her and Ware had now been erased from a lot of people's memory.

Hopefully. Maybe.

She bit her lip as she imagined how Rachelle would take her news. She could just hear her sister's words now: *"Oh, so now you want to come back here, after yet* another *man has rejected you? When are you going to learn, Paige? How much heartbreak are you going to have to go through before you realize that men are selfish pricks? No matter what you do, no matter how much you give, it will never be enough."*

Rachelle was unforgiving when it came to the opposite sex. Unfortunately their father was the root cause of a lot of her internal struggles. Believing their father was dead like their mother, she and her sister had been shocked to discover that not only was he alive, but also living in the same city. Rachelle had discovered by sheer coincidence while reading the local newspaper that their father had another set of kids that he'd been taking care of. He'd been taking care of them while still being complete oblivious and continually absent toward his own children's needs. His picture made the front page as a proud parent, boasting of his stepdaughter success in a basketball game, while he stood next to his other stepchildren and wife. He'd looked happy and content.

And unashamed.

After seeing his picture, Rachelle had attempted to reach out to their father, in hopes of bridging the gap between them. Unfortunately,

34

their father chose to discount them both, opting to ignore the fact that he had two biological children of his own.

The confrontation had occurred during Paige's high school years, where the majority of Paige's time and attention had been spent working to help their grandmother with the household bills. The work had helped to distract her from the hurt of their father's rejection. Rachelle, however, had taken his neglect to heart.

After continued years of paternal neglect, Rachelle's overall attitude, particularly toward men, became extremely sour. After many long, heartfelt discussions with her sister, Rachelle was able to turn some of her bitterness into a positive action, setting out on a personal mission to speak out against child abuse and neglect, both from fathers and mothers. She became an avid spokesperson in many neighborhood self-improvement classes for battered women. The classes she was currently taking were in preparation to transfer to a major university, where Rachelle's ultimate goal was to be a school counselor, assisting troubled teenage kids who'd lost their way to find the strength within themselves to succeed in life.

Paige applauded Rachelle's desire for a higher education; she just hated the motivation behind it. Despite her numerous attempts, she knew she hadn't fully convinced her sister that all men were not like their selfish father. She feared Rachelle's heart and trust had been damaged in such a way that it could never be fully repaired.

Hmmm...on second thought...maybe in my case, Rachelle had a point.

She shook her head to quickly dispel that thought. Misery loved company, but she couldn't go to the extent that Rachelle had taken. She just needed to take a break, clear her mind, and figure out what the hell she wanted to do with the rest of her life.

"RACHELLE!" Paige screamed yet again, bringing her mind back to the present. She walked around the old, creaky porch to view the driveway next to the house. Her sister had to be there, because their Granny's old Cadillac Eldorado still sat in the driveway. The car had been left in Rachelle's care so she could travel back and forth to school.

Glancing back over her shoulder, Paige noticed the mailbox overflowing with junk mail and letters. Grabbing the pile from the bin, she walked back to the door, preparing to bam against the railing once more.

"There's nobody there, child." A soft voice spoke behind her. Paige turned around to face an older woman, probably in her mid-sixties, standing on the sidewalk. The woman clutched the handle of her dog's leash; apparently out for a mid-day stroll with her all black Cairn terrier.

Frowning slightly, she moved toward the end of the porch to get a better look at the woman.

"Do you know the lady that lives here?" Paige asked. Although not a shy girl by any means, Rachelle didn't often allow herself to get close to strangers, always preferring the company of youth versus older adults. Paige, on the other hand, loved the thrill of meeting new people, both old and young. It made the day more interesting and exciting. If this woman had a relationship with her sister, it would be shocking, to say the least.

The woman shook her head. "I don't know her per say, but I live about three houses down from here..." She pointed down the street toward a set of row houses joined together at the end of the block. "...And I see everything. The young woman that lives there hasn't been home in about two weeks."

Alarmed, Paige moved off the porch to stand in front of the woman. She looked vaguely familiar, but Paige couldn't place her face. "What do you mean, she hasn't been home? Do you know where she would've gone?"

The woman shook her head again. "Not sure. One day, a couple of men came knocking on the door just like you're doing. They weren't yelling though. They were real quiet. I saw her open the door, talk to them for a few minutes, and then leave with them in a large van."

Alarm bells were now ringing in Paige's ears. Something was wrong. Rachelle would never go somewhere alone with a man, especially more than one. She didn't trust them, and would never allow herself to be placed in a vulnerable position, especially when they outnumbered her.

Unless she didn't have a choice.

Fear began to grow in Paige's heart. "Please ma'am," she said, trying to push her panic down. "Can you tell me anything else? I'm her sister, and I've been out of town. This is the first time I've been home in a while, and I'm really worried about her."

The woman nodded her head as she studied Paige's face. "I remember you. You used to help Ms. Irene when she got sick. I'm so sorry about your grandmother, dear. Ms. Irene was a really nice lady. I'm also sorry about what happened between you and that football player. My bid whist partners were upset for weeks after he flaunted that new fiancé of his all over the news. I always said you were too good for that boy."

Embarrassment flooded Paige's system, heating her face. Gritting her teeth against the automatic retort that threatened to break free to tell the woman she should get over her sympathy the same way she'd gotten over Ware, she pushed on. Snapping at the lady wouldn't get her any answers as to where her sister could possibly be.

Instead, she nodded her head, deciding to focus on the reference of her grandmother, and plastered on a fake smile. "Yes, I cared for Granny until her transition. Thank you for your condolences."

The woman nodded her head, seeming to also move on. "Unfortunately sweetheart, your sister hasn't been here. Not since that night. I'm sorry. I wish I could give you more information." With a final nod of her head, the woman patted Paige's shoulder before walking away.

Feeling her heart jump inside her throat, Paige ran to the rental car she'd left parked in front of the house. Opening the backdoor, she quickly unzipped her suitcase, rummaging through its contents to final recover her cell phone. She'd left it in an off position shortly after arriving at William Hobby airport last night, fearing she'd get a call or text from Nate that would ultimately obliterate all of her courage to leave.

Now, he was the only person in the world she wanted to call for help. She needed his calm to help her think through this mess.

She needed him.

Slamming the back door closed, she jumped in the driver's side as she dialed Nate's number. She waited impatiently as the phone rang, until Nate's deep, husky voice sounded over the speaker.

"Nate." Paige breathed a sigh of relief that he was still answering her phone calls. "Nate, I'm so glad you answered. I know I left kind of funky, but I swear I thought it was the best thing to do. Right now, though, I need your help. My sister is missing, and I don't know what to do. One of her neighbors says she's been gone for two whole weeks!"

Her voice drifted as her thoughts ran wild with her rising panic. "I don't even know where to look! God, why didn't I try and contact her before?" Full terror now seized Paige's chest and she held her phone in a death grip. She knew she was working herself up into a frizzy, but she couldn't stop herself. She swiped furiously at the tears that now shed from her eyes. Her breath caught as she tried to speak again. "My...my sister...I don't know where she is...oh god! I don't know what to do!"

"Breath, baby. I need you to breath." Nate's calming voice sounded over the speaker. Paige felt her breath slow down at his demand, while she mentally tried to push her anxiety down. She took a deep gulp of air to try and slow her heartbeat.

"I hear you baby, very good. I need you to stay calm. Where are you right now?" Nate asked, his voice sounded like silk over the speaker.

"I'm in front of my Granny's house." She looked down at the mail she'd thrown in the front seat next to her. "Rachelle hasn't been here in a while. Nate, I'm scared. It's not like her to disappear like this. And she wouldn't just up and leave the house without trying to get word to me. She just wouldn't do that." She took another breath as she tried to prevent her angst from choking the life out of her. "Do you know anybody here in Detroit that might be able to help me? I don't want to call the police just yet, but I don't know what else to do."

"Text me the address of your grandmother's house," he replied, his voice still as soothing as buttered cream.

Confused, Paige lifted the phone from her cheek to stare at the receiver, before placing the phone back to her ear. "Did you hear me? Do you know anyone in Detroit that can help me? I know you've got a lot of contacts from all over." She'd seen the various people that had frequented his popular club over the years. Nate knew everybody. The vast amount of celebrities and pop stars that traveled from different cities all over the country just to party in his establishment sometimes floored her.

"I heard you, Paige. Did you hear me? Text me your address," he repeated.

"What in heaven's name for?" Paige asked, bewildered by the request. Was he going to send a couple of his friends over?

"Because I'm already in Detroit."

Chapter Five

"Let's get this party started!" Terri Blackburn shouted, raising her lemon-lime flavored carbonated soda high in the air. After taking a huge gulp, she let out a loud, exaggerated sigh, before collapsing against an overstuffed loveseat, and wiping the back of her hand across her mouth.

Laughing at her friend, Asha Allen shook her head. She then turned to wink at Holley as they sat together on a leather L-shaped sectional directly across from Terri. "You'd think she was chugging a shot of Patrón."

Holley Rune laughed as she lifted her glass of Stella Rosa Rosso to take a quick sip. "She still has a few more weeks before she can indulge in that spirit."

Terri rolled her eyes, and then looked resentfully at the half-empty soda beside her. "A few more weeks my ass," she mimicked drily. "I'm ready for this pregnancy to manifest already. The doctor told me it would get better in the last trimester, but that's complete bullshit. I've had morning sickness, afternoon sickness, evening sickness, and midnight 'til dawn sickness. If it weren't for Levi, I'd have told the doctor to just knock me the hell out until it was time to deliver this little prince." She then affectionately patted her belly. "I must say however, that my husband has been extremely patient whenever I have to wake him in the middle of the night to help me to the toilet."

Hiding her smile behind her hand, Holley unsuccessfully tried to give her friend a sympathetic look. "The doctor told you that as long as you're not dehydrated, and that you're continuing to gain weight, that you and the baby are fine. Besides, it's only a few more months until little Zion gets here."

Terri and Holley had gathered together in Asha's home estate for an early birthday celebration for Holley. Holley was turning thirty years old next week; and since her birthday also fell on Valentine's Day, the friends decided to get together to celebrate the weekend before. They

40

each figured that more than likely they'd be with their significant other on the national day of love, and didn't want to miss the opportunity to celebrate with their friend.

Terri snorted in response to Holley's statement. "I have *three* more months, to be exact. And he better not be late."

A movement in the corner caught Holley's attention. "Hey Jay-Jay! What do you have there, sweetie?"

Holley smiled at Asha's energetic three and a half-year old daughter as she ran into the room and climbed on her mother's lap. "Hi Ms. Holley and Momma Terri! Daddy gave me a Minion toy when he came home last week. He said he'd take me to see the movie when it comes out if I stay a good girl! Isn't that great?" She shook with excitement in her mother's lap as she held the toy up for her friends to see.

Jayme Allen was the spitting image of her father, Delphi. With dramatic blue-green eyes and dark hair, she was already extremely tall for a child of her age, and held all of the sassy humor of her big sister Alanna. Asha recently had Jayme tested to assess her daughter's advanced displays of intelligence, and discovered her feisty daughter scored at a gifted level for her age group. Upon hearing the news, both Holley and Terri jumped at the chance to assist in Jayme's development. Terri was teaching her to speak and write in Spanish, and Holley was sharing her love of 18th British literature, with works like Lord Byron. The advanced learning helped Jayme in sounding like a seven-year when she spoke, rather than someone almost half that age.

"Yes baby girl. That's wonderful." Asha stated, responding to Jayme's previous declaration. "Nevertheless, remember what Mommy told you earlier? This is a big girl's gathering, and some things we might talk about aren't really for a little girl's ears? Now go back to your room and play like we discussed."

Jayme huffed as she climbed back off her mother's lap. "Alanna says I should just wait a couple more years, then I can figure out big girl talk myself without anyone's help, just like she did."

Terri raised a single eyebrow. "Jayme, your mother just told you to do something. She should only have to tell you once, love." Terri was also trying her best to teach her goddaughter etiquette and discipline, but those lessons were still a work in progress.

Jayme pursed her lips together in thought, and then nodded her head, as if she needed to consider the fact on whether or not telling her something once was good enough.

"Ok. The Powerpuff Girls are on TV right now anyway. Bye!" With that, she raced out of the room.

Holley chuckled. "She's going to be a handful when she gets older. The boys will be killing themselves to get her attention because of her beauty, and the girls will hate her because she'll out maneuver them in wit, charm, and personality."

Asha snorted and shrugged her shoulders. "That's her father's doing. I blame everything on him."

Terri continued to rub her protruding stomach as she nestled back in her seat. "Anyway, Zion and I had a long talk last night while I clutched the toilet seat. I figured he could listen to what I had to say, since he was the reason I was puking my guts out for the second time that evening. We agreed that if he arrived according to his May due date, I'd let him puke and shit as much as he wanted without complaint. Of course, I'll make sure his Daddy takes most of the brunt of that cleanup."

"Like that's something you can control." Holley shook her head as she laughed. "You and Levi have no idea what's coming. I've never had a child, but I've read enough to know that you can't plan every minute of every day with a newborn. I hate to tell you sweetie, but you're not in charge, the baby is. Sure, you've had a little experience with having Jayme come over to your house, but I know it's nothing like having a person depend on you every minute of every day."

Asha clapped her hands together in excitement, smirking at Terri with great anticipation. "Jaymes and I CANNOT WAIT until your son is born! It's going to be a day that will go down in history! Levi's going to completely lose his shit, and I'm bringing my recorder to the hospital when you deliver so I can get it all on film. I need to make sure I capture his breakdown frame by frame to playback during holiday parties."

Terri blew off her friend's teasing. "Yea, like Delphi was the epitome of calm during your delivery." She referred to Asha's husband by his nickname. "I distinctly remember him running around the nurse's station like a chicken with its head cut off. Not to mention the poor delivery nurses that you cursed out when they broke your water." She continued to rub her stomach affectionately. "My Levi will do an amazing job. He's much more in control."

Asha snorted. "Yea, ok. We'll see."

Holley grinned. "I think Levi will be fine, and so will you. I can't wait to hold Zion once he gets here." She paused. "And you're sure it's a boy? When Momma St. Claire was here last week, she mentioned how you were carrying like you were having a girl, because your stomach was sitting up so high. You know sometimes those lab technicians can get things wrong." Holley was referring to her own mother's dilemma with having been misdiagnosed during pregnancy. Her mother hadn't known she'd been carrying twins, both Holley and her sister Harmony.

Asha also nodded, agreeing with her mother's assessment.

Terri shrugged. "The ultrasound showed a picture of a tiny penis. Well, I guess it looked like a penis." She frowned. "Honestly I couldn't really tell. It all looked blurry to me. And once Levi heard the word *boy* come out of that lab tech's mouth, that's when all the hooping and hollering began." She then lowered her head in admittance. "I just went with it. It really doesn't matter to me, as long as he's healthy. But for right now, it's just easier to refer to this gigantic bulge in my stomach as a *he* and name it Zion." She then let out a shaky breath. "Makes this whole motherhood thing seem real."

Holley rose from the sectional, and then moved to kneel down beside Terri's seat. She reached up to squeeze Terri's hand, a look of understanding crossing her face. "You'll be a great mother, Terri. I know it. It doesn't matter what type of childhood you had. You have more love in your heart than most people I know. I know from personal experience that you can control your own destiny; and I know that if you set your mind to becoming a wonderful parent, then that's what you'll be."

Asha nodded her head in agreement as she leaned forward on the sectional. "Absolutely. Every woman may not be naturally bred to become mothers, but that's definitely not the case with you. I know you'll be a great mom, but you have to believe that too. I mean, look at how much Jayme loves you. I couldn't have picked a better godmother for my daughter. And I won't even talk about how much Alanna and Austin adore you. You'll be fine, sweetie." Asha then rose from her seat, moving to also kneel on the other side of Terri's loveseat. She reached up to gently wipe the tears that had fallen down Terri's face.

"Besides," Asha added, giving Terri a quick wink and a smirk. "I'm counting on you to hold it together, because I've got money riding on you. Jaymes and I have a bet going to see which one of you will break down in a full-blown panic attack during the first six months after delivery. My money's on Levi, and I need you to hold it together until Levi falls apart."

Terri let out a choked laugh. "You have absolutely no faith in him do you?" She wiped the last of her tears as she let out a shaky breath. "Look at me. Lately I've become a big ball of emotion. It's ridiculous. This isn't me at all."

"It's you. The *real* you. And we love you just as you are." Holley reaffirmed softly.

Terri smiled. "And I love you guys too." She took another breath before shaking her head. "But enough of the waterworks. We're here for a celebration." She reached inside the bag sitting next to her and pulled out a beautifully decorated box. She then handed it to Holley, who stared back at her with surprise. "We're here celebrating you, my wonderful friend! Happy early birthday, Holley!"

"I thought we agreed you guys wouldn't get me anything!" Holley cried, her grin contagious as she accepted the gift from Terri's hands.

Asha rolled her eyes. "*You* agreed. We didn't say shit. And this is just the first celebration. As far as I'm concerned, you still have a couple more gifts that are due to you. After this, we need to plan your engagement party to my brother." She then raised a single eyebrow in chastisement. "Then, we need to host your graduation celebration. Don't think that Killian wouldn't tell us about the online classes you've been taking in secret to earn your Bachelors degree. I'm pissed, and quite honestly personally offended, that you felt like you couldn't tell us."

"Exactly." Terri chimed in, her earlier sadness forgotten as she narrowed her eyes disapprovingly in Holley's direction. "Seriously, what's up with that? I can't believe you've almost completed your degree in Business Administration, and didn't feel the need to tell anybody! That's a great achievement, Holley. You should feel proud, not ashamed."

Holley hung her head, as her face grew red with embarrassment. She knew her fiancé wouldn't keep her secret from his sister. He'd been on her to tell her friends for months, but she'd never felt like the timing was right. She shrugged her shoulders. *Well, the cat's out of the bag, now.*

"Ok, I confess. At first everyone's credentials really intimidated me. I mean, you've got your MBA," Holley began, nodding her head in Terri's direction as she folded her legs underneath her to sit comfortably on the floor.

"Asha's got her degree, and this hugely successful singing career. Killian's got his Masters in Finance, along with his paralegal certification. Delphi and Levi both finished law school. Shoot, Levi's even begun taking classes to earn another undergraduate degree in Accounting and Finance."

She raised her hand when Terri began to interrupt, cutting off any potential argument. "You told me yourself Levi wants to pass his Series 7 exam so he could be licensed to buy and sell stocks himself, instead of using his brokerage firm. I mean, who does that on top of also running a law practice? And then there's his brothers Lafayette and Lucas, who both have Masters in Criminal Justice. They've opened and established their own private investigation firm, and brought Killian on to help them out. My little undergraduate business degree didn't really seem all that important."

Holley then stared wistfully into the distance, a small smile creeping over her features. "Now, however, Killian is showing me that I don't need to be intimidated by anything. Or anyone. Not anymore."

Asha made a snorting sound as she moved back to the sectional to take a seat. "He'd better, because you're damn sure worth it." She gave Holley a serious expression. "I'm really glad he let us know. We think it's fabulous you're getting degreed up. And you should be excited too. Now, enough of the lecturing. Open your present. It's from the both of us."

Holley grinned, then began ripping open her package. She gasped as she pulled out four Royal Caribbean cruise tickets to Jamaica. Her eyes widened as she looked into Asha's grinning face.

"All of us are going: You, me, Terri, and Zaria. We asked Harmony if she wanted to go, but she said she had things she needed to wrap up here, whatever that means. We leave from Galveston in July." Asha explained. "It's a seven night cruise headed to Jamaica, with port stops to Cozumel, Mexico and George Town in the Cayman Islands. Since this is a *Ladies Only* celebration, we're leaving our husbands and significant others here. Terri should be recovered from her delivery by then, and Momma and Evelyn are flying in to help out Levi, since they've deemed themselves as Zion's foster grandparents."

"This trip is perfect." Terri chimed. "It's right before Asha has to go on tour this fall, and right after you finish up with your last classes. I know, cause I've checked." Terri stuck out her tongue playfully when Holley rolled her eyes. "It's going to be fabulous, but hot as hell though. So prepare to be half-naked in your swimsuit during most of the cruise."

"I think this is absolutely wonderful." Holley exclaimed as she bit back tears. Hustling to her feet, she leaned over to give Terri a hug, and then followed it up with giving Asha a tight squeeze, before plopping down next to her on the sectional. She grinned widely. "A girls vacation! This is going to be fantastic! I can't wait!"

"Well I can." A deep voice called from the entrance of the great room. All three women turned to watch as Delphi, Levi, and Killian sauntered casually into the room. Suddenly, the atmosphere of the conversation changed, as each woman took an internal sigh as they gazed upon the love of their life.

Levi Blackburn, with his long, midnight black hair and chiseled, masculine features passed down by his Native American ancestry, stared intently at his wife as he strolled into the room. Delphi Allen followed closely behind, with his cafe latte skin tone, dark shadow beard, piercing blue-green eyes, and gargantuan six foot seven inch muscular frame. His overpowering presence screamed that he was certainly not a man to be taken lightly. Finally, Killian trailed the men inside the room. Killian Devine, with his slanted hazel-eyes and smooth mocha-chestnut complexion so similar to his sister Asha, was the most muscular of the group. He was also the deadliest. His broad chest, strong biceps, and muscular thighs that strained tightly against his dark blue jeans, were developed from years of physical training as a Navy Seal. It also made him the object of desire and fantasy for many women throughout his lifetime.

Each man, however, only had eyes for his *Lady,* as each one strolled into the room toward their mate. Killian leaned a hip next to Holley against the armrest of the sectional, draping his arm casually across her shoulders. Delphi simply picked Asha up and set her gently across his lap as he replaced himself in her seat. Levi stood protectively behind Terri's chair, leaning down to rub a possessive hand across her stomach.

"I'm still not sold on you leaving me for a week to kick it with Asha to parts unknown. There's no telling what you guys will get into. And then you've gone and added Holley and Zaria in the mix, for heavens sake. It's a recipe for mischief." Levi murmured softly as he caressed his wife's stomach. "Besides, my son will only be a couple of months old at that point. He'll still need his mother."

Asha rolled her eyes, leaning into Delphi's chest as she pursed her lips at her friend. "No he won't. He'll be fine. And what makes you absolutely certain it's a boy? You know sometimes those tests could be wrong. Besides, Momma's coming to help you, and so is your stepmother, Evelyn. You'll have more than enough feminine support." She looked at him slyly. "But if you think you can't handle it..."

"He can handle it." Delphi interrupted, looking intently at his friend. "My bet is on him. Levi can handle everything, and if he can't I'll help."

Terri rolled her eyes, and then looked up at her husband. She laughed at Levi's confused expression, patting his hand as his long fingers sprayed widely across her stomach.

"I can handle it. I just won't like it. And it's a boy because the tech confirmed it, and I commanded it to be so." Levi stated matter-of-factly. Asha just rolled her eyes, and then smirked in his direction.

"Where's Jayme?" Delphi asked. He glanced around the great room and noticed his daughter's Leapfrog game that she'd been playing with earlier laying next to the fireplace.

"She's in her room watching her favorite show." Holley responded.

Delphi chuckled. "I forgot the Powerpuff girls are running a marathon today on the Cartoon Network. She'll be in her room for awhile."

"So, how do you like your new body guards, sis? I just left Nate's place to talk about some security concerns with his business, and I want to make sure you're good to go." Killian asked as he grabbed a lock of Holley's bright red hair, absently playing with it between his long, thick fingers.

"Tyson and Reid are ok." Asha responded nonchalantly. "I expected them to be a pain in my ass like the other guys Jaymes assigned, but so far, I don't have any complaints."

Killian nodded, exchanging a knowing look with Delphi before looking at his sister. "Do me a favor and don't give them a hard time. They know how far to push, and when to reel it in. They won't smother you, but you can best believe they'll have your back if they see you in any sort of danger. I trust them with my life, and now with yours, especially after the incident with Tanya."

Tanya Lewis was a former college mate who'd set her eyes on capturing Delphi's heart, while also trying to torture and kill Asha and Holley. She'd been in cahoots with Officer Danny Stevens, and had ultimately killed herself in retaliation for Delphi's rejection of her unrequited love. Afterwards, Killian set out to find better security for his famous sister, people that he knew he could trust.

Tyson Bowman and Reid Cross grew up with Killian in the poorer sections of Detroit, Michigan. They'd both been involved in illegal activity during their adolescence, causing each to do some time in a penitentiary. Killian had hopes that if given the right opportunity, his

48

friends might change their ways. He believed underneath their rough exteriors, the men actually had caring hearts; they just needed a cause, or in this case a person, to believe it. So far, the match seemed to be working.

"They'll be with you when you sing at the Essence Music festival on the fourth of July. After that, they'll fly back with you to Galveston to meet up with the rest of the Ladies before you leave for the cruise." Killian informed.

Asha nodded her head in understanding. Her singing stage name, *The Painted Lady*, always drew in thousands of adoring fans, but sometimes the crowds could be really intense.

"I brought you something, baby." Levi stated as all eyes turned to him. "I knew you guys were celebrating Holly's birthday today, but I wanted to get you a little pre-Valentines Day gift, to remind you of our love and dedication to each other. A small bribe, if you will. The thought of you leaving me for so long is painful. Why can't you guys think of something else to do for Holley's graduation?" A sad expression skated across his features as he attempted to look grief-stricken.

"Nice try, but we're still going on the cruise." Terri stated matter-of-factly, not at all swayed by her husband's antics. She then tried to make her tone softer as her wide eyes blinked innocently up at him. "But if you please, Master, can you please give me the present you brought me?"

"Manipulative brat," Levi murmured. He smiled as he shook his head. "I guess some things will never change." He then reached down to pull a large wrapped gift basket from behind the chair that the ladies hadn't noticed earlier. He then gently placed the gift in Terri's lap.

"Oh My Freaking GOD! I LOVE you so much!" Terri exclaimed, joyfully clapping her hands together. She then wrapped her arms around the basket of assorted treats, pulling it closely to her belly.

Asha and Holley burst out laughing as Delphi and Killian chuckled lightly.

"REALLY?" Holley asked, wiping the tears of laughter from her eyes as she eyed Terri's present. "That's the bribe you brought her?"

Levi smirked. "Hell, yea. What else would you give my pregnant wife to try and win her over?"

They all laughed at the enormous basket full of assorted Oreo cookies, beautifully displayed underneath a thin layer of cellophane. Holley leaned over to get a better view of the variety. After taking a count, she saw that Levi had stuffed the basket with over ten individual variety packets of Oreo cookies: Lemon Twist, Neapolitan, Cookie Dough, Caramel Apple, Pumpkin Spice, Red Velvet, Root Beer Float, Key Lime Pie, S'mores, and Birthday Cake. The cookies were arranged around a beautifully crafted ceramic coffee mug, with packets of flavored hot chocolate stuffed inside. Finally, individual Hershey kisses and Godiva wrapped chocolate truffles were sprinkled throughout the basket's stuffing. It was a chocolate lover's dream.

Terri began to cry. "This is the most beautiful thing you've ever given me," she sniffed, tears drizzling down her face. "Well, besides Zion of course."

Panicking at the sight of his wife's tears, Levi grabbed the basket from her lap and placed it on the floor. He then tugged her to her feet to wrap his arms around her.

"Don't cry, little one. I hate it when you cry. Please, I can't take it." He croaked, as he buried his face in her neck. "I know you're more emotional because of the pregnancy, but I really hate to see you in tears."

Asha huffed as she looked up cockily at her husband. "Who's going to lose the bet?"

Levi looked up as he cradled Terri in his arms. "What bet?"

"Nothing." Delphi, Asha, and Terri, replied all at once. Holley just laughed.

"Where's Zaria? Wasn't she supposed to be here?" Levi asked. He moved and took Terri's place on the loveseat, pulling her down on his lap while she tried to compose herself. Zaria Wilson was a childhood friend of Levi's, and licensed counselor to both Terri and Holley. Over the years, she'd assisted in helping the women find emotional healing through moments of extreme grief.

"She was, but apparently she got held up by Lafayette on her way over here. I wouldn't be surprised if we see them announce themselves as a couple soon." Holley predicted.

"Now that's something to take bets on. Zaria won't go down easy." Delphi said thoughtfully.

"But never underestimate the willpower of a Blackburn." Levi countered knowingly.

"Touché, my friend. *J'Wad* wasn't going to be denied either."

Levi and Killian burst out laughing at Delphi's reference, while the woman looked at them curiously.

"Who is J'Wad?" Asha asked. "I've never heard of him before."

"Oh yes you have, *meu curacao*. You've been up close and personal with him. You saw him last night, as a matter of fact. Haven't I explained who he was before?" Asha shook her head, causing Delphi's smile to stretch even further across his masculine face. Killian and Levi just laughed even harder.

"J'Wad is my dickname. It means *Jaymes' Weapon of Ass Destruction.*"

"Oh My Freaking God! How embarrassing!" Asha cried, burying her face inside her husband's shoulder.

Killian laughed as he now absently moved from twirling Holley's hair to now rubbing her back. "It's nothing to be ashamed of, sis. All guys name their dicks. I think it's a man code thing or something. Just like all guys like to take their woman by surprise, just because they know they can." With that, Killian leaned down and brushed a soft kiss across Holley's lips, causing her face to redden while her silver-grey eyes darkened with desire.

Delphi huffed. "*J'Wad* doesn't need to take by surprise. He'd rather play with his favorite toy, knowing eventually it will bend to his will, just like he likes it." With that, Delphi quickly turned Asha around in his lap so that her legs straddled his hips. Gripping her neck tightly in his large hand to hold her in place, he lowered his mouth to run his tongue seductively across her bottom lip. After hearing her gasp of surprise, he then captured her mouth, swallowing her breath as he tasted and savored the flavor of her tongue. After a moment, he released her,

51

and then quickly turned her back around to face the room. He chuckled softly in her ear as she shifted uncomfortably on his lap, obviously turned on by his display of affection.

Levi snorted, obviously not at all impressed with the displays of ownership being set before him. "And Mr. Satisfaction doesn't need to take by surprise, nor does he need to tease his toy. He simply takes what's his." With that, Levi grabbed Terri's long dark brown hair, wrapped it around his wrist, and yanked her head back, causing her to gasp at the demanding move. He then swooped down to seize her mouth, her moans of satisfaction heard loudly as she purred underneath her Master's touch.

Holley laughed as Levi released his hold, allowing Terri to try and control the shortness of breath his kiss had caused.

"Well, we can see how Terri got in the state that she's in." Holley turned to face Asha. "I think I want in on that bet, but put me down for Levi to win."

Chapter Six

"Tyson," Nate greeted his friend from his cell, after attaching it to the wireless audio speakers of his rental car. He'd said he received Paige's call right as his plane landed at Detroit Metro Airport. After verifying the address, he'd driven straight from the airport toward her grandmother's home to find her nervously perched on the porch steps.

Now, they sat together inside his rental outside of the home. After once again calming her down, Nate decided to call the one person he knew could help. "Hey man, I'm in your hometown of Detroit. I have Paige here with me, and you're on speaker."

"Hey Nate, what's going on?" There was a slight pause on the other end before Tyson spoke again. "And how are you doing today, beautiful lady?" Tyson asked.

Paige smiled, despite her warring emotions concerning her sister. Tyson always had a kind word for her whenever he came into the club. He'd tried to convince her more than once how she was wasting her time waitressing for Nate, instead of going back to school. She felt a close, brotherly affection for both him and his partner Reid, since they all originated from the same city. They'd always watched out for her.

However Nate had never appreciated the close bond they shared, as she caught the side eye glare he now threw at her. She mentally shrugged. *How did that Beyoncé song go? If you like it then you should have put a ring on it?* If Nate didn't like the fact that she'd found single male friends who openly flirted with her, then he should have claimed her a long time ago.

"Hey Tyson. It's good to hear your voice..."

"Look man, I need you to do me a favor." Nate quickly interrupted, frowning as he gave Paige an irritated glare. "I know you're from this area, and I thought you may still have some connections up here. Paige's sister is missing. She's been gone for a couple of weeks, we believe. A neighbor of hers told us that a couple of guys came to her house, and then she disappeared with them shortly after. No one has seen her since. Do you have any contacts you might be able to call to see if they've heard anything?"

"My contacts have got contacts, man. I'm never slacking. I can find out the color of drawers you have on if you give me enough time." Tyson replied cockily. "Paige, what area of Detroit does your sister stay in?"

"She was living in our grandmother's house off Beresford Street." Paige replied. "When I got here, the mail looked like it hadn't been picked up for a while, and her car was still parked in the driveway. I know something's happened to her. Rachelle wouldn't just leave the house unattended like this without letting someone know. She's a bit secluded, but she takes precautions when it comes to her safety. She just wouldn't leave with two strangers, like her neighbor told us. Something's going on."

"Ok," Tyson said over the speakers. "Give me a couple of hours to see if I can dig something up. Can I reach you guys back at this number?"

"Yes, I'll keep this line clear. Let us know whatever you can, man. We appreciate it." Nate stated.

"Will do. I'll talk to you guys in a few." With that, Tyson disconnected the call.

Paige nervously wrung her hands together in her lap. "I wish I'd kept a copy of the house keys before I left for Houston. I feel like a total stranger sitting outside my own grandmother's home, instead of going inside."

She looked out of the window toward the silent residence staring back at her. "Rachelle insisted I leave my set of keys with her before I left town. She'd said if I was going to disappear from the state, she didn't want me just reappearing without any warning. She'd rather have a heads up, just in case she had...company." Paige laughed, but the sound was without any humor. "She said I wouldn't dare catch her ass high and naked in the air without first calling, even if I was her sister."

She turned back around to face Nate, her eyes misty as she looked pleadingly at him. "God, I know something's going on. I should've tried to come back sooner."

Nate took one of her hands and placed it inside of his. He then squeezed it gently to give her reassurance. "There was no way you could've predicted she'd disappear like she did. Tyson's got some strong connections with this city. I'm sure he'll be able to give us some type of direction on where she might have gone when he calls back. Let's not jump to conclusions just yet."

Paige nodded her head once in understanding. She let out the deep breath she hadn't realized she'd been holding. "Ok. We'll wait until Tyson calls back." She then looked down at her hand that was now entwined inside his, her fingers curled around his strong, calloused ones. Bowing her head to hide the confusion on her face, she felt the all-too-familiar pull within her chest triggered by his touch. She slowly withdrew her hand from his, placing it back on her lap.

Remember the reason why you left Texas in the first place, she chided herself.

"Nate, why are you here?" She asked as she tried to reign in her already fragile emotions. Her mind drifted as the hurtful words Isobel had spoken only a few nights ago began ringing in her memory.

^^^

The last of the club's patrons had just left, and Paige couldn't be happier. She was exhausted, and wanted nothing more than to go home and soak in her bathtub full of lavender scented aromatherapy bath salts.

Maybe I could get Nate to stop by and give me a foot rub, *she thought wistfully. She shook her head as she quickly banished that idea. Nate had never visited her apartment before. Every time she'd suggested it, he always found a way to evade her. When she tried to press for a reason, he'd just give her the same blanket excuse he always gave: the time wasn't right.*

Mentally shrugging her shoulders as she rolled her neck in exhaustion, she continued to pick up the empty beer bottles and shot glasses, tossing them into the plastic bin to be washed later. She and the bartender Isobel were now completing their last minute spot checks and trash disposal before shutting down for the night. Nate had locked himself in his office earlier in the evening to go over the night's inventory receipts, so she knew he wouldn't reappear for another couple of hours.

"Hey Paige," Isobel called. "I heard about you and Nate. Well, actually I heard that you've been mooning over him for years, and that he won't give you the time of day. Take some free advice, girlfriend. Nate is never going to settle down with someone like you." The tall, attractive brunette sneered in her direction as she tightened the seals on the vodka and wine bottles behind the bar.

Paige stiffened at the woman's vile words. She turned from the table she'd been cleaning to give the woman an assessing glare. "And what exactly do you know about me and Nate?"

Isobel grinned sassily in her direction. "I know that he won't get serious about someone he's not fucking. He needs a real woman. That's why he's finding his pleasure elsewhere." She tossed her long hair over her shoulder. "And believe me, it's all pleasure, sister. He's just too nice to tell you to stop fawning over him, especially since you won't give up the pussy. He doesn't like a dick tease."

Pain unlike anything she's ever felt sliced through Paige as she struggled to keep her face neutral. Not again. Not again. Not again.

"I'm not your sister, Isobel. And Nate and I have an understanding..." Paige began.

"...He understands that you'll never take the hint." Isobel scoffed, interrupting her. "That's why this morning, while we were having breakfast, he asked me to see if I could break it down for you." Isobel then sneered in her direction, as her steely eyes bore into Paige with disdain. "You do get the picture, don't you?"

"Yes," Paige responded. She then lifted her chin in pride. She wouldn't let this viper see her cry. This bitch was just like those cronies from her neighborhood back home, just waiting to laugh at her misery. "The picture is quite clear."

With that, Paige threw down her dusting rag, and stalked out of the club.

^^^

"What are you doing here, Nate?" Paige asked again, breaking through her flashback. The pain of Isobel's words was still fresh in her spirit. "You didn't need to come to Detroit to help me. You could have stayed in Texas."

Nate frowned when she removed her hand from his grasp. "I came here for you."

"But why? You've got a business to run." *And apparently a woman to screw.*

Nate's frown deepened. "Gena and Tony can handle things while I'm gone. I trust them. Besides, I'm glad I came. Looks like you needed me here."

Paige pursed her lips. She hated the feelings raging inside her right now: desire, confusion, helplessness and resentment. Desire surged at seeing Nate in person once again. Confusion warred because she couldn't understand why he really came to see her, especially when she knew how much he hated leaving the club in someone else's care. Helplessness rolled because she still felt uneasy about what was going on with her sister. And finally, resentment flared at having her perfect fantasy of Nate and she being together for the long haul utterly destroyed by a venomous bitch.

"Nate," she started. Suddenly, Nate's phone began to ring, cutting her off. He immediately slid the bar to answer, making sure to once again set the speakerphone so Paige could hear.

"Nate, it's Tyson calling back. I've got some news for you and Paige that you need to hear. Am I on speaker?"

"Yea, man. Go ahead." Nate confirmed.

Dread raced through Paige. It hadn't taken long at all for Tyson to call back. Which meant he'd found out immediately what was going on...and it couldn't be good.

"I talked to a couple of buddies from my old crew up there. They know what happened to Rachelle."

"Spit it out, Tyson!" Paige exclaimed, throwing her hands in the air. He was killing her.

Tyson let out a deep, frustrated sigh over the airwaves. "The Hunter Group has her. I'm not sure if you know what that is, Paige. HG is a very dangerous organization. They have affiliations throughout the entire country, not to mention various parts of the world. Their main product of distribution is the kidnapping and selling of young girls into the black market. Apparently Rachelle was targeted after she'd become involved in the prosecution of a high-ranking buyer who liked his girls young, including his stepdaughter. She helped the District Attorney's case by giving her testimony. The guy's stepdaughter confided in Rachelle during one of those sexual awareness and assault prevention classes that she teaches.

"Word is that the girl joined seeking help and asylum. HG didn't take too kindly about one of their main buyers being infiltrated, however, so they took Rachelle. She's already been shipped out of Chicago, headed back down here to the Houston area, where she'll eventually be auctioned off to the highest bidder. I also heard that there's a lot of international buyers flying in for that auction, but my contacts weren't able to verify the exact date yet."

Paige began to shake violently in her seat as Tyson's words resonated with her. The thought of her sister being abused and sold.... *oh god!* She couldn't breath, couldn't speak...*Rachelle!*

She felt Nate grab her hand again in a show of comfort. "Thanks Tyson. This is good info. Let me hit you back in a couple of minutes after I talk to Paige."

"Will do, man." Tyson said, his sympathy pouring over the phone line, before Nate disconnected the call. Paige then felt his hand squeeze hers, causing her muteness to break.

"NO!" She cried into the closed atmosphere of the car. "Oh my god! This is all my fault! I shouldn't have been gone for as long as I was. I have to do something!" She turned pleading eyes back to Nate, all earlier misgivings completely forgotten. "Nate, I can't lose my sister this way. She's all I have left!"

Nate rubbed a hand up and down her arm in support. "Don't worry, baby. We'll find her, I promise you. I'll tell you what. Come back to Houston with me. Tyson said they've already sent Rachelle there. I think we'll have a better chance to find her if we head there now. I also have a couple of contacts that I can let know what's going on. It turns out they've actually been monitoring this Hunter Group's activity for a while, so they may be able to help us. In fact, I was talking with them about the possibility of doing some investigations at the club before you left me."

She raised a single eyebrow at his last words.

Taking a deep breath, he quickly looked away for a moment with a pained expression on his face. When he turned to face her again, the emotion she'd thought she'd seen was gone.

"In any case, they might be able to shed some light about that auction Tyson was referring to."

Biting her lower lip, she simply stared back at him. She'd escaped Houston to get away from him. To start her life over again. To reinvent herself. If she went back, she might once again lose herself. Leaving was the hardest thing she's ever had to do. It would kill her to have to do it again.

Nevertheless, her sister needed her. And it looked like this might be the only way she could help her.

"I'll go back with you, but only until we find Rachelle. After that, I'm gone."

Nate nodded his head, his eyes searching her face with an emotion Paige couldn't identify.

"Come on. Let's head to the airport."

Chapter Seven

Standing next to Paige while they waited in line at the Southwest Terminal, Nate was filled with turbulent emotions.

And he hated it. He hated the helplessness he felt.

On one hand he was beyond relieved that Paige was returning back to Houston with him. On the other hand, her reasons for returning were troubling. The uncertainty surrounding her sister's whereabouts were not to be taken lightly. Tyson had said her disappearance was in retaliation for involving herself in HG business. Nate couldn't help but wonder what other sort of ramifications could happen if HG found out about his investigation activities at *Escapades*. And to top it all off, Paige had given him a hard limit that once her sister had been located, she'd be gone for good.

Like that was going to happen, he thought, determination steeling his willpower. He'd allow her to leave again over his dead fucking body. She was going to stay by his side permanently, even if he had to strap her to his fucking hip and drag her everywhere he went.

Glancing over, he took in the way she held herself: stiff posture and reserved mannerism. Withdrawn. Secluded. Paige had never built walls around herself before, especially not around him. She'd always had a smile on her face and a sparkle of mischief in her eye.

Now, she looked as if she wished she were anyplace except standing next to him.

He hated it.

His cell phone began to buzz in his pants pocket. Taking it out and sliding the bar to answer, Nate kept his eyes on Paige as he responded to the call.

"This is Nate."

"Hello sweetheart. This is your mother."

His heart immediately sped up at the sound of his mother's voice. She rarely called, outside of holidays and birthdays, unless there was some sort of issue. Belinda instead preferred to keep in contact with him through letters or emails. She always rationalized that she could savor a word from her remaining son even longer if he put his thoughts into writing and mailed them to her. That way if she grew lonely, she could always pull out one of his letters to read.

"Hey Ma. What's up?" He asked tentatively.

"Nate, I need to see you. There's something I need to speak with you about. I don't want to do it over the phone, nor do I want to send it to you in writing. Is there any way for you to come to Chicago? It's pretty urgent, baby. I really need to talk to you in person."

His breath caught at the worried tone in her voice. Things rarely worried his mother. Usually Belinda *Khan* was the one causing others to stress.

"Hold on for a minute," he responded, attempting to keep his own voice calm. They'd just reached the terminal desk. The ticketing agent looked at him expectantly with a bright smile plastered on his face.

"Hello, we have a reservation for Houston, but I need to go to Chicago instead. The last name is Kerr." Turning to Paige, he looked at her apologetically. "Paige, we need to make a pit stop before we go to Houston. Something's going on with my mother..."

"You don't have to explain. Of course, you need to see how she's doing. I don't mind." She nodded her head to the agent. "When is the next available flight to Chicago?"

"There's actually another flight headed to Houston, but with a four and a half hour layover at Chicago Midway. There's a plane change before it heads down to Houston. Were you just wanting to pass through Chicago, or would you prefer a longer stop?" The agent responded as he checked the online reservation system.

"That's actually perfect. Can you please change our reservation for that flight?" The agent nodded his head as Nate returned his attention to his phone call.

"Hello? Ma, I'm in Detroit right now, but I'll be in Chicago in a couple of hours. Hold tight until I get there."

^^^

61

"Hey, Ma. It's good to see you." Nate greeted his mother as she opened the door to her small condo apartment in the River West neighborhood of Chicago. He watched with concern as his mother's eyes ate him up, before she pulled him into her arms for a tight embrace. After a few moments, she reluctantly let him go to acknowledge the woman by his side.

Nate took a step back as he studied his mother's appearance. Standing tall at 5 foot 8 inches, Belinda Kerr didn't currently display the powerful image Nate was accustomed to seeing. Her cinnamon complexion appeared ashen, while her dark brown eyes looked up at him with seeming relief. Her face contained deep, weary lines around her eyes and mouth, while her short afro-centric haircut, sprinkled with wisps of grey at the temples, was tied in a stylish black and green head wrap, securely knotted in the middle of her neck. Her normal attire of wearing all black, her typical dress since his brother died, was currently exhibited with a black V-neck sweater and black corduroy slacks. A dark look, which also didn't help to brighten her disposition. Overall, she appeared to be a bundle of frayed, restless nerves.

Cataloguing his mother's emotional state for discussion later, Nate placed his hand on Paige's lower back, making his possessive claim evident with his gesture. "Ma, this is Paige. We were on our way back to Houston when I got your phone call." His mother smiled at Paige, but Nate could see the worry lines still echoed around his mother's eyes.

"Hello dear, my name is Belinda. Please, come in, come in! Have a seat." Belinda ushered them inside of her apartment, before locking the door securely behind them. She shook the hand Paige extended to her in a warm greeting.

"It's very nice to meet you." Paige replied with a shy smile, releasing her grip. She then followed Nate down the hall into the tastefully decorated living room, taking a seat beside him on the sofa.

"You as well, dear. Although I wish it were under different circumstances." Belinda turned her eyes toward Nate. "I'm so relieved you were able to see me, son." She frowned as she stared at him in thought. "I'm not even sure where to begin."

She then looked anxiously toward her front door before shaking her head. "I'm forgetting my manners. Do either of you want something to drink? Perhaps something to eat?" Paige shook her head no, but Nate nodded his head. He knew his mother well enough to know that she would feel more at ease if she had something to do while she spoke with them. She liked to keep her hands busy. *Idle hands are the devil's workshop,* she'd always told him and his brother. Belinda believed in staying busy and being productive. Anything less was a waste of God's approval wink toward his conception. Nate knew he could contribute his hard work ethic directly to her.

"I'll take something to drink, Ma."

"Ok. I've got a few bottles of Fanta in the refrigerator. You want Orange or Grape?"

"You already know. Grape, please ma'am." He quickly glanced at Paige before turning back to his mother. He needed to have this conversation quickly so they could head back to the airport. He knew Paige was anxious to get back to Texas, and he didn't want to delay getting her back any more than he already had.

"Now Ma, tell me what was so urgent that I needed to come to Chicago and have a conversation with you in person?" He reached up to accept the soda from his mother before watching her take a seat across from them in her recliner. Twisting the cap on the bottle, he took a swig, and then sat the bottle on the floor before waiting for her response.

Belinda let out a deep breath before she began to speak. "I got an unexpected visit yesterday from an off duty Chicago police officer. He said his name was Gerry. He flashed his badge and asked a lot of questions about you. His face looked mighty familiar, but I can't quite place where I've seen him before."

Nate thought about the name, but drew a blank. "I don't know anyone by that name. Why would he be asking about me? I haven't been back here to Chicago in quite a few years."

Belinda nodded her head. "That's what I told him, but he didn't seem to care about that. He kept insisting that I needed to speak with you, if I knew what was good for you." She wrung her hands nervously in her lap. "Nate, he really got to me, but I tried hard not to let it show. When your brother was killed, there were men asking the same sort of strange questions that this officer was asking, like who Darrick was with when you boys went downtown to that Bears parade." She shivered slightly. "But this man gave me the creeps. He said I needed to tell my remaining son to keep out of HG business. Do you have any idea what that means?"

Nate stiffened as he heard Paige's involuntarily gasp beside him. His temper flared at the knowledge that someone had bulldozed their way into his mother's home, and threatened him by using her as leverage.

He stood up, suddenly needing to release some of the pent up adrenalin coursing through his body. He clutched his hands to his sides as he began to pace back and forth. The same assholes that had taken Paige's sister were now fucking with his mother.

But why? *What the fuck was going on?* This couldn't have been a coincidence. He'd only recently discovered that this so called Hunter organization even existed. Surely he wasn't knowledgeable enough to pose any sort of threat to them so soon in the game.

He remembered Harmony's warning that HG had hubs throughout the world, including a central base right there in Chicago. Maybe Chicago was the connection to everything that was going on. That operative word, however, being *everything.* What else was occurring in this city, besides the shipping of abducted girls, which needed to be protected so fiercely that they needed to send out a warning message?

He turned back to his mother. "Can you think of anything else he said? I need you to really try and remember."

Belinda pursed her lips as she stared at her son. "I remember *everything* that he said. He warned me that if you knew what was best for you, you'd stay out of HG affairs. Otherwise, you might end up suffering the same consequences as Darrick. I don't know what the hell is going on, but I do know that you need to be careful. I sent you to Cincinnati to go to school, so you wouldn't have to deal with the problems and dangers involved on the west side of this city. I wanted to keep you safe. Now you've moved to Texas, and became a successful businessman, just like Darrick and I wanted for you. Part of me misses seeing you on a regular basis, but my heart was still content because I knew you were safe down there.

"Now, this man is threatening to come after you, and I'm terrified for you. I can't lose you like I lost Darrick. Do you hear me? If you're not alive to reap the benefits of all your hard work, what good has it all been? This cop meant business, and he worked for CPD. There's no telling what sort of resources he may have to reach you, to monitor you, and to harm you if he sees fit   That's why I wanted to talk to you in person."

She stared intently at her son as tears began to streak down her cheeks.   "I need you to be careful, Nate. When your father was killed while driving you and your brother to the movies at the hands of that carjacker, I thought my worst pain had been realized. I was wrong. It was the day your brother was killed. I just couldn't handle it if something were to happen to you too."

Seeing his mother's distress, Nate pulled her from her chair, enfolding her within his embrace as he rocked her gently in his arms.

"I'll be careful, Ma. I promise. I promised both you and Darrick that I'd become something for you guys to be proud of, to be better than my circumstance. And now, I'll make another promise to you. No one will ever come to your house and threaten you again. I vow to you this day. I will never let that happen again. Do you understand?"

Belinda nodded her head as she wrapped her arms around him. "I understand. And one way to make certain is if you leave the city. It's not safe if you stay here for a long period of time. They could be watching you right now."

Nate used his thumb to wipe the tears that continued to leak from her eyes. "Ma, trust me. I've got this. However I need for you not to worry. And as far as that cop is concerned, I'm going to make a few calls to see if I can have someone watch *you*, especially while you're here unaccompanied." He kissed his mother gently on her forehead. "My girl needs protection as well."

Belinda waved off his concern. "I'll be fine. There's nothing that my Glock 19 handgun can't handle. I told you, it's you that I'm worried about. And have you been keeping up with your target practice?"

Nate grinned. "Yes, Ma. I still go to the gun range every other week. The 9mm you bought me is still in good shape."

Belinda nodded her head. "Very good."

She then turned and noticed that Paige sat staring wide-eyed at them during their entire conversation. "Oh dear, I'm so sorry sweetheart. That was certainly a lot to take in during our first meeting. Please forgive me."

Paige shook her head, giving her a small smile. "I'm fine, really. And I understand. I definitely understand." A look Nate couldn't quite name crossed her features as she watched them.

"Good. Well, be safe. Both of you." She turned back to Nate. "If anything else comes up, how do you want me to notify you?"

"For right now, I need you to keep off the radar. Don't call or write. If you really need to get a hold of me, call Delphi. You still have his contact information, don't you?"

"Your roommate from college? Yes, I still have his information. Is it still the same?"

"Yes, he hasn't changed that number." He then leaned down to kiss her cheek, then moved over to where Paige sat.

He grabbed Paige's hand and gently pulled her to her feet, signaling that it was now time to go. "Paige and I need to head back to the airport." He guided Paige toward the door, with his mother following closely behind.

Opening the door, he turned and gave his mother one final hug. "I love you, Ma. Take care of yourself."

Belinda patted his cheek as she embraced her son. "I love you too, Nate. And remember, don't start none..."

"...Won't be none." He grinned as he remembered the familiar quote he and his brother would recite with her before they left for school each morning. Belinda taught her sons that although they were to never start or instigate any sort of confrontation, if the streets brought it to them, then it was their duty to finish it.

The streets were now bringing a confrontation right to his front door, and it was now his job to finish it.

By whatever means necessary.

Chapter Eight

Mayor Eugene Penne stared silently at the folder brief in front of him, its contents untouched and unread. His stomach churned in knots as he tapped his fingers along his desk. Turning his head, he peered absently out of the window at the Chicago lakefront view from his downtown office.

Restlessness set in as he stood up to pace within the recesses of his quarters. He had a meeting with the Cook County Board of Commissioners in just over an hour concerning the city's latest budget crisis, and the untouched brief he should be studying outlined specific plan recommendations on how to resolve it. The State of Illinois recently denied his request for a third time asking for a state-funded bailout, citing that Chicago's budget crisis was a local issue, and should not impede on the financial confines of other counties and cities within Illinois. Now due to the lack of funds, his office may be faced with a very real possibility of closing down some of Chicago's highly needed programs, like mental help counseling, in-home care for seniors, and city-funded homeless shelters. He also had to deal with the possibility of closing a few inner city colleges, as well as a potential teacher's strike.

With all of the issues and highly publicized concerns going on around him, there was only one thing that occupied Penne's attention. One thing that kept him up at night. One thing that continued to haunt his dreams.

Nate Fucking Kerr.

Nate had the power to make him lose *everything*.

And he couldn't fucking afford to let that happen.

Penne wiped his sweaty palms down his pants, his unease flowing freely as the ghosts from his past started to creep in. Ghosts he thought he'd gotten rid of, and had finally laid to rest. Agitated, he ran a hand through his thinning auburn hair, his pale skin stretched across his haggard face as a testament of his weariness and frustration. He kicked a piece of invisible lint on the floor, ignoring the slight pain in his knee the action triggered, attributing it to the wear and tear of a man in his late sixties.

His intercom buzzed, signaling that his secretary wished to speak with him. Marching swiftly back to his desk, he plopped back down in his chair and hit the call button.

"Yes, Mrs. Vanderfield. What is it?"

"I have your wife on line two, Mayor Penne. Also, Alderman Spivey is waiting to meet with you. He wasn't scheduled today, but he insists that he be allowed to speak with you. He says it's urgent."

"Tell my wife I'll call her back later. Send Spivey in here." Penne demanded.

"Right away, sir." His secretary clicked off the line.

A few moments later, Alderman Conrad Spivey strolled into the Mayor's office, looking unbothered and completely relaxed. The alderman was an attractive man, appearing to be in his late-forties, who obviously believed in dressing well. The form-fitting Hugo Boss suit was tailor-made for his slim frame, and his thin, dark moustache, which matched his closely cropped hair and chocolate brown skin, was well groomed. Although he was rather short in stature at only 5 foot 5 inches, he gave the appearance of a well put-together individual.

After closing the door securely behind him, Conrad walked over to one of the chairs in front of the mayor's desk and took a seat. He casually crossed his legs in front of him as he coolly assessed the mayor's frantic state.

"You need to calm down, Eugene." Conrad stated.

"How the hell can I calm down?" Penne spit. "Nate's back in Chicago. Who knows what the hell brought him up here!"

"We have people watching him, remember? They told us he was in Detroit with that girlfriend of his. He must have stopped in Chicago on his way back to Houston to see his mother. Don't worry about it. There's no need to ring the alarm on him just yet."

The Mayor pointed a shaky finger in Conrad's direction. "You better be sure about that, Spivey. I can't afford any fuckups."

68

"And you think I can? Relax. We've already given a warning to his mother, which is probably why he stopped by. It's being handled."

"So you say." Penne took a deep, steadying breath. "Any word on that shipment?"

"The last shipment was herded through Chicago a couple of weeks ago. We included that Clarke girl out of Detroit. She was making too much noise up there to be left alone."

Penne nodded his head. "Good. And the buyers...?"

Conrad gave a small smile. "...Are all set for the auction. Our contact at the Houston Police Department told me personally that everything has already been cleared. They're expected to arrive as planned. The Ides of March is on track and on schedule."

Penne drummed his fingers across the top of his thigh. "Good, good. We can't afford to blow this. That idiot Stevens already fucked up our last auction when he went and got himself killed. He almost exposed the entire operation. It's a good thing our other contact got wind of what went down at that hunting log with that singer, and called in a chain sweep to notify everyone to lie low."

He then turned and gave Conrad a pensive stare. "I don't want anymore 'accidents' happening before we can get the last of this inventory unloaded, sold and shipped out. The Ides buyers are coming with millions on hand to spend, so they expect top quality when they get here. Where's the stock being held until the auction rolls around?"

"There's a warehouse just south of Tomball that's secluded, and not too far from Cypress. It's well hidden and highly secured. There's no worry that any of the merchandise will escape."

"Excellent." Conrad walked over and sank back in his chair as he loosened his tie. Wiping the sweat that had accumulated on his heated, reddening forehead, he assessed his visitor once again before he spoke.

"It's good to have a partner I can really trust. You've been a big help to me, Spivey."

"You know I am to please, Sir."

"That you do." He sighed. "These fucking bitches can all go to hell as far as I'm concerned. It's better that we rid the world of their contamination now, before they can infect the rest of us. They're the spawns of Satan, and should be destroyed."

Conrad raised a questioning brow. "Who exactly are you referring to, Mayor?"

"This unruly female population. Anyone woman who isn't cowling beneath our feet should be swiftly dealt with, before they infect the rest of their kind. We are the Lords of the Manner, God's rightful protector of all those who respect and uphold the law of obedience. Females, who display early warning signs that they're incapable of becoming quiet, demure, low-key partners, even in their infant stages or through their maternal lineage, should be handled accordingly. It's also why we monitor women who were too late too turn because of their age, but still have the ability to birth and mold impressionable offspring who could potentially one day become corrupt. The offspring of the spawns of Satan should be taken from her, mentally and physically transformed into merchandise, and rebuilt back up to obey the laws of HG. It's one of the reasons why the Hunter Group was established, to hunt down those who are immoral. It's our responsibility as upstanding men to ensure that our world, our men, has what it needs in a sufficient partner. You believe that, don't you Spivey?"

"Absolutely, sir. It's one of the reasons why I decided to become an Alderman, to assist you in your endeavor."

"Very good. Now, tell me about this latest shipment. Are you sure you've gotten *everyone* that you need? I've received word about one more possibility that might need to be transformed..."

Chapter Nine

Paige stared out of the window of the Boeing jet as they made their way down Midway's airstrip. She was so taken back with the amount of information she'd learned over the past 24 hours, that she didn't know where to start. It was almost too much to take it all in.

Her younger sister, the only immediate family she had left, had been abducted by an underground organization, whose sole purpose was the buying and selling of young girls for human trafficking. The man who'd hurt her by detaching himself from every possible emotional entanglement, had just flown over a thousand miles to see her. Although he still hadn't explained his reason as to why he'd come, from her standpoint, he seemed completely oblivious to the fact that she'd purposely left him to recuperate her broken heart. And last but not least, she'd also discovered that the man she loved had witnessed not one, but two personal tragedies so heinous, he'd built his entire existence on proving that he was better than his past circumstance. She wasn't even sure how to insert herself into his preconceived outlook on life, or for that matter if she even wanted to.

However there was one thing she *did* know for certain. She knew that Nate was dedicated in helping her find her sister. He'd given his word, and Nate's word was bond. For the moment, she would at least have to be content with that.

Glancing at him out of her peripheral vision, she took in his rigid posture and sealed off expression. Leaning back into his seat, his eyes were tightly closed, and his mouth set in a thin, grim line within his goatee. His jaw was locked tight with tension, and his hands were enclosed into tight fists within his lap. He hadn't said much since they boarded the plane, seemingly just as lost in his thoughts as she was in hers.

His emotional distancing hurt. She wished he would share some of what he was feeling with her, because she desperately wanted to talk to him about what was going on inside of her.

She wished he would talk to her.

Hell, just look at her.

But isn't that what she wanted, to be left alone?

She was so fucking confused.

She looked back out of the window, still lost in her thoughts as the plane ascended into the air. His mother had mentioned the fact that Nate's father had been killed when he was younger, along with his brother. How much had those murders shaped the man she now knew? Paige estimated quite a lot.

No wonder why he's so single-minded in making sure his club is a success, she pondered. He had something to prove. To his brother. To his father. To himself.

A man with something to prove, however, could miss the fact that he didn't need to prove *anything* to the woman who already cared about him. He could miss the fact that he was *enough* for her.

She now understood his driving need to succeed; however she also couldn't discount her own needs. Her need to be desired, to be put first above everything else. She needed to know that the man she loved would put her first before anything, as he should expect the same thing from her. Right now, Nate had other things that clearly took precedence in his world, like his club and his need for his business to be the most successful that it could be.

That quote from Maya Angelou kept ringing over and over in her head: *Never make someone a priority when all you are to them is an option.*

Was she just an option for him? It certainly felt that way. Especially when he clearly had other options at his disposal, like that bitch Isobel.

Paige winced as she remembered the woman's scathing words, the hurt still fresh as if they'd just been spoken. How else had Isobel discovered her vow to remain celibate until she'd found a relationship that could truly last, unless Nate told her? The only person Paige conveyed that belief to was him. She'd done it in a weak attempt to explain why it wouldn't be a good idea for him to come back to her place one night after closing. They'd been walking out of the back door and locking up when he'd asked if he could continue their conversation at her apartment.

That was a few years ago. Since that time, she thought they'd gotten closer over the years, enough for her to consider bending that rule. *After all, he did take me to that wedding with all of his friends,* she thought absently. *...Although he really didn't introduce me to anyone...*

She thinned her lips together as the cold truth suddenly washed through her.

What a fucking idiot I've been! He hadn't introduced her because he had no intention of having her stick for any future engagements, just like Ware. He undoubtedly must have told Isobel to try and get rid of her in the heat of passion, just like she'd described. In addition, since he wasn't screwing her, he obviously needed to release his sexual frustration elsewhere.

How could she trust him after that?

And her sister, my god! Who the hell were these HG people? Were the people who'd taken Rachelle mistreating her? Did Rachelle believe that no one knew of her plight, and resigned herself to a life of abuse forever? Her sister already had a tainted, scornful outlook on the world, and this latest tragedy would not make her view any better. How much pressure could Rachelle endure before she finally broke?

Paige twisted her hands nervously in her lap as she continued to stare out of the window. She knew that she was only driving herself crazy by mulling over questions she didn't have answers to, but she couldn't help herself. Her sister was a strong woman, but everyone had their breaking point.

Stay strong, Rach. I'm coming for you. Stay strong.

Closing her eyes as an impeding migraine began to blur her vision, she leaned her head back against the seat, opting to catch a couple of hours of sleep until the plane landed at Hobby airport.

^^^

The jarring of the plane's landing woke Paige from a fretful slumber. She'd dreamt that her sister was crying for help, scared and crying in a dark, damp room. Several masked men stood around her viciously spitting and kicking at her, and all Rachelle could muster was enough strength to call Paige's name.

Rubbing a hand down her face, she shook off the last remnants of sleep and glanced at Nate, who had already unfastened his seatbelt in preparation to depart the plane.

"Come on," Nate said. "I left my car in the overnight lot. I can take you home if you'd like, or we can head into the club and see what my contact has gathered so far about HG. Your choice."

Paige studied the tension etched across Nate's face. The flight hadn't lessened his turbulent thoughts any more than it did hers. Following his lead as they disembarked the plane, she watched the rigidness in his back and the jerky way his bowed legged were working, a far cry from the carefree stroll she was used to seeing on him. Nate was obviously feeling just as restless as she was.

After reaching the terminal entrance, he turned around and looked at her expectedly, still waiting for an answer to his question.

She shook her head slightly, chastising herself for being so easily distracted. Then, upon realizing exactly what he'd asked, she felt her stomach twist.

"Umm," Paige started. How could she explain that she didn't have a home to go to anymore? When she left, she'd already told her landlord to go ahead and lease her apartment to someone else. At the time, she'd had no intention of ever returning back to Texas. Now, not only was she back, she was now homeless.

"I, uh..." Before she could finish her fabrication on exactly where she'd planned on staying, Nate's phone buzzed. Breathing a sigh of relief that she could delay her answer a moment longer, she watched as Nate reached inside his pocket and pulled out his cell to answer. He moved aside as other passengers bustled past them.

"Nate speaking."

74

Paige watched as first shock, and then absolute horror washed over Nate's face. "What the hell!" Nate shouted, startling the few remaining passengers still remaining in the terminal.

Paige reached up to place her hand on his shoulder. Her fingers flexed as she touched the tense muscles underneath his designer suit jacket.

"Nate, what is it?"

His eyes moved to her as a haunting look gripped him. He reached up to place his hand over hers as he continued to listen.

"When did this happen?" He shouted. Pause. "I had my phone turned off because I was still flying back here from Detroit! No! Not that I'm aware of. Last month, and there shouldn't have been an issue. It passed with flying colors! Yea, she's here with me now. Yes, we're on our way."

Nate slammed his phone case shut, his lips thinned with red-hot anger. He then let loose a string of profanities in a tirade that most sailors could respect and admire.

"What happened?" Paige pressed. She'd never seen Nate so angry. His rage had never risen to this level, even when Tony mistakenly dumped a 1997 unopened bottle of L'Art de Martell in the trash. Nate was always the epitome of cool, calm, and collected.

And right now, it looked like he wanted to shoot the next thing smoking.

He grabbed her hand and began tugging her behind him as he walked hurriedly through the airport. Paige struggled to keep up with his long stride, her shorter legs causing her to stumble a few times in order to keep in step.

Finally, she jerked free from his hold, frustrated with being manhandled by someone she supposedly was trying to distance herself from.

"Dammit Nate! Tell me what the hell is going on right now!"

Black fury burned in his gaze as he turned to stare at her, causing Paige to take a cautious step back.

"Some motherfucker just tried to burn down my fucking club," he spit.

Chapter Ten

Nate and Paige pulled up to the parking lot of *Escapades* in his black and white Mercedes Benz Sports coupe, just in time to catch sight of the blazing inferno that was formerly his pride and joy. Skidding his car to an abrupt halt, Nate raced from the driver's seat to pull Paige from the passenger side. Together they ran toward the group of people who stood among the police as they watched the firemen try to control the flames.

Lucas, Lafayette, Harmony and Killian stood around in a circle; quietly talking among themselves as they watched the firemen battle the blazing inferno. Gena, Isobel, and Tony were also huddled together, however they stood closer to one of the police officers. Upon seeing her friend return, Gena rushed over and pulled Paige into her arms, giving her a tight embrace. Nate let out a low, painful moan as he watched multiple firemen trying to contain the damage. Heartache and despair plummeted through him at having to witness his life's work go up in a ball of smoke.

"Goldilocks!" Gena exclaimed, drawing Nate's attention away from the fire. Gena gave Paige a small shake. "I thought you'd left! Well, whatever the reason is that made you change your mind, I'm glad for it. I just wish you didn't have to come back under these circumstances."

"I'm not back," Paige whispered. Nate stiffened as his heart ached with another agonizing bolt of pain. "Not officially. I just have some business I need to take care of concerning my sister. After that, I'm gone." Paige's gaze stayed riveted to the scene before them, while Nate felt as if he were slowly dying inside.

Still huddled within Gena's embrace, Paige stared sympathetically at his former business, and then glanced over her shoulder toward the area where Tony and Isobel still stood. She stiffened as she took in Isobel's direct glower.

"In any case, I'm glad to see you, doll." Gena commented, her losing battle to control her emotion evident in the quivering of her lower lip. Gena then turned her head toward Nate as unshed tears welled in her large brown eyes. "I'm so sorry, boss. I know how much *Escapades* meant to you. Hell, to all of us."

"Thank you, Rodriguez." Nate said, before nodding his head toward Lucas and Lafayette. The two brothers briefly paused their conversation with a couple of firemen to acknowledge his arrival, tipping their head back toward him in response. Harmony just narrowed her eyes as she stared back at them.

I wonder what's that about, Nate thought briefly.

"I'm just glad you weren't here when it started, and that you're safe." Nate stated absently.

Gena nodded her head, releasing her hold on Paige. She reached inside the purse that was slung across her shoulders to pull out her cell phone. She then swiped the screen and scrolled through its contents.

"That security app you installed that monitors the club's activity when we aren't there started sounding off alerts a few hours ago, so initially I called the cops. I then tried to contact you, but I guess you were still on the plane, because I just kept getting your voicemail. I'm so glad that Lucas guy was able to get ahold of you. The fire department got here before I did; however by the time I arrived, the place was already engulfed in flames."

Gena then nodded over to where Lucas, Lafayette and Harmony were still standing. "That new girl was already here too. She said she got here at the same time as the fire department."

Clenching his fists together to prevent them from shaking and giving away how truly rattled he was, Nate watched as Harmony approached them, her sharp focus scrutinizing the crowd of bystanders.

Did she already have someone in mind as a suspect? Nate thought, as a shimmer of hope tried to fight through his current misery. *Maybe she knows more than what she wants people here to believe.*

Maybe she's got some insight. He mentally shrugged. *Best to play along with whatever cover story she's trying to create.*

"Nate!" Harmony cried as she suddenly rushed toward him, throwing her petite arms around his waist.

Whoa...umm...ok. Wasn't expecting that.

"Darling, I'm so glad you're back! I can't believe what's happening right now! *Escapades* was your dream, baby." Harmony spoke with the best imitation of a down home Texas drawl he's ever heard. The unexpected dialect momentarily caught him off guard. Her sudden and bewildering affection also threw him for a loop, but he quickly recovered. He quickly realized that whatever game Harmony was playing, it was strictly for the benefit of the curious crowd now watching their show.

Taking stock of all of the additional eyes now taking witness in his exchange with Harmony, he glanced quickly over at Paige to gage her reaction. His chest tightened as he noticed her eyes had now narrowed with contempt in their direction.

Trust me, baby, he internally pleaded. *Please trust me. It's not what you think. This isn't real.*

He shook his head slightly before patting Harmony awkwardly on her back. He then untangled himself from her hold. "Yes I'm here, but it doesn't do my club any good."

Harmony blinked lovingly in his direction as she touched his bicep. He watched as her face turned down in a look of sadness and regret in an effort to show him sympathy. If he wasn't so upset about everything, he might have found her feigned interest in him amusing. Her antics were so unlike the woman he'd met a few days before.

However right now it was just pissing him off, because Paige was soaking in every intimate touch Harmony was making. He could feel her disdain for him growing with every second.

He gritted his teeth as he tried to hold it together. Whoever Harmony was performing for needed to believe that he was the playboy he betrayed during club hours. They needed to think that the only thing he cared about now rested in a pile of drowned brick and stone underneath the fire hoses.

According to his mother, HG wanted to send a warning. What if this incident was the first of more things to come? He couldn't let Paige get caught up in his troubles. It was bad enough her sister was missing. He wouldn't add his fight to her anguish as well.

Pushing down his anger, he turned to Harmony and gave her a tight smile.

"Thank you Harmony. I appreciate you looking out for me."

"That's why I'm here, sugar. I also completed those other requests you asked me to do for you." Harmony pressed closer to him, reaching up seductively to rub her hand across his chest before wrapping her delicate hand around his neck. She then leaned in to whisper in his ear so only he could hear her next words. "I was able to transfer the data from the security feeds in your office before the place went up in smoke. I sent them to Lafayette so he can take a look at them. There are some interesting conversations that were captured that I think you should see. Meet me at the Blackburn's office tomorrow so we can discuss it."

He glanced over to see Gena and Paige staring at them, both of their mouths hung slightly open as they watched the open display of affection Harmony showcased. Nate's lips tightened even further as he gave a short nod of understanding.

"Thanks," was all he could muster at the moment. He was so far past ready for this day of torment to be over.

"Excuse me, Mr. Kerr?" A hefty man downed in sweat approached. His duck insulated tan coveralls, lined with bright yellow ribbing, was covered in soot. His grey t-shirt was soaked and plastered across his frame, while his thinning, matted black hair lay limply across his forehead. He wiped the sweat from his brow with one hand as he held his black hardhat with the other. Peering through the smoky haze that still clung in the air, he tried to adjust his eyes as he searched Nate's face. "Are you Nate Kerr, the owner of this club?"

Nate nodded in his in acknowledgement. "I am. And thanks to you and your men for trying to salvage my business. I'm eternally grateful for your efforts."

The fireman shook his head. "No thanks required. It's our duty. I'm Lieutenant Oscar York, by the way. Your place sustained some real damage, but we were able to contain most of the fire and smoke damage to the back of the club near that office and bar area. The front bar, dance area, and upper floors were untouched. Initial inspection reports seem to conclude the blaze started from an electrical fire. You'll be shut down of course, until the fire marshal can complete an assessment of the damage. My guess, however, is that you'll be back up and running in a matter of a few weeks. I've seen buildings sustain a lot more damage than yours, and they were reopened in no time."

"What are we supposed to do for work while your club is shut down?" Isobel whined. Nate hadn't noticed that both she and Tony had moved closer to the group, obviously eavesdropping on his conversation with the fireman. "I mean I know I only worked here part time, but I needed this job. Don't you have some type of worker's compensation insurance or something?"

Gena stared coldly back at her and quickly responded back before Nate completely lost his temper.

"Look, you half-wit." Gena snarled. "Nate just lost his reason for living! Show some fucking compassion, why don't you?"

Paige stood silent, her stare toward the brunette venomous enough to kill on impact. Tony was quieter than normal as well. He was watching the scene between him and Harmony with acute interest, the hard sinew of his arms crossed tightly over his muscled chest.

York seemed oblivious to the other conversations around him. He nodded his head in Nate's direction. "Like I said before, you'll be hearing from the inspector soon." With that, he tipped his hardhat toward the group before turning around to walk away.

"According to the police, they don't believe any foul play was at hand. They have to wait for the inspector's report to validate of course, but based on the accounts from the fire department, they think they can rule out arson." Killian informed grudgingly as he, Lucas and Lafayette followed an ominous looking older gentleman toward their group.

The gentleman, dressed in a uniform of dark navy pants, a sky-blue shirt, and a diamond-shaped patch over his left shoulder that was standard dress issue for police officers, frowned as he walked toward them. The four gold stars on each side of his collar displayed his status as

Chief of Police. The surname NEIL was displayed on the nameplate above the right pocket seam of his shirt, and six hash marks were slashed boldly across his left sleeve, indicating the man had been in service for over 30 years.

His time served didn't put the officer in a hospitable mood, however, since he scowled irritably at the crowd around him.

"I'm Chief Harrison Neil," he growled, his granular voice resounded through the air like sand paper against a wood grain surface. "I'm well-acquainted with each and every one of you, although I can't say it's been a pleasurable experience."

Nate startled at the man's obvious distaste for them.

What the hell was wrong with him, Nate thought angrily. *It wasn't like it was* his *business that was ruined.*

Harrison shook his head in disgust. "Ever since you guys came around, I've had to deal with more incidents in my territory than I have in the past 15 years. I'm Officer Jolsten's commanding officer. He's been keeping me abreast of your activities lately," he said. He turned judgmental eyes toward Nate. "Your club has been nothing but trouble ever since you took it over. I knew something like this would happen one day. Good riddance, as far as I'm concerned. This area didn't need another hotshot, slick talking bar owner anyway." Harrison then turned his bile toward the Blackburn brothers. His eyes roamed over the brothers, and made no secret about the fact that he found them lacking. "I'm also not surprised to see you two here. You guys seem to bred trouble with every turn."

Nate's fists once again clenched at his sides as he stared at the officer. He'd had just about enough of yet another arrogant, know-it-all cop speaking negativity into his life. He'd had to tolerate it throughout his adolescence, and during his trial after college. He'd be damned if he continued to just let bullshit pass without calling attention to the stench.

"You *knew* something like this would happen, huh?" Nate stated, raising one condensing eyebrow toward the officer. "And just how much did you know, *Officer* Neil? My building just passed its safety inspection four months ago, after I finished the renovations to the second floor. It passed with flying colors, so there shouldn't have been any possibility of the potential for electrical damage that the fire department stated caused this. This is clearly a sign of some sort of arson."

Harrison snorted. "Anything is possible, son."

Nate narrowed his eyes. "Oh, I am *so* not your son."

Lafayette raised his hand to try and diffuse the tension. "We know the inspector will be out shortly to investigate, so we'll have the full report at that time. Then we'll see what our next action steps will be."

Killian nodded his head. "Yes, we will. In the meantime, I know a couple of guys who could poke around and run security checks to make sure the building stays secure while its under investigation, especially since it's obvious we may not be able to rely on the help of authorities." He directed his last words toward Nate, clearly dismissing Officer Harrison and his ability to protect and serve. He then looked intently in Harmony's direction. "You ready to go? I can drop you back off at your apartment."

"I can drop her off." Lucas volunteered. He reached over to grab Harmony's hand, but she quickly sidestepped him.

Instead, Harmony drew Nate in for another hug, before she pulled away. "Call me later, darling. Let me know if you need anything," she drawled. Then with a quick glance around the group, she followed Lafayette, Lucas and Killian toward the parking area.

"We'll be in touch as well, Mr. Kerr." Harrison informed, his tone evident that he hadn't taken too kindly to Killian's dismissal. "And please try to stay out of trouble." He shrugged his shoulders nonchalantly. "Maybe you should even consider this as an omen that you might not be welcome in this part of Texas."

Nate stiffened as he heard Paige take an involuntarily gasp at the officer's words.

Nate turned his full attention toward the officer. "Is that right? Well, I'd like to see anybody try and make me leave. The last time I checked, and according to my *Magna Cum Laude* business degree, I believe this is still a free country. I also believe in every part of the U.S. Constitution, including the second amendment." He turned to Tony. "You used to work as a parole officer in Dallas. What was the paraphrasing again regarding that particular revision?"

82

"It describes the right for people to keep and bear arms," Tony replied, looking back and forth between Nate and the officer with keen interest.

Nate gave a terse nod. "Yes, I believe you're right." He then turned to Harrison, his baritone voice dropping another several decimeters, ice dripping with every vowel and consonant he spoke.

He'd had enough.

"Don't you *ever* presume to threaten me again, especially as an officer of the law. It was foolish of you to do it in front of witnesses. Even more careless that you didn't recognize the strength of the man you spoke it to. No man, and I do mean *no man*, will ever hold enough power over me to threaten my well being again. I moved to Texas for a fresh start and a better way of life. However, please know this..."

He moved closer to Harrison as he felt his back straighten even further, his shoulders widening his stance in a predatory position. The custom-made suit he wore, like armor against his skin against those who dared to threaten his manhood, suddenly felt tight against the swelling of his chest. His narrowed eyes bore into the face of the officer in front of him as they stood toe to toe.

"I will *never* have a problem showing *anyone* exactly where my roots come from if they choose to threaten me. Recognize the West Side of the Chi in me, because my mother didn't raise a punk, *Sir*." The last word spoken was filled with sarcasm and contempt, with Nate never breaking eye contact with the focus of his stare.

Harrison just sneered in his direction.

"We'll see," Harrison replied ominously. With that, he turned around and walked back toward his patrol car.

Gena let out a long, exaggerated sigh as she moved closer to him. "Go on home, Nate. There's nothing more you can do tonight. I can wrap things up here with the Lieutenant about the inspection. Go home and get some rest."

Nate slowly let the hostility run loose from his body before he turned to finally face Paige. She looked sullen as she wrapped her arms around her torso. Her body language screamed that she was in self-preservation mode. He then suddenly realized she'd just heard him practically threaten a cop.

She must think I'm a typical street thug, he thought gloomily. He sighed as his heart ached at the possibility. The day had already turned to shit. What's one more piece of dung to add to the growing stink pile?

"Paige, can I take you home? I know you must be tired." Nate offered, trying to shake the negative energy from his thoughts. He could at least see that she got home safe tonight. She might hate his very existence, having completely lost his perspective on helping to find her sister in the aftermath of his destroyed property. The least he could do was to see her home.

Paige bit her bottom lip nervously, and then glanced in Gena's direction. "Gena...umm...would you mind if I crashed at your house for a few days? Just while I'm in town?"

Nate narrowed his eyes suspiciously as he studied Paige. Her telltale signs that she was hiding something from him were on full display.

"What's wrong? What's wrong with your apartment?" He demanded.

Paige sighed as she turned toward him. "I gave up my apartment when I left. I had no plans on returning back to Texas. But now with the stuff going on with Rachelle...." She pursed her lips as she studied him, and then crossed her arms defensively across her chest. "I just need a place to crash until I can get in contact with my sister, that's all."

Well. Fuck. That. He was trying to play nice and take her somewhere she'd feel comfortable, even though he knew her apartment was a shithole. Gena's small, one bedroom apartment was already crowded with her and her little boy. Paige wasn't staying somewhere where he couldn't keep an eye on her. And with the events of tonight and the threat from HG...

"You're coming home with me."

"Typical." He heard Isobel murmur into Tony's ear. "Little miss perfect bats her eyelashes, and the boss keels over like a limp dick."

This day had turned to shit, but at least he could try and end it with a positive wash.

84

"Isobel," Nate started, snapping his fingers in her direction as though an idea just occurred to him. "You'd asked about worker's compensation earlier. I just remembered, I got you covered on that. You don't need to worry about a thing."

He watched as Isobel's face lit up with smug satisfaction, right before he doused her fire. "You're fired. I don't need shitty, insubordinate help like you. Now, you don't need to worry about when the club will reopen, because you won't be here to see it."

With that, he grabbed Paige's hand, and then dragged her toward his car.

Chapter Eleven

The ride back to his home was tensely quiet. Paige bit her bottom lip as she stared out of the passenger window at the cars on the TX-99 expressway. The sun had long since set against the western horizon, causing its dusky rays to shine romantically in its afterglow.

And if she weren't so pissed off, she'd actually be able to enjoy its beauty.

How the hell had the day turned into such a cluster fuck? She'd arrived at her grandmother's place fully expecting to reunite with her sister. She'd looked forward to laughing like old times over a cup of chamomile tea and a batch of her grandmother's raisin and molasses teacakes. Rachelle had fortunately inherited their grandmother's talent for baking, and Paige had been craving a small token from their childhood.

Now, the chaotic events of the day were crashing hard into her reality, causing cold chills to run through her body. First, she'd gotten word that her sister had been kidnapped. Next, the love-slash-hate object of her desire shows up out of the blue, demanding answers as to the reason for her escape from his daily interaction. Then, she'd watched as a beloved place of employment and camaraderie burned right before her eyes. She also had to witness yet another attractive chicken head blatantly throw herself all over the previously stated desired object, although she did feel a small twinge of satisfaction when he'd fired that Isobel bitch. And finally, she was now headed to God knows where with said desired object, because she'd been foolish enough not to protest louder when the desired object dragged her away from the only true girlfriend she'd made in the past three years.

Life fucking sucked.

"I know you're probably thinking the worst of me right now," Nate started, breaking into the silence of the drive. "But if you'll just hear me out, I promise you'll understand." She felt his eyes quickly glimpse at her unreadable frown. "Well, I *hope* you'll understand. Will you at least try to listen?"

Paige raised her hand in a defeated gesture, giving a small huff. "What else am I going to do, Nate? It looks like I have no other choice in the matter but to sit here and listen to you, now does it?"

Nate frowned slightly at her before tearing his eyes back to the road. "You always have a choice, Paige. I'm asking you to choose to listen to me."

"Fine, ok. I'm listening, Nate. Speak." Her voice sounded angry and clipped, even to her own ears.

He took a deep breath, then plunged right in.

Paige listened quietly as Nate explained how Harmony, Killian, and the Blackburn twins visited his office a few days ago. He explained how Harmony informed him that HG was monitoring his club, and how he needed to be careful. She listened as he described Harmony's FBI experience, which was also the reason why she was currently acting as a decoy waitress in his bar. He assumed that all of the earlier flirting Harmony had done was connected to whatever information she needed to tell him tomorrow. It was the reason why he'd played along with her ploy, as uncomfortable as it had been at seeing Paige's discomfort.

He went into detail about how his friend Asha, along with Harmony's sister Holley, had gotten kidnapped a few months earlier, with the intent of being sold into HG's human trafficking market. The same group who now apparently had her sister, threatened his mother, and for all intensive purposes, had now just tried to burn his business to the ground.

He explained how his mother and brother were the catalyst in making him want more out of life; and how his best friends Levi and Delphi were the models he used to show him which direction to go, how to finally grow up, and to go after what he wanted.

Finally, he confessed that how now, after everything that's happened over the past week, he felt like he's failed in every single goal he'd ever tried to establish for himself. Everything he's ever wanted was slipping through his fingers, and he didn't know how to stop it.

He took a deep, steadying breath after he finished, staring blankly into the night as he drove. His hands gripped the steering wheel so hard; she could see the tendons in his fingers clearly outlined in the dark of the car's interior.

Her heart squeezed painfully as she stared at his masculine profile, his luscious lips surrounded by the hairs of his trimmed goatee cast down in a frown etched across his face. She realized in that instant that Nate felt so much more than he let on. More than he wanted people to know. More than he'd ever shared with her in the past. He cared, maybe too much, for everyone and everything around him. His heart was the thing that made him the most vulnerable, and was the very thing that caused him the most pain.

She bit her bottom lip as she soaked in everything he'd just told her. She fought the urge to demand that he pull the car over right then so she could take him in her arms and comfort him. Instead, she turned away to stare out of her passenger window, opting to remain silent as she struggled to settle her thoughts and feelings.

They continued to drive until he turned off TX-99, heading toward Northpark Drive. "Your home is quite a distance away from the club." She murmured, breaking into the thought-filled silence as she watched the trees pass by in a blur.

"I wanted to stay somewhere I'd always dreamed," he responded. They drove into an expansive gated community near Lake Houston, until the car finally slowed in front of an impressive lakefront estate. The massive two-story home sat on a 9000 square foot lot, its regal brick structure shadowed by large willowing birch and ash trees.

He pulled into the driveway, hitting the button on his visor to open the four-car garage. After pulling in and shutting off the engine, he turned to look warily in her direction. His eyes slowly scanned her face before he spoke.

"I know today didn't turn out like you wanted. I'm sorry about that. All I want for you right now is to offer you a good night's rest. I'd feel more at ease with having you under my roof. There's too many puzzle pieces at play right now for me to let you stay somewhere alone without any protection."

Tears misted in her eyes as she reached up to touch the protruding bicep of his arm. She felt the tense muscle twitch underneath her fingertips. *God, after all he was going through, he still was concerned about her and her safety.*

"I understand. And thanks for explaining everything to me. It helps...it helps me to better put things into perspective."

He searched her face for a moment before he nodded once in understanding. Climbing out of the car, he walked over to her side to help her from the seat. Together they walked through the garage door into his home.

And Paige halted in her tracks.

Nate's home was utterly gorgeous. The impressive great room was tastefully decorated in variations of blues and creams throughout the entire area. As she continued walking, she saw that a two-story foyer flanked the formal dining and study area near the front entrance. Walking toward the kitchen, she noticed the breakfast area had spectacular views of the lake through the French doors of the rear covered patio. A spacious game room occupied the rear area of the home, shadowed by a massive staircase that lead to the second floor.

Turning toward him, Paige just stared at him, completely dumbfounded. "Nate, your home is absolutely beautiful! And huge! Why on earth do you need this much room? It's just you..." her voice trailed off.

Unless he'd planned on having someone else occupy his space when he got the home. Someone like Isobel...

Nate looked embarrassed for a moment. "I grew up in a cramped apartment back home. My brother and I never seemed to have enough room. We were always bumping into each other." His gaze turned wistful for a moment, before he quickly shook off the melancholy. "Anyway, I always dreamt of living downtown Chicago in one of those fancy condos overlooking Lake Michigan, and feeling like I was king of the world." He shrugged sheepishly as he glanced around his surroundings. "I guess I just switched out lakes when I moved to Texas; and I still wanted more space."

Paige smiled wryly in his direction. "And what about becoming the King of the World?"

He turned back to stare at her for a long moment, before giving her one of the sexiest grins she'd ever seen. "Oh, you mean K.O.W.? Oh, he's still the King, sitting fat and taking notice, sweetheart. He just hasn't had a chance to rule over his kingdom yet."

She looked at him like he'd completely lost his mind. *What the hell was that suppose to mean?*

He chuckled softly to himself before shaking his head. "Come on, let me show you where your bedroom is located."

She followed him as he led the way up the back stairwell to the second floor. Looking around the open walkway, Paige was still in awe as to the grandeur of Nate's home, but now she could see where his bachelor taste had taken over.

Passing each open door bedroom, Paige could see that each room was tastefully decorated to reflect a major NFL football team, complete with artwork paraphernalia and matching bed linen. She passed a blue and white bedroom signifying the Dallas Cowboys, an orange and white room for the Denver Broncos, yellow and blue for the Baltimore Ravens, and orange and turquois for the Miami Dolphins.

The last bedroom located at the end of the hall was the one Nate led her to. Turning on the light, he stepped back so she could follow him inside. The room was just as tastefully decorated as the rest, with its navy blue, plush carpeting. Chicago Bears decal artwork decorated the walls, including signed autograph pictures of Walter Payton, Brian Urlacher, and Lance Briggs. Finally, incredibly soft looking cream and orange bed linen, complete with what appeared to be satin burnt orange sheets covered the massive king-sized bed that sat in the middle of the room.

"You can take my bedroom, since it has the largest bed. I'll bunk down in one of the guest rooms." Nate offered.

Paige looked around the room once more before resting her eyes back to him. Everything in his room was in its perfect place, from the lined cologne bottles of Yves Saint Laurent and Dolce and Gabbana on his dresser, to his collection of Bulova watches on the nightstand.

"Nate, I really don't feel comfortable kicking you out of your bedroom. I can take one of the rooms down the hall."

Nate abruptly shook his head. "No, I want you in my bed." At her surprised expression, he cleared his throat and shifted his feet as he tried to explain his statement. "What I mean is, it would make me feel better to know you're sleeping in my bed, between my sheets." Cringing at how the words still tumbled out, he looked down at his feet for a moment before lifting his head to stare intently into her eyes.

"Look, I'm not saying this right." He then moved from the door to walk closer to her. "I care about you, Paige. More than you can imagine. I don't want to see you hurt, especially with everything that's going on. It killed me when you left. I...I didn't know what to think."

Paige was frozen in place. Her heart pounded in her chest and her breath hitched in her throat. Lustfully, she watched his bowlegged stroll slowly advance toward her.

"There's never been any other woman in my life, besides my mother, who's ever meant more to me than you do. I couldn't take it if something were to happen to you. I know you may not believe that, or even care, but I swear I'm telling you the truth. There will never be another woman in the world for me. You're everything to me, Paige. I... I need you, more than you know." He shook his head sadly. "The club means nothing to me if you aren't there by my side."

He now stood in front of her, and Paige forgot how to breathe. Her eyes moved as he grabbed one of her hands and placed it against his rapidly beating heart. "I swear to you this night, I will help you find your sister, if it's the last thing I do. I want to see you smile again. I don't want to cause you another moment of grief. Once we find her, if you still want to go..." His eyes then slowly roamed over her face.

"You are so beautiful, Goldilocks," he whispered as he leaned toward her. Paige's tongue licked her dry lips, her eyes riveted to his mouth as it leaned in slowly toward her. She felt her own heart pounding within her chest as she felt the heat from his skin brushing against hers. Anticipation of his taste drugged her thoughts, and caused her nipples to painfully harden. Then, taking a deep breath, he quickly stepped back, moving out of her space. Paige felt the dejected loss immediately, like a stream of acid splitting her heart into pieces.

"I need to take a shower and wash off this smoke." He stated hoarsely. Turning around, he opened one of the dresser drawers to pull out a t-shirt and jogging pants. Paige could see his hands shaking as he closed the drawer with a resounding click. Maybe she might not be the only one who was affected by their closeness. *Maybe.*

Nodding toward the adjoining bathroom, he placed the clothing on the bed. "There's towels and shampoo in the closet in the bathroom. Go ahead and get some rest, Paige. It's been a long day, for both of us."

He then lifted a single eyebrow and pointed toward his bed, his intent clear. Finally, he gave her a thin, tight smile, before turning and walking out of the room.

Paige stood there for a minute, grappling with what he'd just confessed. *He cared? Really?* He sure had a hell of a way of showing it. She'd wanted him for years, and now, *now* when she was fed up and ready to leave, he confesses his need for her?

But...what if Isobel's words were just spoken as the result of a jealous reaction? After all, Nate did fire her. Had she misunderstood his actions all this time? It was so hard to tell with that man.

She shook her head in frustration. She was so fucking confused.

If I stand here contemplating much longer, my head will explode. Mull over this in the morning, Paige. Tonight, go shower, then rest.

Marching toward the bathroom, she decided that washing away the lingering soot and ash from her skin, and falling into a deep, coma-like sleep was all that she could deal with for the moment.

Chapter Twelve

The bright morning light woke Nate from a restless night's sleep. He opened his eyes and looked around the interior of the Ravens themed bedroom he decided to crash in. Asha had teased him relentlessly about keeping a child-like decor in his personal space, but to him, it felt more like keeping a happy memory in place whenever he felt lonely or isolated. Football had always been the way he and Darrick had connected, bonded as brothers. After he died, simply enjoying the game quickly transcended into a life-long obsession. A comforting way to relax when his nights got too lonely in his spacious home. He knew his friends used other methods to relax: Levi used D/s, Killian played PlayStation games, Delphi recently started taking culinary classes at a local college, and he, well, he turned to ESPN.

Stretching in the full size bed that was too small for his large frame, he glanced at the clock and noticed the time. He still had a few hours before he needed to get up. He'd received a text late last night from Lafayette, asking if they could meet in the Blackburn office at noon. Since it was just a little before seven, he had plenty of time to lounge around before it was time to actually get up.

Listening to the stillness in the air, he assumed Paige was still asleep. Maybe she might like it if he fixed some breakfast and served her in his bed.

His bed.

He'd been adamant last night that she sleep in his bed for purely selfish reasons, ones that he kept hidden to himself. He'd wanted to make the dream of making love to her in his bed a reality so bad; it had been a physical ache to walk away from her last night. However the conversation they'd had years ago, a few days right after she first began working for him, was one that he would never forget. It was one that he respected. He vowed to honor and keep her wishes, regardless of how much it killed him.

She'd told him that she wanted to remain celibate until the day she found her true and only love.

She'd vowed to stop falling for men who only wanted to take her body, without giving their heart in return. *Selfish bastards,* she'd called them. She'd hoped that by denying her physical urges, it might open her mind to help lead her to the right man. The news had been devastating to his libido, since he'd been physically attracted to her from the moment he saw her.

He tried to tell himself that they were better off not being romantically involved, opting instead to maintain a friendly, yet protective distance. With her words echoing in his brain, he'd jumped back into the dating scene with one stereotypical club head woman after another; while at the same time deflecting would be suitors wanting to approach Paige in his club. It quickly became common knowledge that the "Golden Girl of Escapades" was off limits, and he couldn't help but to be happy about that fact.

To make matters worse, it seemed that every woman he tried to date after meeting Paige turned out to be a complete waste of time. During each rendezvous, the only thing he thought about was how fast he could get rid of the girl, so he could go to the club the next day and see Paige's face. Eventually he stopped trying to date other women altogether, opting to not lead women on unnecessarily.

As time went on, he found that he only wanted Paige. Wanted to be with her. Wanted to protect her. Wanted to love her.

Wanted to earn the right to make her scream his name as she came.

So, he began to use his imagination, as well as his right hand, to dream about what it would be like to finally have her. He'd waited years, literally, to have her in his bed; and last night he couldn't pass up the opportunity to put her right where she belonged.

He'd wanted her scent to coat his sheets and fragrant his linen. He'd wanted to reenact the dream of having her mocha cream skin slide against his orange satin sheets, the color beautifully complimenting her skin tone. The thought of her wild, honey brown hair falling against his pillows made his dick weep so badly, he had to jerk off in the shower last night just to get some relief. And those eyes... the thought of those sexy, golden eyes staring back at him as he buried himself deep inside her body...

Nate reached under the sheets to grab his aching dick as it twitched uncontrollably under the covers. Spreading apart his muscular thighs, he began massaging his cock while thoughts of her penetrated his mind.

He closed his eyes and thought about what it would be like to finally taste her lips, the ones located in the steamy juncture of her creamy thighs. He could imagine sliding his tongue along her seam, and watching the petal of each labia opening softly under his administrations. His mouth watered at the imagined taste of her core, sweet with the faintest hint of tanginess. Once he finally got a taste, he knew he would quickly become addicted to having his head between her thighs and sucking up her juices all night long. He wanted her essence soaking his lips and goatee so thoroughly, that he wouldn't be able to take a breath without inhaling her scent.

Letting out a small moan, he continued massaging his dick, running his thumb over the head to catch some of the moisture that now leaked from the tip. He spread it over his shaft to help in lubrication as he jerked his dick a little more forcefully. His breathing became labored as he felt his balls drawing up close to his body. Kicking the sheets from his heated body, he exposed his heated member to the cool morning air.

His mind wandered back to an image of her lips, succulent and soft. Paige never wore a ton of makeup, opting to only use a light coating of gloss whenever she went out. In his opinion, she didn't need any makeup. Her natural beauty was spellbinding.

"Paige..." he whispered, caught up in his mind's image. "Goldilocks...my baby...my baby..."

"Am I really?" A soft voice called from the hall, startling his fantasy. He jerked, sitting upright to see that Paige now stood in his doorway. The t-shirt he'd given her covered her athletic frame, but couldn't quite hide the heart-shaped ass he's grown to love. His dick seemed to lengthen as he stared at her.

Paige stood looking soft and vulnerable, her eyes searching his before moving to stare at his exposed body. He watched as she roamed over his face, down his chest, and lower to his hardened dick, which seemed to harden even further under her hot gaze.

Taking a steadying gulp, he found his voice. "Yes," he responded hoarsely. His voice sounded strained even to his own ears. "You'll always be my baby."

A lone tear fell down her cheek, and his heart seized. He watched her lower lip tremble, and instantly regretted his words if they caused her pain. He didn't want to be the source of any of her grief.

"I'm so scared," she whispered. "I don't want to get hurt again. I couldn't handle it. Not from you," she whispered.

"I know, baby girl. I know. I'll never hurt you, I swear. I lo...I care about you, more than you know. You're everything to me." He wanted to confess his love for her, but wasn't quite sure she was ready to hear it. Feeling exposed discussing his feelings with his dick hanging out, he leaned down to reach for the sheet he'd kicked off earlier.

"No," she murmured. "Don't cover yourself. I...I want to see you. And...I want you to see me." Slowly, she pulled the t-shirt over her head, revealing the breasts he's longed years to taste. He couldn't tear his eyes away from her round, full orbs as they swung slightly with her movement. His nostrils flared as his eyes slowly ran down the lines of her taunt stomach, over her ample hips and down her toned, shapely legs. He then zeroed in on her pussy, ripe and succulent for the tasting. He could see her swollen folds from where he sat on the bed.

Yep, I'm going to die, he thought lustfully.

"Paige," he croaked. "You told me you wanted to wait..."

She shook her head. "I told you I wanted to wait for the man who would love me unconditionally. I wanted to save myself for my true love. I can't hold it in any longer."

She paused for a moment, seeming to finally come to a decision. "When Isobel told me that you and she decided to let me down easy, I got so upset. I just wanted to get away...from everything. So, I left. I thought you had given up on me."

He shook his head, confusion marring his brow. "Whoa. Wait a minute, what? I don't know what you're talking about. Isobel and I never talked about you. Why would I talk to her about anything? She doesn't mean anything to me. Nor any woman, for that matter. Not like you. The only woman who matters is you."

Her voice lowered and he strained to hear her next words. "I know that now. I *believe* that now." She took a deep breath. "I've always loved you, Nate. I think I fell in love the first day I met you. I was so scared of being hurt again, of being *humiliated* again, I thought that refraining from physical contact would help me think clearer. Except I can't...I can't..." Her eyes swept over him in a lustful glance. "I can't resist you anymore."

He was off his bed and standing in front of her in an instant, crushing his mouth against hers with an agonized moan. He wrapped his arms along her sides, fitting his large palms against her hips as he lifted her off the ground. His cock twitched as she wrapped her legs around his waist, causing her heated core to brush mercilessly against him. He felt the wetness from her bare, shaven pussy drip over his pubic hairs, and he groaned again.

"Then don't," he growled. He carried her over to the bed and gently laid her down. Stepping back, he let his eyes eat up the vision before him.

She was magnificent.

"It's you, Goldilocks. Only you. You're my African *Theia,* the Mother of Light, and Daughter of Heaven. You helped me see the type of man I truly want to be." His eyes reflected the same raw need he saw in hers. "And I want to be yours."

He moved forward to quickly brush his lips across hers, feeling her tremble underneath his mouth. He then slowly slid his finger down her cheek and over her jawline, his eyes never leaving hers. Letting his hand trail over her shoulder, he reveled in the softness of her skin before tracing his tongue where his hand had just led.

Moaning at the succulent flavor of her skin, he kissed his way over to the other side, nibbling and kissing her shoulders as he pressed her into the mattress. He felt her hands slid up to grasp the back of his neck, locking his head in place as she writhed in satisfying purrs underneath him.

Moving lower to trail his tongue over the swell of her breast, he left a path of wetness across her skin as he enjoyed its sweet flavor. She gasped as he latched onto her nipple like a swaddling newborn, sucking and biting the dark brown tip until it stabbed him in the chest. He then administered the same actions on the other breast, before moving his head lower over her stomach. He smiled as he watched her stomach quiver underneath him, reflecting both her anxiousness and excitement.

"You taste so good, but I know what will taste even better." She whimpered as he then lowered himself to the position he's dreamt about for a lifetime.

Spreading her thighs apart, he placed his nose next to her neatly trimmed, golden colored core, and then inhaled deeply.

"Finally..." was all he could muster, before licking his lips. He then let his tongue catch a pearl of moisture that had escaped her pussy. Paige jerked, then let out a loud moan above his head.

"Be still, Goldilocks. Let me have my fill." With that, Nate took her pussy in his mouth and gently sucked. The flavor was both intoxicating and addictive, and he knew at that moment he'd just lied.

He'd never be able to get his fill.

His strong fingers gripped her thighs as they quivered in his hands, before placing his mouth back against her. His tongue speared her opening, rolling around its cavity while her juices coated his tongue.

"Fuck, you taste good," he breathed, coming up for air. "More."

He grazed her protruding clit with his teeth, biting down gently before sucking the muscle in his mouth. He felt her tremble and roll as he sucked, her hand seeking his head as she tried to push her core harder against him.

He ate her pussy with the gusto of a starving man, licking and slurping up all of her moisture. Her taste was so potent, he soon couldn't tell the difference between her wetness and his saliva.

"I'm going to...I'm going to come," she gasped, her thighs shaking underneath his onslaught.

"Let me take you over, baby. I'll be here to catch you when you come down."

"Yes..."

With that, Nate gave one final tug on her clit before thrusting three fingers into her pussy. Tilting his index and middle finger upward, he stroked over her g-spot, while his thumb rolled her clit in a downward rotation.

Paige's resolve finally broke.

"Nate!" she screamed, her fists clawing frantically at the sheets as her body jerked under the waves of her orgasm. He grunted as he watched her body shudder, loving every jerk, bend and scratch she gave to him.

"Damn," was all he could muster as her body slowly calmed. He reached over to the nightstand to retrieve a condom, slipped it over his dick, and climbed over her. Looking down into her eyes, he cupped her cheek to speak the words that resonated within his heart.

"I love you, Paige. Always. My heart, body, and soul is yours forever."

With that, he dropped his hands to her hips to lift them up, and in one sharp movement, thrust deep within her. He held himself still as she tensed, trying to adjust herself to his size. Knowing he was larger than most women were comfortable with, he didn't want to hurt her with his eagerness.

"Are you ok?" he asked, his words choppy as he struggled to maintain his composure. Her pussy was so hot...so hot. She was clamping down on his dick like a vise grip...*Shit.*...

He felt her pussy spasm around him as she threw her legs high on his back. Her hands clawed at his arms as she twisted underneath him.

"Please, Nate. Please take me. Claim your pussy."

"Damn straight."

He fucked her with everything he had, plunging in and out to a rhythm as old as time, while she met his strokes with an urgency of her own.

"Yes, yes! Right there, oh! Right there! Keep stroking me." Paige murmured. Her words echoed in his head, and he was lost to the whirring of blood swirling in his brain.

"My pussy. My pussy. Mine. Mine." Nate chanted over and over, succumbing to the heat and slickness around him. His balls drew up once again toward his body, and he continued to stroke.

Knowing he wouldn't last much longer, he reached between them to stroke her clit with his thumb in the same rhythm as his plunging dick.

Paige exploded once again, crying his name once again. The quivering in her pussy finally pushed him over the edge as well. Sight and sound diminished as he felt himself lost in the orgasm of his life. His hips began to buck uncontrollably as he readied himself to release his seed deep within her body.

He groaned loudly as his cum splashed wetly inside the latex. *Damn, the condom might not hold up,* he thought absently as aftermath shudders racked his body.

Oh well, fuck it.

He laid his head on her shoulder as he struggled to get his breath under control. Finally, he slowly pulled out of her, catching her soft wince as he slid from her swollen folds.

"Are you ok?" he asked. *Please be ok.*

She smiled up at him, reaching up to stroke her hand over his facial hair, and then finally resting her hand on the nape of his neck. "I'm perfect. Everything is going to be ok, as long as you're by my side."

He rolled over to his side, removed the condom to toss it into the nearby wastebasket, and then pulled her back against his chest as he stroked her from breast to hip.

"And I'll never leave it, baby. You can count on me. You and your sister can both count on me." He kissed the back of her neck, tasting the salty sweat that covered her skin. "Get some rest for now. In a few hours, I'll make us some breakfast, then we'll get dressed to meet Lafayette, and see what he's discovered from the surveillance tapes. Hopefully sooner rather than later, we'll find your sister and this whole damn nightmare can be over. Then we'll plan on how we want to start our life together."

Paige nodded her head, indicating that she'd heard and comprehended his instruction. When she then snuggled deep within his arms, Nate felt like he, along with his dick, had finally won the title of being King of the World.

Chapter Thirteen

A few hours later, after another round of mind-blowing sex, they'd gotten dressed in preparation to head over to the Blackburn office. When Paige walked out of his bathroom dressed in a light, flowy blue sundress with a matching pinstriped jacket, he'd whistled long and hard at the image of seduction she portrayed.

There's definitely something to be said about a sexy, voluptuous woman wearing a dress that molds every curve of her figure, he thought, licking his lips as his heated gaze roamed her body.

"You are *Sexcellent*, my *Theia*. Just like that song by *Silk*," he stated. He smiled when she'd blushed under his praise, thanking him for the compliment. He figured if he reinforced his actions with words, she might one day believe him without any misgivings. Her confession about Isobel grated his nerves, justifying even more why he was glad he'd fired the incompetent wench. It also made him more determined than ever to put any insecurity Paige may still have to rest.

Soon after grabbing a quick breakfast of toast, scrambled eggs, and turkey bacon, they headed over to the Blackburn, LLC investigation firm. As he escorted Paige into the office, Nate felt tension rising back up.

Please let them have some answers, so we can put this shit behind us.

"Come on in." Lucas called, walking from the back to greet them in the small, unpretentious lobby. It was a functional and modest environment, with beige walls and furniture to match. The Blackburn brothers hadn't needed much space when they'd first transitioned to Houston from Los Angeles a few years back. After seeing Killian's skills as an astute Navy SEAL intelligence officer, the brothers decided to bring him on as a partner to help sift through the lucrative contracts that now came their way as a result of solving Holley and Asha's kidnapping.

102

Now, they were in process of expanding to a larger, more spacious area in downtown Houston to accommodate all three partners.

"Have a seat. Lafayette will be out in a minute." Lucas said. He gestured toward the sitting area, where Killian was already occupying one of the seats. Killian stood up as he nodded his head to them in greeting. Nate placed his hand on the small of Paige's back, leading her to one of the loveseats. After waiting for her to take a seat, he took the seat next to her while Killian reclaimed the chair he'd previously occupied.

"First off, let me just say how sorry I am about your club, man." Lucas stated as he took a seat next to Killian. "I know that business meant a lot to you."

Nate nodded his acceptance before speaking. "It did. Whoever the bastards are that thought they could scare me into shutting down has another fucking thing coming. I'm made of much stronger stock than that."

"I heard that." Killian supported. "Whoever the bastards were had to be feeling mighty scared that we were getting too close for comfort. It's the only explanation as to why they targeted the club."

"We know exactly who did this. It was the same motherfuckers who snatched Paige's sister. It was the Hunter Group. And now I'm gunning for their asses. I'll be damned if they fuck with what's mine, and think that they can get away with it scott free." Nate spat venomously.

"That's exactly what they think. And I'm also betting the reason why they're being so bold is because they have a lot of local help supporting them, mainly that Chief of Police we met last night." Lucas countered.

"Harrison," Paige murmured. "Yea, but he couldn't have caused that fire by himself. He had to have had help."

"Chief Harrison definitely had help." Lafayette confirmed as he walked in from the back of the office. Nate looked up, and then nodded his head in greeting. Lafayette nodded back, his lips pursed in grim determination as he walked toward them.

"Harmony is running late, but she forwarded me what she's discovered so far." He then tossed a manila folder to Killian, who caught it in mid-air, before looking intently at Paige. "Apparently word has already spread about your sister's kidnapping. Harmony is prepping a couple of her crew members to start surveillance on both you and Nate, to make sure their reach doesn't go any further." He then turned to Nate. "She's also sending someone up to Chicago to keep an eye on your mother."

Nate let out a small sigh of relief, letting out the breath he hadn't realized he'd been holding. "Thanks. I appreciate that more than you know."

"It looks like Harmony's got some really interesting details here," Killian mumbled as he flipped through the folder.

"What did she discover?" Lucas asked.

Killian pulled out a black and white still picture from the folder and then tossed it on the coffee table in front of them. Nate, Paige, and Lucas crowded around the table to get a better look at the still photo.

Nate narrowed his eyes as he studied the two figures displayed in the photograph. He then picked the picture up to get a closer inspection, before letting out a small growl.

"Is that my fucking security guard?" Nate asked incredulously.

Lafayette nodded his head. "It appears so." His eyes studied the two figures in the photo Nate held as he spoke, pointing to the stamped timer at the bottom of the picture. "These pictures were taken hours before the fire. Harmony was able to extract these stills from the security feeds she sent me." He paused before giving Nate a serious stare. "How well do you know this guy?" He frowned as he rephrased his question. "Better yet, how much of your business does he have access to?"

"He's my night manager and security officer. He's supposed to handle any incidences with party guests, help with inventory, and make sure the wait staff and disc jockey report for work timely."

"Does he have access to open and close your club?" Killian asked.

Nate shook his head. "No. Besides myself, only Rodriguez and Paige can do that." Nate studied the other shadowed figure in the photograph. "Who is this other guy talking to Tony?"

"That's what we were hoping you could tell us." Lucas stated. "The facial recognition software doesn't match against any of the databases Lafayette has access to. I wish we knew a good hacker that could do a deeper dive into identifying him. Harmony is reaching out to a couple of members on her team to see if they can decipher who he is, but for right now, we're at a loss."

Nate narrowed his eyes as he peered into the photograph once more. The other man in the photo wore a floor-length trench coat pulled tightly over his expanded mid-section. A black fedora hung low on his head, shielding his face from the security cameras' rooftop viewpoint. He was tall in stature, with wide, intimidating shoulders and a menacing stance. The man gave an ominous appearance, similar to Mickey Rourke's character in that movie *Sin City*.

Nate felt Paige shiver beside him. He turned to give her a questioning look, only to see her quickly lower her head in shame.

"God, I've been so distracted with all these other emotions, I almost lost sight of the real reason why I came back." Nate heard her mutter, the softly spoken words were so faint that he almost didn't hear them.

Except he did.

His gut clenched with anxiousness. He needed to make her see that being here with him served a dual purpose: Keeping her safe while they hunted for her sister, and then becoming his lady permanently.

And he was determined to win on both fronts.

"Do you think he had something to do with Rachelle's disappearance?" Paige whispered as she leaned into him, breaking into his wayward thoughts.

He twisted his lips as he thought about how to respond to her. He wanted to soothe her, but he didn't want to lie either. Instead, he grabbed her hand and tucked it inside his arm in an attempt to comfort her apprehension.

"It's a strong possibility, baby. That's what we're here to find out." When she nodded her head in understanding, he let out the breath he hadn't realized he'd been holding.

"So you don't recognize the other guy?" Killian asked.

Nate shook his head. "I've never seen him before. I sure as hell recognize Tony, though. Were they trying to break into my office?" Nate asked as his outrage bubbled back up to the surface.

Killian nodded his head. "It looks that way. What do you have stored in your office that they may want to take?"

Nate shook his head. "Nothing. I don't keep valuables in there, but I always keep the door locked. When I first opened the club, I hated people freely walking in and out of my office. I like my privacy, and the disturbances always broke my concentration when I tried to tally the receipts at the end of the night. So, I started locking the door. Now it's a habit. Only Paige and Rodriguez have a key to the office, just like with the outside doors."

"And how well do you know Gena?" Lucas posed the obvious question, raising a single eyebrow.

"I've known her for years. I trust her, just as much as I trust Paige. She was with me in the beginning when I first opened *Escapades*. She helped convince the previous owner to sell to me, even though he was really skeptical about selling to a "Northerner", as he liked to refer to me. She was his daughter, and she'd been bartending under him for a while before I came along." Nate shrugged. "She recognized it was time for some new management to rev up some excitement in the place. After I took over and rebranded the name, I gave her a raise to stay on with me. I also pay for her little boy to go to childcare while she works. She wouldn't betray me by trying to burn my place down."

Lucas nodded his head, seemingly satisfied with his answer. "Well, like I said, hopefully Harmony can come through with some of her guys to tell us who this other man is in the trench coat."

"I'm working on it." A feminine voice called out, prompting all eyes to turn in her direction.

Harmony walked in, looking cool and refined in a long t-shirt dress with a matching belt. Her long, brown hair fell in waves down her back as she walked over to the group.

Nate felt Paige stiffen beside him, and turned to look at her quizzingly. Then he remembered the reason for her discomfort. The last time she'd seen her, Harmony was trying to climb on top of his dick.

He turned and gave Paige a small wink. "Remember what I told you last night, baby. It was all a cover."

Paige's lips thinned before she slowly nodded her head. He felt some of her tension leave as her grip on his forearm lessened its tentacle hold.

A small part of him cheered that Paige's jealous flag was flying at high mast. Jealousy meant she cared about what he did, about who he was with, even if it was unfounded. Jealousy meant that after all these years, she cared about him, maybe just as much as he did for her.

And he was fucking obsessed with her.

Last night he'd gotten his first taste, and now he was addicted. More than addicted. What he really wanted to do was crawl inside her pussy, pitch a tent, throw down his *Land of Nate* declaration flagpole, and never leave.

He cleared his throat as he tried to bring his mind back to the present.

Harmony's intense brown eyes studied them as she walked closer. She nodded her head in Lucas' direction, before taking a seat next to Killian.

"Just got a great lead from one of my team members." Harmony said, pausing to make sure all eyes were on her. "The Ides of March is coming soon."

All eyes looked at her with blank stares.

"What does an old Shakespeare saying have to do with anything?" Lucas asked. He wasn't known for his patience.

"The Ides of March is the code name that HG is using to transition their latest batch of victims. It's giving notification to their buyers that the next auction date is scheduled for March 15."

"That's just a couple of weeks away." Paige said, worry tinged in every frown on her face.

Harmony nodded. "My contact told me that's the date when it will all go down. They've got some big wigs from out of the country coming to view the *merchandise*," she said, disgust evident in her voice. "This auction is going to one of the biggest these parts have seen for a while. And that's not all. Apparently my reputation has preceded me.

They've arranged to have that 'bratty, big mouth slut' included in the bidding as well."

Harmony smirked. "I'm being considered for auction, to supposedly teach me a *lesson*." She imitated air quotation marks.

She then turned to Nate, grinning mischievously. "I knew studying that reality star from *Real Housewives of Dallas* would pay off. I've become a total brat while you were gone. HG's plan to take me is just the break we need."

Killian nodded his head. "Good looking out, Harmony. We'll be ready as well."

Nate stared around the room, feeling his stomach roll. He just wanted this shit to be over. Moving to Texas was supposed to better his life, not make it more complicated. He felt Paige grip his arm, feeling the slight tremor in her hold.

I'll find a way to finish this once and for all, he thought glumly.
For us.

Chapter Fourteen

Alderman Conrad Spivey paced the confined quarters of his Chicago Westside campaign office. Glancing at the clock, he let out a huff of frustration, before finally walking back to his desk. Irritation fueled his movements as he picked up his cell phone. After pulling up his contacts, he pushed the button to trigger the call.

"Where the hell are you?" Conrad barked into the receiver. "You were supposed to be here an hour ago!"

"I'm here already, man. Relax." A large, burly figure stated as he walked into Conrad's office. He clicked on the button to end the call before facing the Alderman.

Conrad eyed the visitor with both relief and anxiousness. His eyes swept over the man's dark attire and floor-length trench coat.

"And what the hell do you have on? You look like fucking Indiana Jones." He observed distractedly. The man's appearance always made him cringe. He wished he could bottle and sell his stylish flare to give the man a fashion clue. A man was nothing if he didn't know how to dress to impress.

"Clothes, asshole." His visitor shook his head, removing the fedora from his head. "Don't come bitching to me about my wardrobe. That flight was long as hell, I'm tired as fuck, and I don't want to hear your shit right now."

Conrad rolled his eyes as he sat down at his desk. He nodded for his visitor to do the same, as they both sat back and crossed their legs in front of them.

After a moment of silence, Conrad let out an exasperated huff, throwing his hands in the air. "Well? Tell me what the hell is going on, Gerry!"

Gerry shook his head, annoyance lining his dark, weather-lined face. "That fucking waitress came in before I got a chance to switch out the last of the surveillance tapes. She must be new, because I've never heard Tony talk about her before."

Conrad narrowed his eyes as a sudden dark thought came to mind. "What did she look like?"

Gerry shrugged. "White girl, long brown hair, weird brown eyes, really short."

Conrad contemplated for a moment before shaking his head. "No, the girl Danny snatched a few month's ago had red hair and a lot of tattoos. I thought maybe for a moment that Nate was finally trying to smarten up and put some decoys in his place, but that doesn't sound like her."

"No, this woman didn't have any tats. She was kind of cute, though. If I thought I'd had enough time, I would've snatched her and tried her out first before we turn her over to the buyers coming in a few weeks." Gerry sneered as he loudly cracked his knuckles together. "I love testing out new, older merchandise. Tony told me her attitude is just what a couple of our buyers are looking for: a rebellious spirit to break. My type of woman."

Conrad rolled his eyes. "I'm glad you didn't *take the time* to indulge. We've already got one spirited female in stock. Do we really need two?"

"You can never have too many. Besides, it's good to have a variety for the buyers to select from. Rachelle's like a bit of milk chocolate. This girl would be like sweet vanilla cream. Hell, with any luck, maybe we can score selling them both to a buyer that likes to make Oreo sandwiches." Gerry chuckled at his own perverse humor.

"Get serious. We've done a good job keeping tabs on all of Nate's contacts since he moved to Texas. Leave that girl alone. Pick up that other piece of merchandise we discussed earlier instead. We can't fuck this up."

Gerry nodded his head at his brother, his smile dying on his face. "We won't. Unfortunately the fire didn't do enough damage before Harrison got there. He had to do some damage control. The fucking fire marshal was about to declare arson before he took care of it."

110

Gerry then let out a snarl. "And according to Tony, that idiot cop let it slip that someone was watching Nate's business. I should go back down there and take care of him right now. I could say I was following up on a case for CPD." Gerry also worked as a homicide detective for the Chicago Police Department. His accessibility into other city department's case files made it conveniently easy to detect whenever someone was sniffing too close to where they shouldn't be.

Conrad shook his head. "No, it's not time for that yet, brother. He'll get what's coming to him." He shrugged his thinly muscled shoulder. "Or maybe someone will take care of him for us. They did with Dan Stevens."

Gerry sat back in his chair, folding his thick weathered fingers across his wide mid-section. "You might be right. If not, I'll show him what the end of a .45 looks like."

Conrad smiled knowingly. "I bet you will."

Gerry just nodded, a grim look of determination crossing his features.

Conrad then let out a small, frustrated sigh. "It's just hard not to worry when Nate is still walking around. That man is a walking, breathing piece of evidence I can't afford to let get out. This is election year, for both the Mayor and me. I promised him we'd take care of this, and I need to be able to deliver. I've been trying to pacify him, portraying the face of the cool and collected hand of Caesar whenever we meet, but that won't hold up for long. If Penne loses it, we're both dead. We need to make sure this goes away, for good this time." He worriedly wrung his bony knuckles together.

Gerry stared intently at his younger brother. "I told Momma I would look out for you, and I have so far, haven't I? Don't worry, I got this. *We* got this."

Conrad felt his breath slowing as calmness penetrated his brain. His big brother had always been able to quiet him down. To make him feel safe, and talk him off the ledge.

"Besides, I know if I don't take care of it, our partners in South America will try to do it themselves. And I'll be damned if I let outsiders come here and try to dictate how we run operations in our own house."

Gerry snorted in disgust. "We didn't say anything about how they almost fucked up that Beijing operation a few years back. Leaving the little girl they'd killed out in the open like that for that Navy Seal to find was just plain fucking stupid. They put the whole goddamn operation at risk. I'll be damned if they come here and try to stick their noses in our business."

Conrad nodded his head, his eyes rolling to the ceiling as his thoughts roamed. "Agreed. We can't afford any fuckups. Not this close in the game. The *Ides of March* is almost here. We're going to make several hundred million from this sale. Then we can lay low for awhile, maybe regroup and strategize on other possible location markets, and infiltrate into a new, more dense population pool."

He leaned forward again to study his brother. "That fuckup with Holley also has the Mayor and me reconsidering our strategy in how we obtain new merchandise. Right now our discovery exploits are too random, too risky. We might have a cleaner, more seamless transition, if we solely concentrate on dense, inner city areas with a high runaway population. Nobody would even notice, or care for that matter, if a person went missing. The Mayor told me about some of the troubles he ran into involving babies when he first got in the game. He's agreed that waiting until the merchandise has aged a few years is a much cleaner way to go."

He then shrugged a thin, careless shoulder. "Our clients seem to like that age better as well."

Gerry perked up at that bit of news. "How about starting up a site in Los Angeles? I heard they have a pretty high teen runaway population."

Conrad thought about that possibility. "Maybe. We'll see. In any case, we can't even think about transferring the Houston branch until after the Ides of March."

Gerry nodded. "Understood."

Still feeling restless, Conrad stood and began to pace. His nerves were still on edge. He and the Mayor had too much riding with this auction. It could either go extremely well, where he, his brother, and the Mayor could be sitting pretty for years to come, or it could all go to hell in the blink of an eye.

All because of Nate Fucking Kerr.

"Dammit. We need to take care of Nate before the *Ides*." Conrad repeated, his anxiety once again overwhelming his sense of reason. "I think there's just too much at stake to just let him walk around like he is. He's still a loose end, and I want it burned. It's why I had you plant those drugs in his car all those years ago. We tried to get him convicted and sent to Statesville prison down there in Joliet until he finally died of old age." He growled in irritation. "Wouldn't you know that the one time the fucking justice system worked right was when we didn't want it to? The bastard's charges got dropped. And then when he turned around and sued the city..."

Gerry nodded his head in complete understanding. "I thought the Mayor was going to have a fucking heart attack, for sure. Both of you thought it would come out then that you had his brother Darrick killed." He shook his head negligently. "But we couldn't get rid of him at that point. Two murders in the same family that close together would have looked too suspicious. We would've gotten more press than we needed at the time."

Conrad grimaced. "And now, the bastard is still causing problems." He stopped pacing and turned sharply, his eyes unwavering. "He needs to go away. Permanently. I think he knows something. I think that's why he took that trip to Chicago. I think that prior trip to Detroit was just a farce, something to throw us off his scent."

Gerry pursed his lips. "That warning visit I gave to his mother should've been a clue." He paused. "I can send another one if you want. A more permanent calling card."

Conrad shook his head. "No, let's not give Nate another reason to visit Chicago. Let's keep him in Texas. We can take care of him from there." He then smiled wickedly, an evil glint catching his eye as he spread his arms across his chest, like a bird expanding its wings. "After all, our hands span across the whole fucking country."

Chapter Fifteen

"Come on, little Celine. Just let me make it a few more miles until I get to the office. Then you can stop kicking my bladder and let me use the washroom so we can both get some relief." Terri murmured as she patted her rounded belly. She then smiled as she felt the pronounced kick against her abdomen, her baby's response in being told to be patient.

"I think you've got a little too much of your father in you, little girl. I said *wait*."

She chuckled as she pulled into the parking lot where her office was located. After parking her truck, she retrieved her designer tote bag from the backseat, and then proceeded to walk inside as she absently rubbed her stomach. She'd secretly begun addressing her new bundle of joy by the name of *Celine,* hoping and praying that God would bless her with a little girl, despite what the lab technician predicted. Although she naturally wanted her baby to also be healthy, she also secretly desired a little girl. She wanted to bestow all of the love she felt for her sister into her tiny bundle of joy.

And if she believed hard enough, anything could happen. Her Master convinced her of that.

She snorted softly to herself as she thought of Levi's ironclad belief that she would deliver a bouncing baby boy, simply because he willed it to be so. Every time he rubbed her belly, he would lean down and whisper next to her stomach, "Your Papa is so excited to meet you, little Zion. My strong baby boy."

She would just have to silently agree to disagree with him on this one.

After getting off the elevators, she threw a hand of acknowledgement toward her receptionist's direction, before hurrying past her toward her office. Switching on the light, she threw her purse on top of her desk, and then rushed over to the adjoining bathroom to relieve her bladder.

114

"Yeeesss..." Terri exhaled, feeling relief of the pressure she'd been holding for the past 30 minutes.

After washing her hands, she walked back into her office to find her receptionist and friend both grinning knowingly back at her.

"Little Zion giving you problems this morning, eh?" Kay acknowledged.

Terri rubbed her belly, once again mentally apologizing to her baby for people addressing her by the wrong name. "Oh my god, yes. It seems like I'm pissing up Lake Houston every hour. It's getting ridiculous." Terri exhaled after plopping down in her seat.

Holley laughed in her direction. "Don't worry, little mama. You're in your last trimester. It's supposed to be easy sailing from here."

Terri snorted, lifting one of her hands to flap together, like she was imitating a quacking duck. "I hear you talking. I also know it's harder to sleep, because I can't roll on my stomach like I used to. I'm tired and cranky and can't seem to stop eating."

She then looked lovingly down at her stomach. "But in between the cookie cravings and the late night trips to *House of Fries*, I have completely fallen in love with this little hormone wrecker."

"Ooh...I can't wait until the baby gets here." Kay exclaimed as she clasped her hands together. "I haven't had grandchildren to play with since my son and his family moved to Arizona. It will be wonderful to spoil a new little honeypot. And anytime you and Levi need a break, you let me know."

Terri nodded her head, smiling at her boisterous, caring friend. "Thank you, Kay. Did anything come today that I need to be aware of?"

Kay nodded toward her open mail basket. "I put everything in your bin there. Some notices from the NPO, a certified letter from Mr. Salzmann, and one legal notice. It was just addressed to Ms. Terri Cortes." She shrugged her shoulders. "Strange. I thought everyone knew you'd gotten married a few years ago."

Terri shrugged, unconcerned. "We kept the name *Cortes Marketing,* remember? I'm sure whoever sent it just wasn't aware."

"Well, let me know if you need anything else." She winked at her before walking out of the office to return to the reception area.

Holley smiled indulgently in her direction. "Just so you know, we're having lunch catered in today. A driver from the Cheesecake Factory should be here around noon. I know how much you love their Shepard's Pie and Oreo cheesecake."

Terri sighed as she glanced at her hips. "She just doesn't care about how wide you're getting, but we love her just the same."

Holley laughed outright. "You'll be fine. Your glow is radiant, and that killer body will snap back into shape in no time, you'll see." With that she gave her a quick wink before leaving to return to her own office.

Yumm...Shepard's Pie and an Oreo Dream Extreme slice of cheesecake. Terri salivated.

With a half smile, she absently picked up the legal notice Kay had referred to. Glancing at the return address, she noticed the large manila envelope had been sent by an attorney's office from her hometown of Vicksburg, Mississippi. Curious, she ripped open the seal, pulled out the introductory letter, and began to read.

If she weren't already seated, she would have fallen to the floor.

She reread the contents again, disbelief and confusion surmounting every following thought and action. Her heart felt like it was going to jump straight out of her chest.

The letter confirmed that the firm contacting her was the acting legal representation for a Mr. Samuel Cortes.

Her father.

Terri's hands began to tremble as she held the document, her ears thumping to the white noise that surrounded her brain. Tears blurred her vision as the grief she thought she'd buried long ago came roaring to the surface. Wiping the tears from her face, she took a deep breath as she tried to focus in on the letter once again.

Dear Ms. Terri Cortes,

We are sorry to inform you that your father, Mr. Samuel Cortes of 202 Railroad Avenue, Vicksburg, Mississippi 39180, passed away quietly

*in his sleep on Friday, January 29th, 2016. Prior to his death, he
contacted our office and asked that we act as the Executor of his Estate.*

*Mr. Cortes left specific instruction in the event of his death, which
is outlined in the attached notarized copy of his Last Will and Testament
for your review. We have also included a copy of a letter he also
requested be included with this notification.*

Our condolences go out to you and your family.

Sincerely,
Robert J. Morris, Esq.

If you have any questions, please contact our office at....

Terri's lower lip began to tremble as she fought off the urge to
scream in anger and despair. There'd been so much that had never been
settled between her and her father. So much pain and agony.

*Papá is gone...*Terri thought, still in disbelief.

A huge, gaping hole began to settle in her chest, as regret filled
her soul. She rubbed a shaky hand absently over her stomach.

You'll never get to meet your el abuelo Celine, she whispered,
tears streaming silently down her face. The finality of the words she'd
just spoken caused even bigger tears to swell and escape from her lids.

Wiping a hand across her face, she placed the lawyer's memo on
her desk, and then reached inside the large envelope to pull out the sealed
letter addressed to her attention. Tearing apart the seal, she began to read.

Mi querido Terri,

*I don't know quite where to begin, but I wanted to start this letter
to you by first telling you that I am sorry. I'm so sorry for how I've
treated you all these years. I humbly ask, no beg, for your forgiveness.*

*Let me also begin by letting you know that I've always known that
you're my daughter. My blind hatred for your mother, along with my
grief for Marcelina, caused me to make you a victim of my rage as well.
I'm so sorry, mi angél. I'm sorry I lost my way.*

I can never forgive myself for isolating you like I did. The guilt and pain has lived with me until my last breath. One daughter has already died, and I killed the other with my words and neglect.

I want you to know that your mother and I have not been together for several years now. Paulina left me shortly after your last visit to Vicksburg, after finally giving up on trying to steal my inheritance. I am alone with my thoughts as I write this letter; which has given me the time I needed to finally come clean and to try and appease my sins.

I was diagnosed with pancreatic cancer about six months ago. If you're reading this letter, know that I choose to forgo any treatment or remedy that the doctors recommended to me, and I am now at peace. I believe my suffering is the penance for my sins, and I choose this path to try to become whole again. I ask the Heavenly Father's forgiveness, as well as yours.

As you know, the estate your mother was trying to steal was my inheritance, left to me from my abuelo, your bisabuelo. I knew what your mother was doing, but my stubbornness and pride wouldn't allow me to rid myself of her selfishness. Instead, I allowed our poisonous relationship to spill over into other aspects of my life.

I can, however, try to make amends to you, my last blood.

I am leaving you with the remainder of my inheritance passed down to me, estimated by the last assessment I had completed at roughly three point four million dollars. I had the money stored in an offshore account in Marcelina's name only, but I amended that authorization so that you also now have access. I can admit now that my foolish pride made me enjoy holding on to that money, instead of spending it. I'm ashamed of the satisfaction I relished at the expense of your mother.

I pray that your heart can be open enough to put this gift to use. If not, can you please set it aside for your future children? Or perhaps your children's children, if you find yourself unable to forgive me at this time. Maybe one day they'll be able to prosper from this wealth. It would make this old man extremely grateful as he passes on to a new eternal life.

I understand that my actions have caused you so much pain, both physically and emotionally, and that you may not have it in your heart to forgive. I understand, more than you know. Again, I am so sorry. I love you, my beautiful Terri. Hija preciosa. *My precious daughter.*

Love eternally,

Your Papá

Unable to hold on to her reactions any longer, Terri let out a pain-filled cry, throwing her head back against the back of the chair as she shook with emotion.

Footsteps quickly sounded in the hall, as Holley quickly reappeared in the doorway to see what all the commotion was about. Upon seeing Terri's grief-stricken face, Holley rushed to her side and knelt down beside her chair. She pulled Terri in her arms as she rocked her grieving, anguish-filled friend.

"What is it, love? What's the matter? You were fine fifteen minutes ago. What's happened?" Holley asked, her voice full of panic as she tried to wipe Terri's tears. The rush of wetness still continued to flow down Terri's cheeks, despite her efforts.

"It's my Papá..." Terri said, her voice strained with emotion. She pointed to the letter that had fallen out of her hands onto her desk. "It's a notification letter from his attorney. He's.... he's dead!"

Another painful blast of realization hit Terri square in her chest.

"Oh God, he's dead! Oh God! Oh God! HE'S DEAD AND I NEVER GOT THE CHANCE TO SAY GOODBYE!" She screamed to the top of her lungs, before collapsing back into Holley's arms. Painful sobs wretched from her chest as she struggled to control her gasps.

"I need Levi. Please, Holley! Please call my Master. I need my husband!"

"Of course, sweetheart. Of course you do."

Chapter Sixteen

Nate awoke to the musical chime of his ringing cell phone. Rolling over, he gently removed Paige's head from his shoulder before reaching over to grab his cell from the nightstand. Glancing at the caller id, he knew immediately that this was the call he'd been waiting for since last night.

Everyone continued to brainstorm in the Blackburn's office well into the late afternoon hours yesterday, trying to figure out a strategy that could predict HG's next move. After learning of Paige's sister, Harmony and Lucas decided that expanding their current recon team might be a good idea. Killian agreed, especially when the disappearance of Rachelle made the urgency to disband HG's reign increase expeditiously.

Killian then decided to call in the best men he knew, Tyson and Reid, to join in on their discussion.

After the two men had arrived, Killian explained how they would need as many street ears to the ground as possible, and that Tyson and Reid were their best offense with underground intel. It seemed even Harmony's reach was limited compared to the data Killian's childhood friends could extract. Tyson and Reid had been eager to assist in bringing down HG's operation, especially since they knew HG had taken Rachelle. They considered Detroit *their* territory, and felt personally insulted that HG dared to invade into their terrain. Harmony then provided them the name of one of her undercover agents that they could filter information to undetected.

After agreeing to meet once again after they'd gained some insight into HG's next move, the group dispersed. He and Paige had arrived back at his place, after grabbing a quick bite to eat, to wait for further instruction. Nate had helplessly watched Paige tremble with anxiety all day. She'd listened to their discussions and strategies with wide, shock-filled eyes, her golden stare unfocused in the distance as she sat in silence. Nate knew Paige's thoughts had been on her sister, and that she was silently torturing herself as to what Rachelle could potentially be going through. Wanting to comfort and reassure her that he would be there every step of the way until Rachelle was found, they'd lost themselves once again in the safety of each other's arms, until they both fell into a coma-like sleep.

He shook his head as he brought his attention back to his phone call.

"Nate speaking." His scratchy voice called over the speaker. Rubbing his face to wipe away the last remnants of sleep, he glanced over to his right to see Paige still fast asleep next to him. She was flat on her stomach, her body relaxed as she breathed deeply in her slumber. Her long legs were slightly parted, and her head was turned to face him. One of her arms was draped possessively across his bicep, as if she'd reached out to him in her sleep to hold on tight. His orange, silk sheet had slipped away from her frame during the night, revealing her heart-shaped ass as it poked up from the mattress.

That ass was calling to him now, inviting his fingers to mold themselves along its curve, to relish in its softness, to drag his tongue along the valley separating each globe...

"Nate, this is Killian. I just heard from Tyson, man. The word is out. The auction date is finalized." He snorted in disgust. "They're calling it the Ides of March, not only because it's happening on the 15th of March, but because someone who calls himself Caesar is running the operation. Can you believe it? It's supposed to be symbolic. The head of the Northern HG believes that death should come to any woman who doesn't recognize a man's authority."

Nate grimaced as he removed himself from the bed. He didn't want Paige to accidently ear hustle on any of this conversation. She was already in a panicked state, and rightly so. Hearing about how her sister's tormentors intended to punish strong, independent women who didn't succumb to threats would not do Paige any good at this point.

He walked out of his bedroom into his hall, adjusting the phone to his ear.

"So March 15 is definitely the day?" Nate asked.

"Yes, and that's not the kicker." Killian paused for a moment. "Tyson told me they found out that HG is planning on using your club to hold the auction. I'll bet any amount of money that your club has been the focal point all along. I'm also willing to bet that whatever past HG activity has occurred in the Houston area, your club has been involved. It's probably why that fire was set, to distract attention, and to have the place shut down for repairs until after the auction. The tapes Harmony extracted already showed Tony as an accomplice to some shady activity. She's still investigating that other person, though. She's waiting on a callback."

Nate bristled as Killian's words resonated with him. Once again, it seemed as if he'd been set up to be the scapegoat for someone else's bullshit. It was his worst nightmare all over again; just like the time he'd been accused of those trumped up charges years ago back in Chicago.

His nostrils flared angrily. He'd beaten those charges then, and he was damned determined to beat whatever bullshit was circling around him now. He gritted his teeth, willing his mind to stay focused on the conversation at hand.

"In the meantime," Killian continued. "Harmony has been continuing to keep an eye on Tony. She followed him and his girlfriend last night to a bar off Brazos Street, and thinks it's a good possibility that HG will target her. She overheard Tony telling that Isobel girl how Harmony needed to learn some *proper behavior*, as he called it."

"Great. That's good to know."

Nate gripped the phone a little tighter as he thought about whatever horrors Rachelle could possibly be facing. They needed to find her, and fast.

Killian let out an exaggerated breath. "We have to bet that Harmony can be picked up. It looks like it's our best shot on penetrating the operation from within. Then, while she's undercover, she can help identify if Rachelle is a part of this last auction. She can also give us assistance from the inside to help release the other girls that are being held."

"Agreed." Nate paused. "Hey, thanks Killian for calling with this information."

"Not a problem. These assholes have caused more than their share of pain and grief to numerous families around the world. I can't wait to take down every single one of these motherfuckers."

Nate nodded his head at the phone, oblivious to the fact that Killian couldn't see him. "Absolutely."

He disconnected the call and stared blankly into the distance. He needed to let Paige know what was going on, but how could he phrase it in a way that wouldn't make her panic?

"Any news right now, except for the words *your sister is free* is not going to come lightly. So be a man and suck it up, Kerr," he muttered to himself.

Pushing his shoulders back in an all-too familiar, man-up fashion, he walked back into his bedroom to find Paige wide-awake. She sat upright waiting for him in the middle of his bed, her face a blank mask.

"Tell me what's going on, Nate." She said softly.

Nate searched her face for signs of distress. After Paige slowly raised an expected eyebrow in his direction, he smiled slightly as he moved toward her. The bed sheet had fallen into her lap while she sat Indian-style, openly displaying her mouth-watering breasts to his hungry gaze.

God, she was so beautiful...

"You are so beautiful," his voice echoed. He couldn't tear his eyes away from her.

Paige smiled in his direction, before shaking her head. "Nice try, Mister. You can't distract me with flattery this time. Who was that on the phone? Did they tell you anything about what's going on with Rachelle?"

Nate nodded. "That was Killian. The auction set up for March 15th is a go. Apparently it's supposed to happen at my club. He thinks they may have used the fire as a distraction to get rid of people so there wouldn't be any witnesses while they set up the sale. Harmony's getting things set up to try and infiltrate their group. If she can get in, she'll be able to identify your sister, as well as the rest of the hostages, and help to get them out of there."

Paige frowned. "Set up how?"

"I told you, baby, she's FBI. She has training. She's posing undercover to paint herself up as a good kidnapping candidate."

Paige wrinkled her nose. "I know you've said that. But I also remember you telling me that HG likes to focus for the most part on younger girls. Isn't Harmony too old to gain their interest?"

"It's her behavior that will gain their interest." He didn't want to remind her that it was also Rachelle's behavior that made her a target as well. "We're hoping she's putting out the same vibes that your sister did before she was snatched. Young girls are the main course for these predators. However a nice, belligerent female that they can break would be a nice dessert. Something to smack their lips with."

Paige visibly shivered at his words.

Cursing himself for being too blunt, he crawled over the top of the bed to pull Paige in his arms.

"We'll find her, Goldilocks. I promise you that."

Paige stroked his chest, her slim fingers playing in his soft, curly chest hair as she pressed a soft kiss to the side of his neck.

"I know you will. And from what you've told me of your friends, I know they won't stop until Rachelle is back where she belongs."

Chapter Seventeen

"I feel so bad for Terri. She's hurting something awful." Asha murmured as she walked into the great room to join her husband. "I know she and her father had a strained relationship, but I also know she didn't want it to end without at least trying to reconcile some of the broken pieces of their relationship."

Delphi nodded as he reached out his hand to pull his wife closer to him.

"I just spoke with Levi. He said it's been rough for her, but that she's managing. Terri's strong. She just needs some time." He wrapped his wife in his arms, relishing in the feel of her within his grasp. "And he specifically told me to tell you to let him console his wife first, before you go busting in over there." He bent his head to playfully nudge the side of her face with his nose.

Asha smiled ruefully. "Busting in? I wouldn't describe it quite like that. I would call it going over to lend a supportive shoulder for my best friend."

"Regardless, he said it's his time to be her rock against the storm right now."

Asha let out a huff as she rolled her hazel eyes to the ceiling. "I know. It's just hard to stay still when I know she's hurting."

"I know, *meu coracao*. However the best thing for Terri right now is the love, security, and protection that her husband can bring. Once Levi has given the green light, I will drive you over to their place myself." Delphi promised, running his nose across the top of Asha's head.

"You're distracting me," Asha said, sighing as she felt her husband's hand run across the small of her back. Delphi then raised the bottom of her silk blouse to run his fingers lightly across her skin. "I can't think straight when you touch me like that. You know my back is sensitive."

"I know," he whispered, before placing a light kiss on the nape of her neck. He then traced the tip of his tongue lightly along the curve, lighting up every sensitive nerve along its wake.

"Jaymes..." She shivered as she moaned his name.

He quickly dropped his hand and pulled away from her, giving her a condensing frown.

Asha lifted the corner of her mouth knowingly, before bending her head slightly in his direction, giving him the honor that was his due as her Master. "I apologize, Sir Jaymes, my Nubian King."

"Much better." Delphi replied, before spinning her around and grabbing her waist. He lifted her easily, placing her legs around his lean waist as she locked her ankles together. He then walked them backwards toward the fireplace, where he'd already started a small, kindling fire.

Lowering them both slowing to the floor, he captured Asha's mouth in a hungry kiss as he laid her down on the plush carpet. He hummed with satisfaction at her body's automatic softening toward his touch. It amazed him that every time he tasted her lips, he felt like he'd died and gone to heaven all over again.

He couldn't get enough of her.

Would never get enough of her.

Itching to touch more of her softness, Delphi ran his hand along the slim line of her waist. Even with her hectic singing schedule, as well as also delivering three children into this world, Asha still managed to maintain the body of a sultry seductress, putting most twenty-year olds to shame. Her hips were shapely and luscious, solidifying the fact that his wife was still in her sexual prime. Her plump, ample breasts beckoned him to have a taste. And that pussy...

He ran his hand slowly over her breasts, caressed the taunt skin of her stomach, before finally lowering it to massage the plumpness of her sex through the skin-tight leggings.

Upon hearing her gasp of pleasure, he grinned mischievously into the side of her neck. He loved how responsive she was, and savored the fact that only he got to trigger that reaction from her. On more than one occasion, he'd been forced to exude his position to overly excited male admirers. He'd been astounded, then irritatingly annoyed, at the sheer number of misguided fans who mistakenly believed they had a chance at seducing *The Painted Lady*, just as she'd seduced them with her music.

The territorial *King Lion* in him had come out more times than he was comfortable admitting. After a few encounters with some overeager admirers, her fans were now well aware that the muscled 6 foot, 7 inch muse for the *Lady's* lyrics didn't take kindly to strangers pawing his wife. Having Tyson and Reid as her permanent bodyguards whenever she had to tour had been both a blessing and a soothing balm to his itchy 'punch first, ask questions later' trigger.

Bringing his attention back to his wife, he let his eyes rake adoringly over her face. "I love you, *meu coracao,"* he said as he bent down to brush his lips along her jawline.

"My heart." He repeated. "You and the kids are my life. I can only imagine Terri's pain. Although I'm sure it's different for a parent, I don't know what I would've done if I hadn't found you again."

Emotion ripped his heart at the thought that he'd almost lost her. Not once, not twice, but three times. Once due to his own stupidity, another at the hands of her ex-husband, and the final blow was due to his deranged ex. Times had not always been easy for the two of them; but through it all, they'd always found a way back to each other.

And they always will.

Asha cupped her hand along his cheek, her fingers lightly grazing against his beard. He closed his eyes as he savored her touch.

"I love you too, My Sir. Always." She then craned her head to run her tongue along the outline of his full lips, causing him to shred his feelings of melancholy and replace them with instant lust. Heat caused his blood to sizzle, making his dick stiffen at the thought of that same tongue running along the pulsing veins of his cock.

"Little one, I have something specifically made for that mouth of yours."

She smiled at him cockily. "Do you now?"

"Damn right. How about a little taste test right here?"

^^^

Asha stared lovingly up at her husband. The man never ceased to make her heart race with his breathtaking good looks. Those blue-green eyes alone were enough to make her panties drip with moisture.

She shook her head as she smirked mockingly back at him. When her husband got his freak on, he also had a habit of becoming incredibly tunnel focused. He was forgetting one important detail.

"I'd love to savor the sweet taste of your delicious dick in my mouth, my beautiful husband." She whispered huskily. She smiled when she felt his member jerk against the damped folds of her leggings. Her husband did love his dirty talk. "However, might I suggest that the taste test wait until after I check in with our daughter? She's still up. I told her to brush her teeth and braid her hair before I put her to bed for the night."

Delphi let out a loud, frustrated groan, before rubbing his pelvis against her heated core. *Damn*, Asha thought. The smirk quickly left her face, replaced by heated desire. *I know exactly how you feel.*

He then placed a light kiss on her nose, before standing back up. He lowered his hand to assist her from the floor, and then playfully swatted her ass.

"Go and take care of my daughter. She asked me earlier if you could tuck her in bed instead of me this time. She said she didn't want you to feel like you were being left out, since she spent such long periods in *Daddy time*," he chuckled.

Asha grinned as she shook her head. "I resigned myself to the fact that Jayme is a Daddy's girl a long time ago. I love it. A girl needs to have the love of her Daddy to know how her future husband should treat her."

A shadowed thought came over her as she thought about her own father. It saddened her that she would never get a chance to meet him, since he'd died before she ever got a chance to get to know him better.

Shaking off her remorse, she smiled. "I love it. In fact, I'll make sure to tell her that when I sing her favorite bedtime song tonight, just in case she's honestly worried about it."

Delphi nodded as he leaned over to run his fingers along her jaw. "That's my girl. And when you're done, come back here. We have unfinished business we need to handle."

Asha winked as she walked out of the room, her hips swaying seductively in her wake. Upon hearing her husband's low growl, she laughed softly to herself. She knew full well the fire she was causing within him, and savored every minute of it.

Humming softly to herself, she strolled down the great hall toward Jayme's room. The hallway was dark, and she felt a slight breeze drifted around her bare feet as she walked.

Frowning, she tried to remember if she'd accidently left a window open. Glancing at the wide bench seat that sat underneath the large bay window near the foyer, she confirmed the bottom panes were indeed closed shut.

Asha's frown deepened as she reached Jayme's room. Her daughter's door was shut. Lately Jayme hardly ever left her room door closed, insisting that she needed the hall lightening as well as her nightlight to make sure the evil vampires from that *Underworld* movie didn't attack her.

She shook her head as she turned the bedroom knob. She'd given both Alanna and Austin hell for scaring their youngest sister a few weeks ago when the two came home for a weekend visit. They'd forgotten that Jayme liked to sneak out of her room at night, turning herself into a midnight cookie thief when she thought no one would notice. The sneaky little girl had screamed bloody murder when she'd walked into the kitchen to see Alanna and Austin having an *Underworld* movie marathon on the mounted wall television set above the breakfast nook. The vampires had frightened her so much; it took a full week to convince Jayme to go back to sleeping in her own bed.

So why was her door closed now?

Asha erased the frown lines on her face, and replaced them with a smile. She didn't want to alarm Jayme unnecessarily. She then opened the door.

And felt her breath leave her body like a bolt of lightning.

There was broken glass everywhere she looked. Jayme's books, stuffed animals, and Leapfrog games, previously stored neatly in her book cabinet earlier in the evening, were now strolled carelessly all over the floor. The Minion lamp her father had given her for her birthday lay broken next to the open window.

A window Asha knew for certain had earlier been closed.

Asha's terrified eyes quickly moved over to Jayme's bed, her feet frantically following. She strained to hear any sort of sound coming from her daughter's bed, but only silence greeted her. Her heart dreaded to acknowledge what her eyes and ears were screaming at her. Ripping the sheet covers from the bed, Asha's heart came to a complete stop.

And she let out a blood-curdling scream.

Jayme was gone.

Chapter Eighteen

"And you think HG is behind my daughter's kidnapping?" Delphi roared, his temper barely in check.

Killian nodded grimly at his brother-in-law. "Jay-Jay's disappearance screams retaliation to me." He then turned to his sister. "You're sure you've checked all over the house? I know sometimes she likes to play hide and seek."

Asha nodded her head, her shocked, teary-eyed expression panged Nate deep within his chest. It killed him that his friend was faced with yet again another tragedy in her life. She'd suffered enough already.

Grinding his teeth together, Nate felt his own blood pressure boiling. Volcanic rage over the injustice of it all threatened to choke his very breath away.

And to top everything off, there was a cop in the room. Cops spelled trouble. He felt his back straighten in an all-too familiar predatory stance as he sized the grey-eyed police officer talking quietly with Harmony. His gaze then slid protectively over to Paige when she came in close proximity to the officer as she walked over to Asha.

"I'm so sorry HG has targeted your daughter, Asha. We'll get her back, just like we're going to get my sister. You're not alone in this fight," Paige said, wrapping a supporting arm around her shoulders.

"That's right. From what the Blackburn twins have discovered, I think it's best that we don't call in the local authorities just yet." Officer Ron Jolsten surmised when he heard Paige's comments. He turned back to Harmony. "And from what you've also shared, my Commanding Officer is also questionable at this point?"

Harmony nodded her head in confirmation. "The FBI has been on to Harrison for awhile. Lucky for us, the Chief has gotten too comfortable over the years. I really think he believes he's unstoppable.

Those careless words he'd tossed when Nate's place was burning pretty much sealed his fate."

"And what makes us so sure we can trust *this* cop?" Nate spit as he continued to size Jolsten up. "After all, his C.O. is dirty. This guy could be just as grimy."

Asha pinned Nate with a blistering stare. "Ron Jolsten is more than trustworthy. He's been there for me more times than you could possibly imagine. I trust him. And so should you."

"But how do you know for *sure*?" Nate continued. He wouldn't want to take the chance that his friends might suffer the same negative experiences that he's had over his life. Their daughter was at stake, along with his sister-in-law.

He shook his head slightly. Future sister-in-law. *What the hell kind of thought was that?*

Killian placed a hand on Nate's shoulder, obviously sensing the tenseness in his stance. "Jolsten is the real thing, believe me. He's one of the good guys. Unlike his boss, he's here to help."

"I know a way he can fucking help! He can help by bum rushing that motherfucker Harrison to get him to say where the fuck the girls are being kept!" Delphi roared, his expression thunderous as he approached Harmony and Jolsten. Jolsten stepped up beside Harmony, as she leaned back in the midst of Delphi's tirade.

"You know he can't do that," Killian said, still trying to be the voice of reason. "We have to handle this delicately if we're to try and put a stop to this whole operation."

"This is complete bullshit! My baby girl is out there scared to death. There's no telling what the hell they're doing to her." Delphi continued to rage. He pointed a long finger toward the officer. "If you won't go after your boss and wrangle some information out of him, and I mean *right now*, I swear to God I've got a .45 that will help him with his fucking memory!"

It was time to intervene. Nate knew from their NSU days playing football that once Delphi's temper peaked, there was no stopping the aftermath until it had completely boiled over. Setting his dislike for the law enforcement authority to the side, he tried to reason with his friend.

132

"Brother, I promise we're going to get her back. You know we wouldn't sacrifice Jayme's safety. However we've got to treat this situation very carefully. There are also more victims besides Jayme that are at stake. Besides, Harmony doesn't think they've set out to harm her. They'll probably wait until the auction to try and sell her. The key is to get them before that fucking auction takes place. After that, the chances of finding her..."

"...Are slim to none." Asha finished, choking back sobs. She turned pleading eyes to her husband and brother. "*Please*..." she cried, her body quivering in shock and agony. "I can't...I *can't*...I can't take it! Please find my baby. Find my baby..." She grabbed her chest, clutching a hand full of silk above her heart as she rocked back and forth in misery.

Delphi's face paled at the sight of his distraught wife. He quickly rushed to her side; hot tears cascading down his own chiseled cafe latte shaded cheekbones. He picked Asha up from her lounge chair and placed her in his lap. He then wrapped his arms around her, whispering softly in her ear as he tried to quench both of their fears.

Paige moved discreetly out of their way to allow the couple time to compose themselves. Walking over to Nate, she gently placed her hand inside his, apparently seeking the same reassurance Asha needed.

Instead of squeezing her hand back, Nate released it to slip his hand around her waist, turning her around to face him. He then wrapped both arms around her, pulled her close, and then crushed her to his chest.

Paige initially tensed in his embrace. After a second, he felt her body sag in his arms. She then let out a small, shuddered sigh as she accepted his console.

I got you, baby, he thought. Nate's heart rejoiced that Paige accepted his comfort so easily.

Killian stood, crossing his bulking arms across his chest. Asha lifted her head from her husband's chest to look beseechingly at her brother.

Siblings stared at each other, identical hazel eyes sending and receiving the same message.

Killian then turned to Officer Jolsten, a deadly expression crossing his features. "We'll find my niece, along with Paige's sister. Nobody fucks with what's ours." Killian vowed.

Nate couldn't have said it better.

^^^

"Tell Spivey to get his ass in here," Mayor Penne barked into the speakerphone of his downtown Chicago office.

"Right away, sir," his secretary responded.

Penne loosened his tie as he leaned back in his chair. He'd just completed the last round of press conferences for the day, and he was fucking exhausted. He hated reporters. He hated the media, period. They were always sticking their noses exactly where he didn't want them-- where he tried to hide his deepest, darkest secrets.

Fucking vermin.

He rolled his neck as he tried to loosen the tension building there.

Reflecting on the frustrating aftermath with the reporters, *So What* had been the recurring words of the day, playing over and over in his mind.

So what that he couldn't explain why the city's crime rate had exploded with drive-by shootings, felony drug arrests, and police assault charges?

So what that the city hadn't seen an increase in high school academic test scores for the past six years, placing Chicago among the lowest cities in the state for college entrance admittance?

So what that the city's budget was so overblown, he had to increase property taxes by 24% over the past year, just to cover the Chicago Teacher's Union pension payments?

So what that the verbal brawl he'd gotten into a couple of days ago with the President of the CTU was so heated and overblown, that now the Union threatened to strike in the upcoming school year if he didn't resign immediately?

So fucking what?

All that mattered for the moment was Spivey, and what he had to say when he walked through those fucking doors.

Alderman Spivey strolled in at that precise moment, once again looking calm and collected in his custom-made Ralph Lauren suit. His thin frame appeared almost anorexic, as the slim fit of the material shaped his body like a glove.

Penne narrowed his eyes as he watched Spivey enter. *It wasn't normal for a man to never get riled up,* he thought. Spivey never, ever showed signs of being stressed, and that bothered the shit out of him.

Although Penne was *Caesar* in North America, his counterpart in South America, The *Herne of HG,* often replaced his right hand every few years. He'd once stated that a change in ranks helped to keep his soldiers from becoming too complacent. Spivey had been with him for a long time; however maybe he should take his mirror's advice, and reconsider cutting off his Right Hand to spite his face...

Spivey immediately turned, pulling Penne's thoughts back to the situation at hand, and locked the door behind him, before turning back around to cross his thin arms across his chest.

Spivey frowned, and Penne immediately felt his anger spike.

"You need to calm down, Eugene. We handled it." Spivey said softly. He raised a censured eyebrow toward the Mayor.

"Don't fucking tell me to calm the fuck down! I've been waiting on goddamn pins and needles up here while you're out playing with your dick!" He felt like snapping Spivey's all too cocky neck. *Who the hell did he think he was talking to?*

Spivey rolled his eyes. "I wasn't exactly playing, but I *was* handling business. My brother made sure that last piece of merchandise was picked up last night. The Allen girl is secured. The blue-green eyes on that one will make us a fucking fortune. She's also the perfect lure to bring Nate out. He'll tell his friends of course, and in the chaos to find her, we can get him alone, and finally take care of him once and for all. We can put an end to this problem permanently."

Penne nodded his head as he let out a short breath. *One problem at a time.* "All right, I'll take you at your word, for now. I've been a fucking ball of nerves all fucking day about taking that Allen girl, but I know it had to be done. Those parents of hers needed to be taught a lesson for Stevens. He was one of my best soldiers."

Spivey pursed his lips together. "Yea, I know. I also heard about your television spat with the CTU President, which is now probably caught on *YouTube,* and getting thousands of hits. You need to control your temper. We don't need anymore unwanted attention."

This time is was Penne who rolled his eyes.

Spivey nodded his head at the unspoken confirmation. "In any case, I called that Houston police chief. He's a fucking imbecile." He snorted. "A useful imbecile, but an imbecile nonetheless. That security plant we posted at *Escapades* let it leak that Harrison almost told Nate what was going down."

Penne's eyes flared as he jolted out of his seat, his earlier calm quickly forgotten. "WHAT!"

Spivey rolled his eyes. "Relax. I said, *almost*. Nate still doesn't suspect a thing. I spoke with Harrison shortly after that, and cursed him out for being so fucking careless." Spivey shrugged. "Seems like that plant is a nice check and balance system in place for us. In any event, Harrison confirm that he's sending his district lieutenants to Corpus Christi on the day of the auction to attend some sort of training drill, so interference from actual authority figures should be at a minimum. The only other crew that should be there are some local street thugs he'd tossed a few coins at to assist with the sales. We should be good."

Penne nodded once as he studied Spivey, trying unsuccessfully to push down his irritation. Tilting his head to one side, the Mayor narrowed his eyes.

Spivey's eyes widened as he quickly realized he'd become the focal point of the Mayor's discontent. He then shifted uncomfortably as he slowly backed against the closed door.

Still eyeing Spivey with scrutiny, Penne moved in a predatory fashion from behind his desk. His lips curved in a sneer as he slowly progressed toward the alderman.

"When Nate's little brother saw what he did all those years ago, I thought both of our careers were over," Penne reflected softly as he moved closer to his prey.

Spivey nodded his head, his eyes wide with uncertainty. "I did too." Penne watched with satisfaction as Spivey lowered his eyes toward his clenched hands. Hands that were now balled into hard fists as he approached. He bit back the smirk at the thought of the alderman feeling off center by his approach, just like he'd been feeling for months.

"Over the years you've proven to be a very useful tool to me, Conrad." He shook his head in disgust. "In the past, I was just a naive alderman, like yourself. That Bears parade was the turning point in both of our careers. It gave me a chance to get close to the previous mayor, learn about his secret addiction to heroin when that packet slipped from his back pocket, and leak his addiction story to the *Chicago Tribune.*"

Suddenly Penne took one hand and slapped it firmly on the nearby wall, physically startling the alderman with the abrupt sound. "WHAM! Easy path straight to the Mayor's office."

Spivey stood stock still, watching as the Mayor then continued to advance in his direction. Penne could see Spivey swallow a large gulp of air, before lifting his chin as a sign that he wouldn't easily be intimidated.

Good.

Spivey swallowed once again before he responded. "It was a turning point for me too. My brother was just starting out on the police force, and I was interning at the Cook County clerk's office."

He gave the mayor an arrogant smile. "Gerry was able to take care of Nate's kid brother pretty easily, but we also knew we had to take care of Nate as well. We couldn't be certain about what his brother confided to him before he died, and we're still unsure. However it's best to be safe than sorry." He shook his head slightly. "Unfortunately, Nate's been a harder fish to fry. When Gerry planted those drugs in his car, we thought for sure we'd had enough evidence to send him to Statesville Prison for the rest of his life. When the fucker got off on that technicality, I should have had Gerry put a bullet in him then."

Penne shook his head, still slowly approaching the alderman. "No, we made the right choice. We needed to watch him. We couldn't kill two family members so close together like that. Remember, this was back in the 80s. Things would have looked suspicious back then. Nowadays it's an entirely different story." He shrugged nonchalantly.

"Family members are getting killed all the time now, sometimes days apart."

"Well, we can end this tragic little tale once the *Ides* is over." Spivey reassured.

"Will we?" Penne said all too quietly as he now stood toe to toe with his alderman. "Will the tale end there?"

Spivey swallowed again. "Where else would it go?" His eyes widened even further as he watched the Mayor's every movement. Penne watched as Spivey's shaky hand reached up to wipe away a bead of sweat from his shining forehead.

"It would go wherever the hell I wanted it to. I'm the fucking Mayor, and the Northern *Caesar* Commander of The Hunter Group."

With that he unclenched his fist, and then reached across to wrap his long fingers around Spivey's neck, relishing in the surprised gasp that escaped from the other man.

And then he pulled Spivey's head forward to thrust his tongue down his throat.

Chapter Nineteen

Rachelle Clarke looked around the dank, musty confines of the warehouse where she, along with the other captives, were being held. The evening light from the moon cast an eerie glow through the broken shutters on the old window frame. A cool breeze blew in from underneath the cracked window, causing a shiver to run through her body. Rachelle drew her knees up to her chin and wrapped her tied arms around them to ward off the cold.

As she took in her surrounding again for the thousandth time, she wondered again about what was the intent of the men who'd taken her from her Detroit home.

Did the men mean to kill them? She let out a shaky breath. She doubted it; otherwise they would have died days ago. Instead, their kidnappers sustained their life by feeding them rations of dried jerky and bottled water. The rations were enough to keep them alive, but not enough to give them the strength they needed to fight back and escape.

Would the men rape them? She bit her bottom lip as ice cold fear shivered down her spine, unsure about the answer to that question. Day after day she'd watched the men's lustful stares, causing both fear and dread to skyrocket within each captive girl. They were all uncertain as to how their fate would end. The men's discerning, hungry looks didn't help their squash their fears either, as they continually raked over each victim from head to toe. Rachelle could practically hear the sexual assaults taking place in their minds.

Would they eventually be set free? Rachelle already knew unequivocally the answer to that one.

Absolutely not.

She looked around once again at the other girls that had been captured. The youngest little girl looked to be about nine years old, while the oldest, besides her, looked to be in her early teens. Rachelle guessed she was probably the oldest among all of the captives.

There were a total of five girls, including herself, that lay shivering and cold together on the wooden floor. During times they'd been left alone, they'd spoken and shared only their first names with each other. They were too scared to share anything more, just in case something tragic happened to one of them. An unspoken understanding had already been painfully communicated. Each girl understood that the pain of losing someone they'd grown close to while in captivity would just make the loss even more profound and shocking.

The steel door locking them inside the room was suddenly jerked open, bathing the room in the bright light from the hallway. The large, menacing looking cop, sporting a long trench coat and tan fedora, appeared in the doorway. Rachelle shuddered uncontrollably. He was also the same person who'd lured her from her home a couple of weeks ago, after promising to take her to her estranged father with hopes of reconciliation.

Stupid, just stupid Rachelle, she'd chastised herself once again as she reflected how naive she'd been. *You* knew *better. Your father's forgotten all about you and Paige. He's clearly moved on. Just like you'll be eventually forgotten as you rot in this hellhole waiting to die. You haven't seen or heard from Paige in weeks, so she'll never miss the fact that you've disappeared. The life you knew will go on, without so much as a ripple to even acknowledge your absence.*

Rachelle shook her head to spell away her dark thoughts as her eyes swung back to the man entering the room. She needed to stay focused on what was going on around her.

Stay focused, so she can stay alive.

She pulled unsuccessfully at the extremely tight, painful bindings around her wrists and ankles, but the coarse, synthetic fiber was cutting into her skin. Her frustration swelled as she tugged once more. The cop had secured her tighter than the other victims, probably because of her age and size. It didn't matter, though. She would find a way out of this hell one way or another. She had no intention of sticking around for whatever twisted future these criminals had in mind for her.

The swarthy officer strolled into the room, carrying in his arms a trembling, terrified little girl. The other girls in the room whimpered

140

softly at the sight at the scary looking man, but Rachelle's heart fell at the sight of the scared little child in his arms. Rachelle guessed that the girl was the youngest victim so far that had been kidnapped. The child was crying and shaking uncontrollably; her wide blue-green eyes searching frantically around the room.

I know exactly how you feel, sweetheart. Stay strong, baby girl, she thought, willing her thoughts to the child.

The message must have been received when the little girl's eyes finally fell on Rachelle. Rachelle watched in surprise as something within the small child instantly calmed. The child's cries slowed, and then turned into soft hiccups.

"Got another piece of merchandise here. Move over and make some room." The gruff-looking man barked at them.

He moved next to Rachelle and placed the little girl on her feet. He then tied the girl's hands and feet together in the same manner as the rest of them, and then promptly shoved her to the ground.

The girl cried out as she fell roughly to the wooden floor, but quickly tried to mask her hurt. She sniffed loudly, and then used the back of her tied hands to wipe her running nose.

The man backed up toward the door, looking at each little girl with a lust that would frighten even Muhammad Ali.

"Tomorrow is the last day you'll be here. Then we're shipping you bitches to an auction, where you'll be bought and sold like the little sluts you are."

An anguished cry sounded from the back of the room. Rachelle couldn't turn her head to see which girl had made the sound. The cry was shut down when the cop quickly marched past Rachelle. She stared straight ahead as his foot absently kicked her side when he moved behind her, stiffening at the offensive, dank odor that followed in the man's wake. Suddenly, a loud smack sounded against flesh near the back of the room. Rachelle knew at that moment that one of the girls had just been viciously slapped.

"Shut the fuck up! I didn't fly all this way to hear your fucking whining! Keep it up, and I'll give you something to cry for! Fucking cunts."

With that, he looked at all of them disgustedly, before marching back out of the room, slamming the door behind him. Once again the room was draped in shadows.

Silence cascaded once again in the dark room, as each girl let the man's words sink in. Tomorrow. They only had one day left before they would discover what the future held in store for them.

Or if they even had a future.

Taking a deep breath, Rachelle turned her head to assess the little girl sitting beside her. Her eyes narrowed as she studied the girl's face. The child was utterly gorgeous, and surprisingly strangely familiar. She had deep blue-green eyes, with a slight slant that made her gaze all the more captivating. Her wavy black hair was tied into two long pigtails streaming down her back. She wore a pair of Minion pajamas with fuzzy yellow socks, and a small gold chain was draped delicately around her small neck.

The child had stopped shaking, her face holding a unique hidden strength as she turned her face toward Rachelle.

Rachelle sent her a tentative smile, trying to appear as calm as possible. For her sake as well as the girl's.

"Hello, my name is Rachelle. What's your name, sweetheart?"

"Jayme." The girl answered, still staring back at her.

"Hi Jayme." Rachelle took a deep breath. "I know you're scared, but we're going to be all right. You have to believe that."

Jayme nodded her head, but said nothing.

After a few moments, Rachelle decided to engage the girl again.

"How did you end up here, sweetheart?"

Jayme closed her eyes, lowered her head, and took a deep breath. Shaking her head slightly, she opened her eyes, and then turned her face toward Rachelle, examining her just as closely as Rachelle had done to her.

"Momma told me not to talk to strangers."

Rachelle bit back a smile. The little girl had spunk, even during a time like this.

"I understand, honey. Your momma taught you well. But I was kind of hoping you and I could be friends."

Jayme nodded her head. "Ok. We can be friends. Mama Terri told me that friends are the best relationships a girl can have."

Rachelle nodded her head, although she had no clue who Terri was. Her sister Paige had been her best friend, before she moved away. The pain of their strained relationship still hurt at times. She shook her head to clear her thoughts. *Focus on the here and now.*

"How did the bad man take you, sweetheart? Were you by yourself?" Rachelle asked as she studied Jayme's clothing.

Before Jayme's arrival, each girl had previously professed in shadows how they'd been snatched. One girl confessed she'd been taken as she was walking her dog. Another had been snatched while she played at the park across the street from her home. Rachelle figured if she could figure out similarities in their abduction, it might help to give some sort of clue as to the reasoning and patterns of these assholes. The jackoff cop had sneered to Rachelle a few nights ago that her own kidnapping had been in retaliation for giving testimony against a high-ranking pedophile back in Detroit.

Rachelle's chest squeezed as she thought about the shame the victim had carried before seeking help from what her stepfather was doing to her. If her actions helped at least one young girl spare the shame and humiliation of being victimized from the hands of another rapist, she'd gladly endure her current situation a thousand times over.

Jayme sniffed loudly, bringing Rachelle's attention back to her, before she finally answered.

"I was getting into bed like Momma told me, when he and another big man came into my bedroom. They were like that Werewolf Man in that *Underworld* movie. That big, scary one."

Rachelle nodded her head. "I agree. I think he's a big scary werewolf too."

Jayme nodded as she turned to look at the other girls. Her eyes widened a fraction before turning back to Rachelle.

"What are they gonna do with us?"

Rachelle shook her head sadly. "I don't know, honey. I just don't know."

Rachelle watched in curiosity as Jayme abruptly straightened her small shoulders. She then took a deep breath and lifted her chin in defiance.

What just ran through her head? Rachelle wondered. She decided to ask.

"What did you just think about, love?" Rachelle asked.

"I thought about my Daddy. My Daddy will come for me. I can ask if he can come for you too, since you're my friend now."

Rachelle shook her head. She didn't want to squelch the girl's hopes, especially if they were being moved to another location tomorrow. The chances of being found were looking slimmer and slimmer. She knew she wouldn't go down without fighting back, but she also knew a small child had little protection against men four times her size.

"I don't know if your Daddy will be able to find us by tomorrow, honey."

Jayme's keen eyes stared back at her. Her chin lifted a little higher. "He will. And when he finds me, he's going to kick their ass, cause my Daddy don't play that shit. He'll probably bring my uncle Killy to get me, too. Uncle Killy don't play either. That's what Miss Holley says, and I believe her. Uncle Killy is strong."

Jayme then turned a serious, pointed stare in Rachelle's direction. "So we've gotta be strong too, until they get here."

Chapter Twenty

It was close to midnight by the time one of Harmony's agents contacted her. They'd finally heard from Tyson. Tyson informed the agent that he'd discovered information that could potentially give them an edge in their investigation.

Apparently the search into Tony's extracurricular activities resulted in discovering new details that Harmony needed to know immediately, but couldn't be discussed on an open phone line. Her agent thought it would be best if she accompanied him when he extracted the information from Tyson. After taking the call, and still needing to keep the identity of her team confidential, Harmony decided to take Jolsten with her as backup. Killian decided to stay behind at Delphi's to console his sister.

After the meeting with her team, Harmony and Jolsten decided it would be best to meet with Lucas and Lafayette in the Blackburn office the following morning, instead of going back to Delphi's place. They agreed that any news outside of 'we've recovered Jayme' would not settle well with her already agitated, mountain-of-a-man father.

Now, as they all gathered together in the conference room the next day, Jolsten felt no closer to discovering HG's current whereabouts than he had hours before. Running a frustrated hand through his thinning blond hair, he studied the report the agent had provided. A million possibilities ran through his mind.

"I'm telling you, I think they're still here in Texas. I can almost guarantee you they're being kept somewhere close. Today is March 15th. HG isn't going to want to have a high transition delay prior to the sale," said Jolsten.

"And you're certain that the auction will occur today?" Lafayette asked, turning to Harmony.

Harmony nodded her head. "That's the word from Tyson, at least. He confirmed it when he met with my man. I have to say, his intel has been a lot better than mine when it comes to getting word from the streets. People will talk to him a lot faster than they would talk with my people. Nevertheless, I assigned a man from my unit to stay parked outside of *Escapades* to keep watch. He'll alert me immediately if he sees anything foul occurring. I also had a man following Tony for the past few days, especially since we've seen he's a part of all of this. He was able to get a wiretap into his apartment."

She shook her head in disgust. "In addition to the illegal meth business he's got going on the side, that security guard is about as crooked as a dog's hind legs."

"We still need to figure out who that other person was in the photograph with him." Jolsten reminded the group. "He's the key to all of this."

Harmony tapped her finger to her chin as she thought. "I think my sister may know someone. Lafayette, I know you're good, but I think Holley's got someone a little better. Someone who could run checks that might be considered sort of a grey area in legality."

Lafayette grimaced as he nodded his head. "I think I know who you're referring to. Yea, that kid doesn't have any problem at all diving into the black web. Hell, he's also got access to monetary resources that could shake up a few feathers, just in case anyone decides to ask any questions."

Jolsten looked up from his reports. "Then let's get him involved. We need all the help we can get. In the meantime, I need to go into the station to run some analysis against other city's homeless statistics. Maybe I can find some sort of link as to how they've been able to cover up some of their disappearances. Houston can't be the only city that HG has targeted."

A soft vibration began to echo in the room, causing everyone to check their phones. Lafayette paled as he confirmed the call was for him. He quickly glanced at Harmony before turning toward the others.

"Excuse me, I need to handle this," he said abruptly, before leaving the room in a hurry. Lucas shook his head as he watched his brother leave.

"We'll go with you to the station. We still have some contacts with the Los Angeles police department that might prove useful. If anything, they could give us insight as to whether or not HG's been active on the west coast." Lucas stated.

Harmony nodded her head. "Sounds like a plan."

Just then, Lafayette walked back into the room. He looked disheveled and completely out of sorts.

"I know there's a lot going on right now, but I need to leave."

Everyone turned to look at him, completely taken back.

"And where the hell do you think you're going?" Lucas spit.

Lafayette stared at him for a long moment, a tense, unspoken communication passing between them. Lucas then let out a loud sigh as he shook in head.

"I hope you know what you're doing."

Lafayette just pursed his lips together. "Yea, I finally do." He turned to give a pointed look at Harmony. "Call me and let me know the next steps." With that, he nodded his head at Jolsten, before darting out of the room.

"I need to just make a quick call to my field agent surveying *Escapades*, then we can leave." Harmony stated. She then quickly walked into the hallway, closing the conference room door behind her.

"What the hell is going on?" Jolsten muttered. Lucas gave a blank look, and then shrugged his shoulders in confusion.

Harmony walked back in the room, closing her cell phone with a determined look across her face.

Jolsten let out a frustrated huff. "Well, are we ready *now*?"

Lucas and Harmony both nodded their head.

"Then let's go."

^^^

After piling into Lucas' car, Harmony, Jolsten and Lucas headed toward the police station. During the ride, Harmony contacted her sister Holley, placed her on speakerphone, and solicited her help. After hearing about HG's involvement, and still reeling from her own turbulent history with the group, Holley eagerly agreed. Holley then conferenced her newly hired digital media forensics analyst on the line, completing their three-way call.

Justin Salzmann had been more than happen to join in the operation. The sort of subterfuge required in identifying patterns with HG's communication completely called upon the young man's hacking impulses. In addition, the fact that the FBI and local police were given him permission to let his hacker freak flag fly was an added bonus.

Justin agreed to meet Harmony at the station within the hour, making sure to contact her upon arrival so they could all go inside together. They didn't want to raise suspicion with anyone if Justin walked into the station solo, asking questions to the wrong people.

They arrived at the police station shortly before noon. Jolsten felt a sudden unease curl up his spine, prompting him to look around the outside of the precinct with caution. He then spotted a white Camaro and grimaced.

"What's up, man?" Lucas asked, sensing his nervousness.

"There's Chief Harrison's car over there. I could have sworn I thought he was scheduled off today, but it looks like he's still here. We'll need to go through the side entrance so he won't notice us. His office is near the front, so I think we should be good to enter unseen."

Lucas and Harmony nodded their heads in understanding. They then turned to see a 1998 Hyundai hatchback pull alongside them. The driver shut off the engine and got out of the vehicle, looking wide-eyed and expectant. His tall, lanky frame emphasized his youthful face and lean physique. Long dark hair hung low around his shoulders, and his clean-shaven face and wide dimpled grin smirked knowingly in Harmony's direction. He watched her slip from the passenger seat to greet him, holding out his hand in greeting.

"Hot damn! You look just like Boss Lady! It's great to meet you." His smile wavered a bit as he saw Lucas' massive frame, along with Jolsten's stern expression as they exited the car behind her.

After a quick second, Justin quickly recovered. He then leaned over and said in a low voice, "I hope you're a lot nicer than she is. Boss Lady can be extremely high-handed when she gets worked up." He shuddered. "I try my best to make sure I'm on her good side each and every day."

Jolsten could see Harmony fighting back a smile. "That's good to know." She nodded her head toward her companions. "This is Lucas and Jolsten. They'll help in getting you access to the classified Uniform Crime Reports of cities we suspect have been infiltrated by HG. Hopefully it will be enough to put together some critical pieces for us."

She held up the picture of Tony and the man cloaked in a trench coat. "We need you to help us identify who this other man is in the photo. Think you can do that?"

"Piece of cake," Justin replied haughtily.

Jolsten studied the young man with a skeptical look as he and Harmony exchanged words. If Harmony trusted him, he knew he should as well, but he had to admit that the young man's appearance was disconcerting. He looked more like a grungy partier, with his black jeans, black t-shirt, and worn converse sneakers, than a highly technical analyst. Jolsten then mentally shrugged. If Harmony and Holley trusted the kid, then he would too.

"Ok, let's head inside." Jolsten said, leading the way toward the side entrance.

^^^

They made it safely into Jolsten's office without being detected. After putting in his security clearance in his computer, Jolsten moved out of the way to allow Justin complete access to the classified UCR reports, Department Directive Systems, and confidential Special Investigation Unit files.

They worked well into the late evening hours trying to decipher and unravel any trail of evidence they could find. Jolsten peeked his head out a few times to make sure their activities continued undetected, while Harmony practically blew up her cell keeping tabs with her *Escapades* lookout. Her agent repeatedly confirmed that the club was quiet with lights out, but Jolsten knew that time was working against them the longer Jayme and Rachelle stayed missing.

"I don't mean to sound too cocky, but I could definitely call myself a modern day genius," Justin said arrogantly as he finally ripped pages from a report he was printing from the inkjet.

"You got a hit on the unidentified man in the photo with Tony?" Lucas asked as he leaned over Justin's shoulder to peer at the report.

Justin raised a singular eyebrow as he narrowed his eyes in contemplation. "Just to make sure, this was a pro bono job, correct? Meaning, you guys weren't planning on paying me anything? I'm doing this for free?"

Harmony swiftly smacked Justin in the back of his head with her hand.

"Ow! Man, you hit like your sister," Justin whined.

"She's the one who told me to smack you if you mouthed off." Harmony chastened. "Now, what did you come up with?"

Justin rubbed his head as he soothed his ache. "That dude in the picture is five-o. Straight out of Chicago." He nodded his head toward Lucas. "That facial recognition software you loaded worked good in capturing his profile, but after a few of my tweaks, I was able to enhance the programming. Chicago PD had his face hidden underneath layers and layers of security. A normal tech would have taken weeks to find out what his true identify was." He snorted. "Luckily for you, I'm not a normal tech."

Jolsten raised his eyebrows in surprise. "He's out of Chicago? Go figure. Isn't that where Nate said he's from? If so, that makes perfect sense."

Lucas nodded his head. "Yea, he is."

Justin pointed at the trench coat figure in the photograph. "His name is Gerry Spivey. He's been on payroll with CPD as a detective for like 25 years, although his name has never been associated with any actual real cases. It's probably why he didn't come up in any traditional searches." He gave a dry snort. "It's like he's a ghost employee, but instead, he's walking around in the flesh. I also dug a little deeper into a few redacted files. This guy Spivey also has a brother who's a big wig politician from the west side." He let out a low whistle. "Chicago politics is one of the shadiest games of deceit in the whole fucking country. And it looks like its dirt has trickled down here to Texas."

This time it was Jolsten who let out a rude snort. "I think it's been down here for awhile, son."

Harmony narrowed her eyes. "In any case, this is good info, but it still doesn't give us a hint as to where HG is keeping the girls right now."

Suddenly a string of curses sounded from down the hall. Jolsten placed his finger to his mouth, indicating for the team to be silent. He, along with Lucas and Harmony, quickly extracted their weapons, released their safeties, and then slowly moved forward to open Jolsten's office door.

"Harmony, you stay with Justin. Lucas and I will see what's going on." Jolsten indicated.

"Already on it." Harmony indicated. She then pulled a shaking Justin to his feet, and all but shoved his tall frame inside the office closet before closing it firmly behind her.

If Jolsten's anxiety weren't already nearly choking the life out of him, he would have found the image of the petite woman manhandling the lanky 6 foot 2 youngster quite comical.

Mentally preparing himself for anything, Jolsten felt his adrenalin pumping as he and Lucas silently walked down the hall towards Harrison's office. The station was now noticeably void of officers, the majority of which had been sent to Corpus Christi for diversity refresher training. How the Chief had managed to get his whole unit sent away at the same time, without causing suspicion, was beyond him.

Great way to vacate the premises and ensure there aren't any viable witnesses, Jolsten thought grimly.

They reached Harrison door to discover it was closed, however they could clearly make out Harrison's gravely voice from the other side of the panel. Moving to opposite sides of the door, they leaned in to try and listen better.

"Did you get that last piece?" Harrison growled from the other side of the door. There was a slight pause. "If she gives you any problems, just knock her ass out. That Cuban buyer is particularly interested in that one. He's making a special trip out here just to see her.

If things go as planned, we might have a chance at moving the U.S. Operations hub to the south, like it needed to be all along. Those northern idiots have been fucking up for awhile."

"He must be on his cell," Lucas whispered. Jolsten nodded in agreement.

"Fine. That's fine. Make sure no one follows you. I'll be there shortly. The Ides starts in a few hours, and I need to get a couple of things prepped before the sale starts. Start transporting the merchandise now. By the time I'm finished, you should already be there." Pause. "They're hoping to get Nate if he shows up asking questions. Yea, I know. I guess the man has too many loose ends for them, but I agree with them on this one. He and his friends have been a pain in my ass for years." Pause. "Who the hell knows? Yes, motherfucker! Of course this line is secure! Stop sniffing that fucking meth you're dealing and get your head out of your ass! Fine. At any rate, I'll see you when I get there."

Jolsten nodded to an open office door next to Harrison's office. He and Lucas quickly slipped inside, leaving a crack open in the frame so they could see what was going on. A short time later, Harrison opened his door and sauntered out. He looked suspiciously back and forth in the hallway for a moment, casting a curious look toward the cracked door Jolsten and Lucas had just run behind.

Jolsten held his breath.

He watched through the peep as Harrison withdrew his weapon, checked the clip, and then shook his head. Giving a loud huff, he then turned and walked out of the front door of the station.

Jolsten and Lucas opened the office door and ensured they were alone before letting out the breath they'd been holding.

Lucas then pulled out his cell, a determined look crossing his features. "I think it's time to round up the troops."

∧∧∧

"I let Nate and Killian in, since the station doors were supposedly closed to civilians." Jolsten informed as he walked in, the two men in

152

reference hot on his heels. Nate and Killian nodded grimly to the team as they now assembled in Jolsten's office, ready for orders.

"I've called in Captain Franklyn Bernard to let him know what's going on. He and his team of SEAL agents are boarding a plane as we speak. They've been on standby since last night, and they'll be here in less than an hour." Harmony informed.

Lucas turned to Killian. "We didn't want to alert Delphi or Asha just yet. We need Jayme secured first."

Killian nodded his head. "I agree. My sister's pretty shook up. She's been through a lot over the years. I don't want to cause her any more pain."

Harmony turned to Justin. She'd released him from his closet cell shortly after Harrison returned. "I need for you to stay locked in this office." She pointed to the seat behind the desk, indicating for him to take a seat. "From what I understand, all of the trustworthy police personnel are in Corpus, so anyone trying to get into the station tonight is with HG. And that means..."

"...Letting them in would be my ass. I know, I know. I'm a tech nerd, not a fighter. I get the point." Justin said as he slid into the desk chair, seemingly annoyed at the obvious increase of testosterone in the room.

"Good. For right now, staying here is the safest place for you to be." Harmony informed.

Jolsten looked at Lucas. "You and I can follow Harrison after he comes back. He left his car out front, which means he took one of the unmarked vehicles to do whatever dirty work he's trying to take care of before the auction. He'll come back here to pick up his car before he heads to *Escapades*."

"How do you know he'll be back?" Nate asked.

Jolsten nodded his head toward the Chief's open office door. He walked out of the room, returning a moment later with a folder in his hand. He then handed the folder to Nate. As Nate flipped through each picture in the file, a low growl escaped his chest through bared teeth.

Inside the folder, mock profiles of each kidnapping victim were showcased, including full, scantily clad body photographs, facial close ups, and personal background profiles. There were a total of six featured profiles, including two recently dated additions that caused curses to spew from both Nate and Killian's lips.

"Shit," Lucas rumbled.

"Fucking hell," Killian growled.

"Motherfucker," Nate spat.

Jolsten grimly nodded his head. "Yea, it's Jayme and Rachelle. I knew Jayme, but wasn't sure about Rachelle until this very moment. The Chief is slipping. He's gotten too arrogant, too sloppy. He'll soon realize he left critical evidence just lying around, and will be back to pick it up. When he does, Lucas and I will follow him. I don't want to make an arrest until he leads us to the hostages."

"I'll go to the airport to meet up with Capt. Bernard." Killian said, looking menacing as he rolled his gigantic shoulders. Jolsten could tell the big man wanted to hurt something. He was just glad it wasn't him.

"Sounds good to me." Harmony agreed.

"I need to tell Paige what's going on. I left her when Lucas called, and I know she's crawling up the wall with worry right about now." Nate said, his eyes never moving from the picture of Rachelle's face.

"I'll go with you," Harmony said. "After that, we can head over to *Escapades* and wait it out. Don't call her, though. You're hot, Nate."

When he looked at her with a confused expression, Harmony actually blushed and rolled her eyes. "I didn't mean it that way, *geesh*. Men. I meant that HG is all over you. They could be tapping your cell phone. I can gear up on the way over there."

Nate still looked at her confused for a moment, but said nothing.

"Alright everyone. Let's move." Jolsten commanded.

Chapter Twenty One

"Good call with Harrison coming back to the station." Lucas said as he and Jolsten followed the Chief toward Cypress. "Even better call for us to use Justin's car to pursue him with."

Jolsten nodded as he discreetly navigated a short distance behind the Chief's Camaro.

"I told you, he's gotten sloppy. He's probably gotten so comfortable over the years that he doesn't believe anyone will call him out on his shit. His defensive barriers down."

"Well, let's hope we can bring down all of those motherfuckers."

Jolsten nodded in agreement. Casting a quick glance at his partner, he asked a question that had been bugging him for a few hours.

"Where the hell did Lafayette go? We need all the trustworthy hands we can get on this. There's no telling how much extra muscle the Chief has stored waiting in the wings."

Lucas's face fell into a complete mask as he responded. "He had something he had to take care of. I promised him I'd leave him alone and let him handle it. I just hope he doesn't fuck it up." He then took on a determined look. "And it's not about the quantity of men, it's about their quality. I'd put us against any group that believes they can continue to black market women in our city any day. We have more of a reason to fight. More integrity to maintain. Don't worry. We've got this covered."

Jolsten sure as hell hoped so.

Finally, they slowed as they watched Harrison pull into the club's parking lot. Jolsten pulled off the side of the road, and then killed the lights so they wouldn't be seen from the half-mile distance they'd maintained.

When the street sign was lit and the place was open for business, the *Escapades* marquee could usually been seen from several miles away. Right now, the sign was eerily dark. The boarded windows and front door gave a haunting illusion, casting a shadowed circumference for several yards out. The sun had already set, making the night air dense with unforeseen expectancy.

This entire maneuver would end tonight, one way or another.

Lucas spotted several low hanging elm trees along the parking lot's boarders near the back of the club. "Let's hike over there and lay low so we can see what's going on. Those trees can make for excellent cover."

Jolsten nodded his head. "Agreed. Let's go."

Holding their guns firmly in hand, they moved silently toward the covering of the trees. Jolsten clicked his phone to silent, nodding to Lucas to do the same. The last thing they needed was for an unexpected call to give away their location.

Noting that the front of the club's parking lot was empty, and anticipating that any activity would occur toward the shaded back area, they positioned a perfect spot to view any activity.

Jolsten let out a deep breath and knelt down, grimacing when his foot accidently snapped a twig in the tall grass. Turning to assure Lucas that he was ok and to apologize for the sound, he watched as Lucas' eyes widened with apprehension as he stared past him. Raising a single eyebrow, Jolsten silently posed a questioning look toward his partner, when he suddenly felt the cold barrel of a gun pointed directly at the back of his skull.

"The safe word is *Prince*." Jolsten quickly hissed, remembering Harmony's earlier communicated security passwords.

The gun was quickly lowered as a lone figure neither man had noticed before suddenly appeared from the dark shadows. He was dressed completely in black, including a black mask covering everything on his face except his eyes and mouth. The man nodded his head in Jolsten's direction.

"My C.O. said you'd be here shortly. Nothing has occurred so far. The place has been completely dead silent, but I suspect not for long." The man informed in a husky voice. He nodded toward the back entrance, where a large white caravan that Jolsten hadn't noticed before sat parked. "That van arrived about 10 minutes ago. No one has gotten out or walked up to the van as of yet. I suspect that whoever is driving was waiting on that man right there."

All three men turned to watch as Harrison walked around the side of the building toward the van. He knocked expectedly on the side panel of the vehicle four times, then stood back and waited. Seemingly satisfied, he then turned and walked to the back door, and gave the same repetitive four knocks, crossing his arms impatiently across his chest.

"You're the field agent on Harmony's team that's been supplying her with intel all evening." Jolsten said matter-of-factly as he continued to stare at Harrison. Understanding finally dawned as to why the cloaked man was out here in the shadows.

The man slowly nodded, his eyes still glued to the van. "Yea, something like that," he said mysteriously. Jolsten thought the man's voice was distinctly familiar, however he didn't have time to ponder as he saw the door of the van burst open.

The man then quickly held out two blue tooth devices, indicating for Jolsten and Lucas to each take a set.

"I placed small recorders near the back door a couple of hours ago while I was waiting for you guys. We should be able to track everything that they're saying, as well as have sufficient recordings of any activity that's going on."

Lucas nodded his head as he placed the blue tooth in his ear. He glanced hesitantly at Jolsten before speaking. "Good job. And just to let you know, we also have another team in route. A Navy Seal unit. Your boss should also be here shortly, but for right now, we're it."

The cloaked man nodded his head in understanding.

Jolsten frowned when he noticed Lucas' hesitancy. *What was that about?* He wondered briefly. He didn't ponder for long, as the back door to Escapades suddenly slammed open, revealing an all too familiar face.

^^^

"It's about fucking time you got here," Tony snarled as he held the back door of the club open. "The Chicago crew arrived almost an hour ago."

"Don't worry about when I get here, asshole." Harrison then held up a 9mm Beretta and pointed it toward the van, a warning signal to whoever was watching from inside, before turning his head to Tony. "Did you make sure the place is secured? We can't afford to fuck this up."

The security guard rolled his eyes as he held the backdoor open. "I'm not an idiot. Of course I did."

Harrison grunted in disbelief. "The jury's still out on that." He then waved the gun, beckoning to whoever was inside the van to get out.

After a bit of shuffling, a line of six girls slowly descended from the elevated stairs of the van. Their heads were lowered, and their hands tied securely behind their backs as they lowered themselves to the ground. They then lined themselves against the van for Harrison's inspection.

Harrison moved to stand in front of each girl, lifting her head, running a hand slowly along their back, before moving on to the next. Each girl shook so hard that Jolsten could literally see their quivering fear from his perch in the distance.

Harrison pointed to Tony as he gave a cruel sneer to the captives. "Follow him inside, and don't make a fucking sound. The first girl that cries will regret it, I guarantee you." Jolsten could hear the girls uncontrolled whimpering through his headpiece as they turned around to walk in a single file line toward the open door.

Jolsten heard Lucas let out a soft curse.

"There's Jayme. I'd recognize those pigtails anywhere," he muttered.

Jolsten was silent as he watched each girl disappear inside the building. The last girl, well more like young lady, walked the tail end of the formation.

"That's got to be Rachelle. She's taller and looks older than the rest." Jolsten observed.

"I think you're right." Lucas agreed.

They then fell silent as a woman suddenly appeared from the side of the building, hustling swiftly toward Harrison and Tony. She wore tight jeans and a pullover sweater, the hood pulled low on her head to cover her face and hair.

158

"What do you want?" Tony scowled.

"I came to talk to Harrison, you jackass." The woman rebuffed. She then turned to the Chief.

"Look, I did what you wanted me to do. I erased the rest of the tapes that hadn't been destroyed in the fire before Nate got a chance to see them. I've been erasing those feeds for the past fucking year. You finally got him where you want him. I want out of this right now. I did my penance. I'm done." The woman exclaimed with a shaky breath.

Harrison snarled in her direction. "You're done when I say you're done. You don't get to come around here giving fucking demands."

Jolsten could hear the woman choking down a sob. "But I've already done what you asked me to do," she repeated. "Please...I need you to keep your word and leave my son alone. I couldn't take it if anything happened to him. He's all I have." The woman cried, pulling off her hood in frustration.

"Fuck," Lucas cursed again. "That's Gena. She's one of Nate's bartenders. His entire club is infiltrated with goddamn spies."

"If we wanted your son, we'd take him, you stupid cunt. However, lucky for you we don't have a demand for boys right now. If we did, your son would be at the top of the list." Harrison spit cruelly. He then grabbed Gena's arm, twisting it at an odd angle. Jolsten stiffened as she cried out in pain.

"Get out of here." Harrison snarled. "Before I change my mind and decide to make you part of tonight's sale." He then roughly pushed her away from him, causing Gena to falter a few steps before regaining her balance. Glancing quickly toward Tony, she turned and ran toward the opposite side of the building.

"You should have let me take care of her as soon as we lit this place on fire." Tony muttered, as he watched her leave. "We didn't need her anymore after that."

Harrison tilted his head in thought. "Maybe we should add her to the mix tonight. She's a loose string that needs to be tied."

Tony let out an exasperated sigh. "We don't have the manpower right now to handle any more merchandise. Most of those guys you usually use for extra security bailed. I can't do everything. Hell, I even tried to help you out by telling Isobel to make Paige believe Nate was fucking somebody else to try and get rid of her. With all that's going on, Paige would have done nothing but get in the way when her sister got shipped here. Plus, I could have sworn she saw me in Nate's office a few times. She wouldn't question Gena, but she sure as hell would question me. Now, it turns out she still showed up anyway. And I won't even get into how close Gerry and I got to being made when we took that Allen girl." He gave a loud huff. "Shit, Chicago isn't paying me nearly enough for the amount of work that I do. I can't fucking juggle everything."

Harrison seemed like he was tired of the whole conversation. He slowly reached in his pocket, pulled out a cigarette, lit it up, and then took a long drag of nicotine before turning an irritated scowl toward Tony.

"Don't worry, you'll get what's coming to you. After all the merchandise is sold, we'll have some free time to clear up all of these loose ends. Paige and Gena can be at the top of the list, right after we take care of Nate." Harrison then threw the cigarette to the ground, snuffed it with his boot, and followed Tony inside the club, closing the door soundly behind them.

^^^

Jolsten turned, a look of determination on his face.

"We've got to stop that auction, no matter what. If the girls disappear tonight..."

"...We'll never find them again. And Nate, Paige, and whoever else, will be a walking target." Lucas finished.

Jolsten pulled out his cell, quickly dialing Harmony's number.

"How far out are you and Nate?" He asked, cutting straight to the point. "The girls are here, and we need backup. We know they have extra security on the inside of the building, but we can't tell how many guys are stationed outside..."

"...None. Not anymore. I took care of them. They're full of Rohypnol, so they'll be asleep for awhile." The cloaked man advised.

Jolsten narrowed his eyes at the informer. *There was something about him...*

"Exactly how many men are posted outside again?" Harmony asked on the line, disrupting his thoughts.

"Apparently none. Not anymore." Jolsten replied as he looked at her agent. "However we're still not sure how many are inside. Your man set up recordings around the backdoor, and we were able to confirm the auction is still being held tonight. Harrison is here, along with Tony. It also looks like that bartender Gena is involved, but she left the scene."

Harmony snorted. "I figured as much about her. Things weren't adding up when I was undercover. I was keeping a close watch on her as well. Glad my instincts panned out."

"Well, I'm not too sure how long we've got before the buyers show up. What's your ETA?"

"Nate and I are headed back from his house now. We should be there in about thirty minutes. I just hung up with Killian right before you called. He's already got his Captain and the rest of the SEALS in route. It might take them a little longer to get there, since they're headed straight to you from the airport. Hang tight until we arrive, and *don't* go in alone."

Jolsten gritted his teeth. He hated waiting outside when he didn't know what was going on inside with the girls. They could be in danger, and he'd be outside sitting on his ass, doing absolutely nothing to prevent their assaults.

"Yes ma'am. We'll keep watch here to make sure no one comes out that shouldn't. If anymore people show up before you get here, I'll give you a call." With that, he disconnected the call.

Jolsten took a deep breath and looked pointedly at the stranger. "I told her we'd make sure no one comes out. I didn't say anything about us moving in. Look, I understand you have a loyalty to your boss. Feel free to wait out here until she gets here. In the meantime, I'm going inside. Lucas, are you with me?" He steadied his weapon, preparing to defend himself, and anyone else he saw fit.

"Damn straight. Let's go." Lucas said, following closely on his heels.

Chapter Twenty Two

Weapons raised, Lucas and Jolsten slowly moved toward the van as they approached the back door of *Escapades*. Lucas walked to one side of the van, while Jolsten checked the other.

"It's empty," Lucas called as he circled back to stand beside Jolsten. "Let's check the back door."

Jolsten nodded his head as he followed Lucas toward the closed metal door. Lucas gently turned the handle, raising surprised eyebrows as the door pulled open.

"I'll be damned," Jolsten commented. "What idiot leaves the backdoor open when there's so much as stake?"

"A man who thinks he's above the law," Lucas replied disgustedly. He glanced at the broken keypad next to the door and narrowed his eyes. "I know Nate has security codes he enters into this security pad to open the door, but it looks like somebody broke the touchscreen." He pointed to the slivered tracks across the digital interface. "Come on. Harmony and Nate should be here any minute, but I want to check out what's going on in there now. Those little girls might need our help."

Jolsten couldn't agree more.

"Lead the way," he replied as he followed Lucas inside. He glanced up briefly to notice the normal camera above the door had been turned to point toward the highway, ultimately preventing any activity from being captured. A new, inconspicuous blinking light was partially hidden behind the low hanging branch of a nearby tree. The agent's planted recorder. Jolsten assumed the old security feeds weren't running since the club was closed for repairs, and was thankful for the agent's earlier foresight to set up new recording devices of their own.

The two men were greeted with silence as they headed into the darkened hallway of the club. Peering into the distance, Jolsten noticed movement near the far end of the room near the open dance floor. Nodding his head toward Lucas, he pointed to the line of girls slowly climbing the stairs toward the VIP lounge.

Jolsten raised his gun, glancing around the room for signs of Harrison, Tony, or any other potential threat, when suddenly the distinctive boom of a loud gunshot vibrated through the air. Jolsten felt himself immediately knocked down when Lucas threw him on the floor, shielding him in self-defense.

Both men quickly recovered, hurdling themselves into the taped-off office to scrounge for cover. The smell of acrid smoke still clinging to the charred walls assaulted Jolsten's nostrils as they crouched behind a large storage cabinet.

"Are you all right?" Lucas asks, keeping his eye out for signs of incoming danger. He moved like a panther to get closer to the door as he peered into the distance.

Jolsten nodded his head, rolling his now sore shoulder that he bruised during his fall. "I'm fine. What can you see?" His question is instantly answered when he hears the granular voice of Harrison sounding through the club. He silently crawls to cover Lucas' back as they look inside the main dance hall.

Several men had now gathered together and were staring up the club's staircase. Conrad Spivey now joined Harrison, Tony and one other man, whose tall, lean frame was turned away from the office. They lounged against the bar area as Harrison stared angrily up the staircase where the girls had earlier disappeared.

"What is the fuck is going on up there?" Harrison screamed from the bottom of the club's staircase. His hand rested on the revolver by his side as he stared into the darkness.

Gerry Spivey slowly descended the stairs, wiping his bloody hands across the back of his jeans as he walked. He gave the Chief a dismissive glance, the challenge evidence in his gaze.

"I had to silence one of the packages, because she wouldn't shut the fuck up."

Jolsten stiffened, and then shifted his stance as he prepared to barge into the room. He felt a hand on his arm swiftly pull him back.

"Not now," Lucas whispered. Jolsten could see the barely contained rage boiling below the surface of his face, his jaw ticking in agitation. "We need to wait for more backup. We're outnumbered, and we don't know how many more are upstairs."

Jolsten felt his nostrils flare in anger. "He just murdered a girl!" He snarled from clenched teeth.

"And they'll kill even more, including Rachelle and Jayme, if we barge in there blind."

Jolsten gritted his teeth in anger. He nodded his head once, and then lowered his body back behind the shadows of one of the filing cabinets.

"You two go upstairs and watch the girls," Gerry nodded toward Tony and the other gunman. "Make sure they stay quiet. That fucking whimpering is getting on my nerves." Tony and the other gunman soon ascended the staircase as directed, disappearing out of sight.

A distance ring chime sounded in the room, and the alderman reached inside his pocket to answer the call.

"Conrad speaking," he announced into the speaker. "Good, we're getting everything lined up now. We'll be ready by the time you get here." He then clicked off the call.

"Our South American partners have arrived. They'll be here within the hour." Conrad said, a small smirk creeping over his lean face.

"Good. I'm excited to meet with them." Harrison stated.

"Are you now?" Conrad raised an eyebrow as his eyes slowly roamed over the officer's face. He leaned against the back of a chair as he carefully weighed his next words. "Tell me, Chief Harrison. Were you able to take care of Nate Kerr? He had critical intel that would not favor anyone in this room if his knowledge were to be leaked."

Harrison leaned against the bar counter as he sized up the slender alderman. He then gave a condescending grin, folding his arms across his chest.

"The blaze Tony started took care of those security cameras and all that footage. Everything's covered from our end."

Fury stole over the alderman's face as he angrily jerked upright. "I wanted you to take care of NATE! Fuck the damn security feeds!

How many ways do I have to spell it out for you country hicks! I wanted *him* taken care of, not just this fucking club! You're just as incompetent as Stevens! *Fuck me!*" Conrad then ran an angry hand over his face.

Harrison stiffened as he met the alderman's angry glaze with an arrogant one of his own.

"*We're* the incompetent ones?" Harrison sneered back defensively. "That's rich coming from you! Chicago has been fucking up for a while now. Word on the street is that you guys can't handle the reigns anymore." He pointed an accusing finger in the alderman's face. "You've been letting too many close calls slip through your fucking fingers, risking exposure to everyone."

Conrad's lip twisted, not backing down from the obvious implied threat the Chief was making. "And what exactly are you referring to, Chief Harrison?"

"I'm talking about the fact that your fuckups started a long time ago. From that New Orleans contact who got busted years ago when he swiped only one of those twins, to Stevens getting greedy and trying to sell two adults instead of sticking with our trademark girls. You have no idea how hard it was to keep the press out of the fact that a famous international superstar almost got her ass sold into the slave market." He straightened his broad shoulders as he towered over the alderman.

"Maybe *our* South American partners feel like it's time for some new management around here. Someone who could give a fresher perspective on things. Maybe they think that moving the US hub from Chicago to Houston would be a better all-around move for everyone involved." Harrison mocked, raising a contemptuous eyebrow.

The sound of another bullet whizzing through the air caused Jolsten and Lucas to duck once more behind the cabinet. The sound of heavy footsteps running down the staircase caused Jolsten to peer once again around the doorframe.

"What the hell is going on?" cried Tony, as he gripped the railing. He stared disbelievingly at Harrison's lifeless body as it lay on the ground. "Are we killing everyone now? What the fuck?"

"He was getting to be too much of a burden. And I didn't like his fucking attitude. Too cocky." Gerry replied, casually replacing his pistol back into his holster. He then gave a challenging look at Tony. "Now, I'm going back upstairs. Maybe I'll entertain myself a bit and sample some of the goods before the buyers come. I've been riding coach planes all day, and need to fucking unwind." With that, he pushed past Tony and started to make his way back upstairs.

Conrad shook his head as he looked at this brother, before turning to the now slain Harrison. He jerked his head in Tony's direction. "Move his body over to that corner over there. We'll dispose of it later, after the sales. And bring that other body from upstairs down here, and pile it on top of Harrison. When you're done, meet me back upstairs. There's a couple of things I need to talk to you about, mainly about taking care of Nate for good."

He nodded his head nonchalantly toward the dead officer. "Obviously he was incompetent to handle the job. Hopefully you can do better. Hurry up." With that, he made his way to the upper level to follow his brother.

Tony watched the alderman ascend the staircase before releasing a visible shiver over his large, muscled frame. He then bent over, picked up Harrison's body, and dragged it off to the side before following the alderman up the steps to retrieve the other body.

^^^

I know something's going on, Paige thought as she paced the recesses of Nate's bedroom. She chewed her bottom lip as she glanced at her cell phone for the thousandth time that evening.

"Why the hell hasn't he called? It's been hours, almost a full day, since he's gotten that call from Killian. Why hasn't he kept me in the loop?" she asked rhetorically. She nervously rounded the area around Nate's bed once again. Noticing a pair of car keys next to the nightstand, she stopped dead in her tracks.

Why didn't I notice these before? She thought as she marched over to grab the keys.

"Because you've been too busy rolling around in Nate's bed, smelling his scent, and rubbing yourself all over his house like a bitch in heat marking her territory." She muttered out loud.

She jogged down the stairs and walked through the house toward his garage. After turning on the light, she let out a low whistle. She'd discovered that Nate had a four-car garage when she first arrived, but never dreamed that he actually had that many vehicles at his disposal, since he normally rode around in his Mercedes. She pushed the alarm on the set of keys and was mildly delighted to find herself in the driver's seat of his jet black Range Rover.

Pulling out of his garage, she headed back down Northpark Drive to begin the long trek to Cypress.

Hmm, Nate mentioned before he left that he was headed to meet Killian.

Although she had no idea where their meeting had taken place, she knew one thing for certain. Nate would be checking in on his club to see how the repairs were coming along. He'd want to know how soon he could reopen.

And that's exactly where she would be heading.

As she approached the exit marker on the highway indicating that TX-99 was just ahead, Paige felt even more solidified in her decision to head toward *Escapades* for answers.

Glancing at the gas tank, Paige cringed.

I'd better fill up so I won't be stranded trying to get those doggone answers.

Spotting a gas station up the road, she decided to pull over before continuing on her journey. After running inside the Exxon station to pay for her gas and a bottle of vitamin water, she walked back outside to fill up the truck, when suddenly the flash of a black and white sports coupe caught her eye. Frowning as she held the nozzle to the tank, her eyes followed the familiar vehicle as it zoomed past her. She then gasped at the next sight that assaulted her vision, causing her to almost spill gas all over the cemented ground.

I know *that wasn't Nate with a half naked female in his car that I just saw,* she thought disbelievingly as she watched the Mercedes race down the highway.

What. The. Fuck!

Her eyes couldn't deny the woman she saw sitting in the passenger side of Nate's Mercedes, pulling a shirt over her head as Nate drove speeding past. Her long hair covered her face, but her bare, pale skin shone brightly against the dark bra covering her breasts.

Shock and outrage soon engulfed Paige, spurring her feet to move quickly to jump in the truck to race after them.

Now she could see why it had been so long since she'd heard from Nate. What a fool she'd been!

I'm such a fucking idiot! She thought darkly. She'd vowed when she left Texas that she would never be played for a fool again, and yet here she was, watching yet another man she loved play her with another woman.

Her foot pressed harder on the gas pedal as she sped to catch up with Nate's car.

She *wouldn't* be played again. *Not again. Not again. Not again.*

Chapter Twenty Three

"What the hell are you doing?" Nate barked as he watched Harmony disrobe unashamedly in the front seat of his car.

"I'm gearing up. Relax, I'm sure it's nothing you haven't seen before." She shrugged the bulletproof vest over her slim shoulders and over her lace bra. "Besides, I'm gay. I have absolutely no interest in anything you have to offer. Didn't I tell you that before?"

Nate kept his eyes glued to the highway to distract him from the woman sitting next to him. "No, but that doesn't matter. There's something called discretion that I would appreciate being shown in my direction."

"Sorry. After years of working undercover with a team full of alpha male FBI agents, I've learned to not be wary of a little thing like modesty. You remember that *G.I. Jane* movie with Demi Moore? Yea, FBI training can be rough just like that, especially for a woman."

She tugged her grey and white shirt back over her head. "Where do you think Paige went? You said she should've been waiting for you back at your house."

Nate shook his head in frustration as his hands tightened painfully around the steering wheel. "She should have been. I have no idea where she went. I need to find her."

"Negative. We need to get to *Escapades* first to help her sister. We know exactly where Rachelle is at the moment, and we can't afford to lose that momentum. We'll just have to regroup with Paige later."

Nate gritted his teeth as he turned onto TX-99, paying no attention to the Rover racing fast a few miles behind him.

^^^

Jolsten and Lucas stood up, moving slowly out of the *Escapades* office as they observed the staircase for any sign of incoming trouble.

"We need to move, with or without backup." Jolsten said. "Those other girls could be in danger."

He pointed to the still body of the young girl Tony had tossed down earlier. "That officer already murdered one of them." The lifeless girl looked to be about ten years old. Regret and anger coursed through him at the young life that had been so brutally taken.

Lucas' lips thinned as his eyes narrowed at the bodies. He then gave a quick nod. "Fuck it. Let's roll."

They cautiously approached the staircase, weapons drawn in defense, when suddenly Lucas cursed. Reaching inside his pocket, he pulled out his vibrating cell phone and checked the message.

"It's Harmony," Lucas acknowledged. "She just sent a text. She and Nate are outside."

Jolsten looked around the darkened club with apprehension as indecision warred within him. They needed backup in order to ensure they took down Tony and his crew, especially since they didn't know how many additional men were also waiting in the VIP area. However time was of the essence. They needed to get to the girls...and quickly.

Lucas read through the next series of texts. "She's basically demanding that we meet her outside. She said she has a plan that won't involve us martyring ourselves, since she knows we don't have sufficient backup."

"The girls..." Jolsten started. He didn't like the thought of what the girls were going through at this moment, especially with a proven killer among their midst. However he also knew that as of this moment, Harmony had jurisdiction over this case, especially since his own superior was involved.

"The girls would fare much better if we gathered some extra gun power. Come on." Lucas said. Grudgingly, Jolsten nodded his head as he followed Lucas out of the backdoor. He wasn't sure if Lucas was trying to convince him with his words, or himself. He silently sent up a prayer that everything would work out.

The cool night air met them once again as they moved back toward the lines of trees where Harmony, Nate, and Harmony's agent waited. Jolsten raised an eyebrow as he watched Harmony check and load her Smith and Wesson 610 revolver, a weapon even he considered to be too powerful to carry on a day-to-day basis. Harmony Rune had obviously come prepared.

Jolsten gave the group a grim expression. "They've already murdered one of the girls. The rest of them are being kept on the second floor."

Harmony cursed.

"And they're showcasing them in the VIP lounge? Shit, they really don't have any limits." Nate muttered darkly.

Lucas clenched his fists together. "And that cop we saw in the picture with Tony just killed Harrison."

"What?" Nate said incredulously.

Jolsten nodded his head in confirmation. "Yea, Harrison is dead, but we did see Rachelle and Jayme among the girls they're holding. We need to get them out of there, like now."

"We don't know how many additional guys they have on the second floor. When we initially arrived, Tony told Harrison that a lot of their extra help bailed on them tonight. That's not to say that they still don't have a sufficient number helping them out, but we just don't know for sure." Lucas informed.

"Speaking of help, I thought you told us not to become martyrs. Where the hell is this extra help? The girls could be in serious danger right now, and we're standing out here gabbing away!" Jolsten snarled, narrowing his eyes at Harmony. He was growing antsier by the minute. The tall, cloaked man narrowed his eyes as he stood silently beside her while she adjusted her bulletproof vest.

Harmony's eyes darted behind Jolsten and lingered for a moment toward the darkness, before moving back to his concerned expression. She then gave a small smile, but it was void of any humor.

"I think we'll be ok. Believe me, no one wants to see the Hunter Group shut down more than me. They've put my family through more hell than you could possibly imagine. Now, the rest of my team has barricades set up a couple of miles up the road to watch for any supposed buyers wishing to make an entrance. We just need to be concerned with the muscle they have right now watching the girls. Follow me, and watch your six."

Harmony then stalked back toward the club like a silent panther, with Jolsten, Lucas, her agent, and finally Nate following closely behind. She gently turned the handle and scooted inside, her gun held high to readily take out any potential threat. Seeing none, she glanced over her shoulder.

"Nate, I need you to man this door. Make sure no one we haven't already identified comes lurking through here. Can you do that?"

Nate grimly nodded his head. "Yea, I can handle that. I could handle a lot more if I could get to my office and get my 9mm. I'm sure it's still in my desk. Harrison was more concerned about rubbing the loss of my business in my face than making sure this place was secured."

Lucas nodded his head. "And now we know why. Go ahead and grab your piece." He then turned to Harmony's agent. "But I'll need you with him. Nate's still a civilian here. I'd feel more comfortable if both of you were covering our six."

"I have to agree," Jolsten chimed in.

"Don't worry, I got him. Get the girls." The rough voice sounded through the mask.

Jolsten, Lucas and Harmony slowly made their way over to the staircase. Jolsten held up a finger of silence as he strained to hear what was going on upstairs.

"Go check it out," a distinguished voice sounded from above.

"Take cover," Jolsten hissed. They quickly moved behind the bar with seconds to spare before Tony came barreling down the steps, weapon drawn.

Jolsten could see Tony's eyes frantically searching around the room for any sign of movement or unrest. His stance widened as he prepared to confront the burly guard. However, before he could move from his hiding place, Harmony jumped up behind Tony, and smacked him hard on the head with the butt of her heavy pistol.

Tony's eyes immediately closed, his body going completely limp with unconsciousness as he began to fall. With lightening speed, both Lucas and Jolsten ran over and grabbed the big security guard before the sound of him hitting the floor could alert someone.

"Shit," Lucas huffed as he helped to drag Tony off to the side. "Next time, can you give a warning before you knock somebody out? This guy weighs a ton."

Harmony shrugged. "Sorry. I couldn't have him alerting the guys upstairs that we're down here."

"Hey, are you guys all right?" Nate called anxiously from the office. Jolsten turned to see Nate slowly approach, staring angrily in Tony's direction. If looks could kill, Tony would have died three times over.

"We're fine. I thought we told you to man the door." Lucas stated.

Nate rolled his eyes. "Look, this is *my* club, and that means that this is my issue to deal with as well. Don't expect me to stand around quietly while you hunt these motherfuckers down." He then pointed toward Harmony. "Besides, her agent is covering the door, and he looks more than capable of handling it. I'm going with you, so lead the way."

"We don't have time to debate about this. Just stay in the back and out of the way." Harmony hissed.

Jolsten then turned to follow Harmony and Lucas, with Nate closely following on his tail up the staircase.

Suddenly a loud boom sounded through the air, causing the building to shake and the walls to rattle. Seconds later, gunfire erupted in the distance, along with the shrill sound of girls screaming. Jolsten cursed, and then pushed past Lucas and Harmony as he sprinted up the staircase.

"POLICE! FREEZE! Drop your weapons and get down on the ground!" Jolsten screamed as he ran into the room. Nate also managed to follow closely on his tail as they reached the upper level of the venue. When they reached the top, they both momentarily paused to stare up at the ceiling.

A huge, gaping hole now appeared in the roof, displaying the night skyline and stars above. Someone had released a smoke bomb into the room, as the air was now pungent with the burning stench of smoke. Several men covered in all black, and sporting gas masks over their noses and mouths, eerily similar to the mask that Bane wore in *The Dark Knight Rises,* slid down a long rope that had been lowered into the room. Upon hitting the ground, they then pointed their weapons toward the back of the lounge.

Jolsten's eyes searched frantically for the girls through the thick haze, finally spotting them near the raised stage area near the back wall. The girls were gathered together in a terrified huddle. He also saw Rachelle trying her best to shield them from the chaos and possible gunfire, her arms stretching around them as much as she possibly could.

Peering into the distance, Jolsten recognized the meaty face of Gerry Spivey, and immediately pointed his gun in Gerry's direction. There were also two other figures standing alongside Gerry, in addition to Conrad, but they were donned in shadows.

Suddenly one of the men, sporting thick, curly black hair and a baseball cap, moved protectively beside Gerry to point his gun in the girls direction. The other man stayed in shadow, looking wildly around the chaos in front of him.

Jolsten tried to swallow down his fear. He couldn't let the girls know how terrified he was for their safety. His eyes then darted to the agents that fell from the roof. He watched as the men worked in harmonized fluency, reflecting years of conditioned training. The men quickly moved to surround the girls within a protective huddle, ultimately resulting in each masked man standing directly in front of each victim. They formed a protective shield with their body as they raised their weapons toward Gerry and his crew in defense.

Upon seeing the influx of armed resistance now pointing in their direction, the suspect still donned in shadow quickly raised his hands to his head, and then lowered his body to the ground in surrender.

Conrad and Gerry however, would not be taken down as easily. Conrad looked wildly around the room, spotted Nate, and let out a wild, inhuman snarl.

"Shoot him!" Conrad squealed, pointing at Nate, who was looking at the scene with paralyzing astonishment. His lowered weapon had fallen to his side as he stared up first at his demolished ceiling, and then at the agents who had fallen through. Upon hearing Conrad's cry in his direction, his eyes looked over in confusion as he regarded the alderman.

Gerry then raised his gun in Nate's direction, preparing to shoot Suddenly another single gunshot whistled through the air. Gerry then dropped his own weapon as his body went rigidly still.

Upon hearing the shot, the girls whimpered softly as they clung to each other, reassuring themselves that no one had gotten hit. All heads, except Jolsten, then turned toward the curly-haired man alongside Conrad, who had delivered the shot to Gerry's chest.

Instead of watching the shooter, however, Jolsten watched with smug satisfaction as Gerry touched the red stickiness that quickly spread across his torso. Pulling his hand away from his chest, Gerry glanced at the blood covering his fingers, before turning a questioning stare toward his own man.

"What the fuck?" Gerry groaned, blood spitting from his jowls. He then looked around frantically for his gun, but Lucas quickly kicked it out of the way.

"I wouldn't try it if I were you," Lucas stated darkly. He then pointed his gun toward the curly haired suspect still standing next to Conrad.

"I second that," Harmony said, rounding toward Conrad with her S&W pointed straight at his head. "I'm going to need your hands in the air, you miserable piece of shit." Conrad's chest moved in small shudders as he slowly raised his hands, allowing Harmony to effectively throw him to the ground alongside the man who had already surrendered.

Jolsten raised his head toward the ceiling, sending up a silent prayer of thanks. It looked like this HG nightmare would finally come to an end. For all of them.

^^^

"Drop your weapon!" Nate heard Jolsten call, as he pointed his weapon toward the man who'd fired the last shot.

The last remaining suspect in the baseball cap slowly moved his hand toward his head in a sign of surrender. However instead of conceding, the man removed his baseball cap, along with the black curly wig he was sporting.

"It's about time you motherfuckers showed up, because they already shot one of them," the man called in a distinguished mid-western drawl. He looked at the agents surrounding the girls. "I thought I was going to have to put a bullet in every motherfucker in here to stop them from raping one of these girls. It would've ruined my reputation as an uncaring bastard." He nodded grimly toward Gerry, who was clutching his chest as he heaved heavily. "I guess seeing that fat bastard get shot is satisfying for now."

Nate let out a relieved huff, realizing just how close he'd gotten to become the next murder victim within his own establishment. He then turned a huge smile at the familiar face.

"Motherfucking Reid!" Nate exclaimed. "God, I'm glad to see you, man!"

Reid gave his signature cocky surfer boy smirk, his long blond hair now flowing freely around his shoulders as he tossed the cap and wig to the ground. "I know you are. Tyson and your boy let me know what's been going on. You had to know that we had your back, as well as his. And we damn sure couldn't let them take his niece."

Nate frowned in confusion. "Who are you talking about?"

One of the agents guarding Jayme pulled off his gas mask.

"*My* niece." With that, he turned around and picked up Jayme, cradling her gently in his arms.

"Uncle Killy!" Jayme squealed, clutching her uncle for dear life. She then turned to Rachelle, giving her a wide, knowing smile. "See, I told you we just needed to be brave for a little longer. Uncle Killy came for us." Jayme then turned to Killian. "Will you take me to my Daddy now?"

"Yes, baby girl. Your daddy is waiting for you." Killian said, his voice hoarse with emotion.

Another agent pulled the mask from his face, revealing a sprinkling of salt and pepper hair sharply contained within a military buzz cut. He stood tall and menacing as he looked over the scene with the eye of a predatory hawk, searching for any additional signs of danger. Seeing Harmony, his grim expression turned into a soft smile.

"Agent Rune, so good to see you." His rough, scaly voice boomed through the room.

"Captain Bernard, it's been a long time." Harmony replied, smiling as she stared up at the imposing man.

Feeling like the nightmare was finally coming to a close, Nate walked over to Rachelle, cautiously holding out his hand in front of her.

"Hello, Rachelle. My name is Nate Kerr. I'm a friend of your sister, and we've come to take you home."

A loud commotion broadcasted from the lower staircase, and all heads, along with their guns, turned toward the sound. Rapid feet running up the steps soon revealed Paige rushing frantically up the stairs. Harmony's discombobulated field agent tried his best to refrain her from entering, but it was obvious that Paige was not to be deterred.

"NATE!" Paige screamed as her eyes frantically scanned the room. He turned toward the sound of his love's voice as she came barreling into the lounge. Her gaze then immediately fell upon her sister.

"Rachelle?" Paige said in a choked whisper as she stopped abruptly in her tracks. She clutched the railing in obvious disbelief.

"Paige?" Rachelle said incredulously. As recognition slowly dawned on her, Rachelle pushed herself to her feet and past Nate's outstretched hand to run toward her sister.

As all eyes turned toward the reunion, Conrad chose that moment to jump to his feet. He quickly knocked the gun from Reid's hand, and pushed the young surfer roughly to the ground. Swiftly snatching the fallen weapon from the ground, he pointed it at Nate.

Nate felt his whole world spinning as he stared death in the face for the second time in his life.

"You will NOT WIN! Die, you miserable piece of shit! JUST FUCKING DIE!" Conrad screamed. Nate's eyes grew wide as the barrel of Reid's gun pointed square at his chest.

Conrad fired.

Somewhere in the distance Nate heard the sound of high pitch screams and anxious calls to take cover. The distant sounds of his own pain escaped from his lips as hot, liquid fire burned into the flesh of his left shoulder.

Looking down at the lapel of his suit jacket, he saw a small bullet hole peering back at him through the material. Momentarily frozen in shock that he was indeed shot, Nate grunted when Lucas knocked him to the ground in an effort to thwart any additional harm, while Harmony held a screaming Paige away from the crossfire.

He turned his head as he struggled to breath under Lucas' weight, just in time to see Capt. Bernard raise his gun and fire a retaliation shot toward the alderman. Mixed emotions flooded the room as they all watched the alderman fall to his knees from the fatal shot, then close his eyes as death consumed him. A still resolve soon followed, the only sounds to be heard were Jolsten on the phone speaking with paramedics, and the girls crying in the background.

Nate felt himself shifted as Lucas turned him around to apply pressure to his wound and elevate his head. Gritting his teeth against the pain in his shoulder, his eyes watched as Capt. Bernard kept his gun on Gerry.

Gerry slowly dragged himself toward his brother, tears cascading down his grief-stricken face. He then picked Conrad's head from the ground to cradle in his arms, the whole time sobbing as he looked at his fallen sibling.

"I got you, Conrad," Gerry sobbed into his brother's shoulder as he held him tight. "I got you, man."

The next sound Nate heard was the distinct wailing of sirens in the distance. Not able to withstand his consciousness any longer, and knowing that at last his woman, his mother, his friends, and his business were finally safe, he closed his eyes and let darkness consume him.

178

Chapter Twenty Four

"We were able to successfully remove the bullet. Luckily it was a clean entry, and hadn't hit any major arteries. We cleaned and dressed the area, and prescribed some mild painkillers. You said he's not allergic to anything, correct?"

"Correct. I'll make sure he takes whatever medications he needs. You just make sure you do *your* job, and we won't have any problems. He will *not* suffer a moment longer than he has to, do you understand me?"

The sound of an irritated grunt was heard loudly in the room, right before a door opened and closed to signal someone had just left.

Nate internally groaned in amusement at the sound of that voice, as he slowly regained awareness.

Who in the hell had contacted his mother?

He knew from experience that the doctors and nurses on call better make damn sure that whatever treatment was administered to him, was done so with efficiency and effectiveness. The last time he'd been in the hospital for any type of injury was his freshman year in high school, when he broke his leg playing football. The treating nurse had literally been a shaking, frightened ball of nerves after Belinda's antics.

"Ma," he managed to mutter. His voice felt scratchy and hoarse, like he'd swallowed a glass full of sandpaper.

He grunted softly when his bed was momentarily shaken as his mother crowded over him. She placed a cool hand over his forehead, and then leaned down to kiss his cheek.

"Hey baby boy. How are you feeling?" Belinda asked, concern lining her voice.

"My shoulder," he started. He glanced down to see that the left side of his chest and shoulder were now wrapped in ace bandages, and cradled in a sling.

"You were lucky, honey. The bullet went clean through you. However I *am* pissed off that a bullet even touched you to begin with. I *know* I taught you how to shoot. What happened to the duck and cover method I showed you?" Brenda scolded.

Nate grimaced. "I wasn't thinking at the time, Ma. I was trying to making sure..." he strained to turn his neck around the confining view from his bed. "Where is Paige?"

"I'm here," her soft voice called from behind his hospital bed. He tilted his head upward to see her pale face smiling faintly. She reached over to lightly brush her fingers over his goatee as she walked around the other side of his bed. "I'm here. I'm so sorry for what happened to you."

Nate frowned. "What are you talking about? This wasn't your fault. None of this was your fault."

"But I distracted you by rushing in there! I should have trusted that whatever you were doing, that you were trying to take care of me, in whatever way you thought was best." She sadly shook her head, and Nate could see the regret lining her face. "I just saw a half-naked woman riding with you in your car, and I lost it."

"You saw a *what*?" Belinda cried incredulously.

Nate winced at the memory. "Yea, umm, sorry about that." He then frowned. "Wait, how did you know?"

Paige gave him a soft smile. "I'd just left your house. I was filling up your truck at the gas station when you guys drove past me. I saw Harmony in the front seat."

She shrugged sheepishly, her gaze falling ashamedly to the floor. "Harmony explained everything to me downstairs in the waiting area. I should have known better that you wouldn't play me. I let my insecurities take hold and steer my thoughts. And then when those guys with FBI jackets wouldn't let me through the roadblock they'd set up while I was trying to follow you back to the club, I panicked even more. I didn't know what to think. I got out of the truck and ran on foot to try and see what was going on."

Her beautiful golden eyes pleaded for him to understand as she beseechingly looked into his gaze. "It's why I came rushing up those

180

stairs. Unfortunately it was also the cause of distraction for everyone, and allowed that man an opportunity to try and kill you."

She then let out a long, regretful breath. Nate felt his heart stop at being the center of her intense focus.

"I'm so sorry, Nate."

He reached out with his uninjured arm to clasp her hand. "There's nothing to apologize for, baby. I understand. I would have done the same thing if I had seen what you had."

Paige's eyes filled with tears of relief. She leaned over and brushed her lips gently across his. Nate closed his eyes, his heart pounded in his chest like a bass drum. His blood surged as her familiar scent washed over his senses. Peaches and cream. So fitting for his sweet African *Theia*.

"My baby," he murmured, gripping the back of her neck. He crushed his mouth against hers as raw need drove him to devour her taste once again.

The sound of a throat clearing reminded him that they were not alone in the hospital room. He smirked as he pulled away from Paige, but still held her close, moving over slightly in his bed so that Paige could sit beside him.

Belinda regarded Nate with amused annoyance. "You're supposed to be recuperating, not making out."

Nate shrugged his uninjured shoulder. "What can I say? I love her."

Belinda's eyes grew wide as the impact of his carefree words resonated with her. She then turned a warm, affectionate gaze toward her son.

"Well," she said, satisfaction humming within her expression. "I'll be damned. I think you'll be all right after all."

"Yea, I'm good. Paige can take care of me." Nate looked around the hospital room and let out a small grimace. "All the more reason I need to get out of this hospital room. A hospital bed is just like a parked taxi cab with the meter left running."

Brenda's satisfied hum quickly turned into a storm fire of agitation. She pointed a reprimanding finger in his direction. "You will stay in this bed until you're fully healed, Nathaniel Alastair Kerr! Or I swear to God I'll give you something to warrant this bed *really* being necessary!"

Nate turned a lopsided grin toward Paige. "I'm a grown ass man, yet Ma still has the ability to make me want to go to my room with my head hung low."

Paige winked at Belinda before giving him a chastened kiss. "That's because you respect her. I love the fact that you honor her so much. It means that you're more than capable of showing the woman in your life that you can honor her as well."

"You're damn straight. And don't you forget it again." Nate growled softly.

Paige bit her lip and nodded in response. "I love you too."

Belinda placed her hands on her hips as she frowned in thought. "I still don't understand why you were shot in the first place." Belinda stated.

At that moment, Killian, Harmony, and Delphi walked into the room. Delphi held Jayme tightly in his arms, as the little girl clung to her father's neck.

"We can probably shed some light on that for you." Killian stated.

"And who are you?" Belinda demanded, moving a little closer to her son.

Nate smiled at his mother's show of protection. "Ma, these are the men who helped me save Paige's sister, as well as my club. And you remember Delphi. He used to be my college roommate back at Natchez State."

"Of course!" Belinda smiled, her face transforming into a gratified grin. She walked over to embrace Killian and Harmony. "It's very nice to meet the both of you." Finally, she stood before Delphi and patted his cheek. "Delphi sweetheart, it's good to see you again. And who is this precious little girl?"

"This is my daughter, Jayme." Delphi responded, rubbing his cheek against the top of Jayme's head.

"Hello, baby girl." Belinda smiled with affection. "I've got some candy in my purse. Would you like a piece?"

"Yes ma'am." Jayme replied softly, studying the woman from underneath her lashes. Jayme watched Belinda as she search for the candy in her handbag. She then shyly accepted the piece of *Werther's Original Caramel Coffee* candy from Belinda's hand, and popped it quickly in her mouth.

Nate chuckled lightly. His mother had always been a sucker for little children.

"We've just found out some interesting information, Nate. We thought you'd want to hear about it as soon as possible." Killian informed.

Nate stiffened. Killian's expression indicated that the news he had to share wouldn't exactly be good. "Any news would be helpful. When that man began yelling my name, it was obvious he intended on killing me. I'd love to know exactly why."

Delphi looked down at his daughter. "Sweetheart, do you think Ms. Harmony could take you downstairs to the hospital cafeteria and get you some ice cream? Would you like that?"

Jayme's arms briefly tightened around her father as she stared wide-eyed at Harmony in a moment of thought. Finally, she eased her arms from his neck and allowed her father to lower her to the ground. She looked up at him for reassurance before slowly nodded her head.

"Ok, Daddy. I'll go with her. She looks like Miss Holley, and Miss. Holley is my friend, so I guess that means she's ok." Jayme reasoned. She then turned to stare at Harmony with assessing eyes. "Are you nice?"

Harmony bent low so that she was at eye level with the little girl. "Yes love, I'm very nice. And I'll protect you while your Daddy stays here, I promise."

Jayme nodded her head, before slipping her small hand inside Harmony's. "Ok."

Harmony stood and looked at Delphi, sympathy lining her face, before masking it to give Jayme a quiet "*Thank you for trusting me, honey.*"

Delphi bent to give his daughter a kiss. "That's my baby. I'll see you in a few minutes, ok?"

Jayme nodded again, before she followed Harmony out of the room. Delphi turned to Nate, emotion warring over his features at his daughter's obvious trepidation, causing his chin to quiver.

"I'm sorry about that. She's been extremely clingy since Killian brought her home." Delphi explained as he physically tried to reign in his emotions.

Belinda waved off his concern, understanding evident in her expression. "It's obvious that little girl has been through a lot, and that she knows her Daddy is a safe place." She then turned to Killian. "Now, explain this *interesting information* to us."

Killian took a deep breath, crossed his muscled biceps across his wide chest, and began to restate everything Gerry had confessed while being treated a couple of hospital floors down.

He explained how Conrad and Gerry Spivey were originally from the West side of Chicago, growing up not too far from where Nate and his family had lived. Their mother died when Gerry was just 18 years old, leaving the care of his younger grade school brother solely to him. He'd pledged to take care of his brother as part of his mother's last dying wish.

Killian described how Conrad had been a closeted homosexual for years, and how his older brother often guarded him against physical threats and harassment--even throughout his adult life.

Apparently meeting the then city alderman, now Mayor of Chicago Eugene Penne, had helped Conrad deal with his hidden desires. Alderman Penne had taken the young man under wing, and began a longtime affair with Conrad for years, while he also worked his way up the power grid within the Hunter Group's organization. Killian explained how one day during a celebration parade, a little boy by the name of Darrick Kerr walked down a side street to use one of the porta potties, and inadvertently witnessed Penne and Spivey exchanging a deep, passionate kiss.

An observation that ultimately resulted in Darrick's homicide.

Furthermore, Killian explained how Spivey and the Mayor had been watching Nate, along with anyone associated with him, for years.

184

They'd feared that Darrick might have previously leaked information about their relationship, which was their main motivator in trying to take Nate down. The men would have stopped at nothing to make sure their secret stayed hidden.

Finally, Killian shared the good news that as a result of the road barricade they'd erected, the FBI had been able to detain several international buyers that had arrived for the auction, placing them all under arrest. In addition, Mayor Penne was currently being indicted on over 120 counts of bribery, extortion, murder, solicitation, rape, and kidnapping. The counts ranged from his involvement with HG, to his recent troubles with Chicago politics. Penne had been wailing like that prison guard from the movie *The Shawshank Redemption* when FBI authorities scooped him up from his home.

Nate sat in his bed, completely numb as the shock of Killian's words rang through his head.

Darrick was killed because of this? This bullshit? This was why he'd been targeted? This was the reason why their mother had been threatened? Why his club had been torched? All because some bigwigs in Chicago didn't want the public to know they were on the down low?

Belinda cried openly, sobbing into her hands, as the truth of her son's murder was finally revealed. Killian placed his arms around her to offer comfort while he continued to speak.

"I was surprised that Gerry confessed to all that he did." Killian stated. "But he said that since Conrad was gone, there was no further need to hide anything."

"Tony, Isobel, and Gena are now all being held without bond down at the police station. Officer Spivey will join them once he's released from the hospital." Delphi added.

Paige gasped next to him as Nate squeezed her hand in comfort. "Why is Gena being arrested?" She exclaimed.

Delphi looked at her unflinchingly. "For her part in helping to take down Nate's club. She was erasing surveillance feeds that captured girls being taken and sold within *Escapades* walls. She knew what she was doing."

Paige shook her head unconvincingly. "There has to be more to that story. I *know* her. She wouldn't do something like that without a good reason."

Nate threaded his fingers with hers.

Killian's lips thinned. "Lucas overheard her ask Harrison to relieve her from his hold on her. Apparently he'd been threatening to take her son in exchange for her erasing the feeds. Right now she's facing lesser charges than the others, since she wasn't directly involved with the kidnapping. However she's still in a lot of trouble."

Paige turned a victorious scowl toward Delphi. "See, there's your explanation."

Delphi's nostrils flared. "She still did it! She could have reached out for help. From Nate. From you. From *anyone*. She could have let someone know what the fuck was going on! Instead, she risked my daughter's life, hell your sister's life, for the sake of her own child. She should have gotten *help*!"

Killian raised his hand up. "Let a jury decide her guilt or innocence. We certainly won't be able to today."

Nate looked grudgingly at Killian. His heart was aching at the thought that his beloved friend could betray him like this. However he knew how much Gena loved her son. She would do anything to keep him safe. And, it seems, she had. Bad decisions and all.

"Who has her little boy now?" asked Nate.

"Her father came to the station to take custody of him. The old man was clearly distraught that his daughter was caught up in this fiasco."

Nate could only imagine. The previous owner of *Escapades* was a quiet, reserved man, who'd been looking forward to his retirement years. Now it seemed his early retirement might be cut short in order to raise an infant grandson.

"You're right. Gena's fate is now in a jury's hands. Thank you very much for coming to tell me, Killian." Nate let out an exaggerated huff. "It's so much take in..."

"I know, and I'm sorry..." Killian gave Belinda's shoulders a supportive squeeze. He then discreetly handed her some tissues to blot

186

her tear-stained face. "...For all of your losses. Learning that the reason why a family member was gunned down was because of pure political selfishness and greed is a hard pill to swallow. We're here for you; in whatever capacity you need us. Both of you."

Nate felt the true, honest intent of Killian's words. "Thanks, man. We appreciate it."

"I'm kinda upset that you never told me you had a brother, Nate." Delphi chastened, getting his temper back under control once again. He pursed his lips at his old roommate as he rubbed his hand over his beard. "You know what that means now, don't you?"

Nate furrowed his brow in confusion. "No, what?"

Delphi shrugged nonchalantly. "It means now I'm going to have to become your brother, man. We were already friends for life, now your status was just raised a notch. Fair warning: Asha tends to treat people we consider family with an iron fist. That means no more disappearances around the holidays, no more 'I got to see about the club tonight' nonsense. She'll expect to see your face front and center around her dining room table on every holiday occasion from now on."

He then smiled apologetically at Paige, silently asking for a truce. Paige responded with a hesitant smile of her own. "And make sure to bring your girl. The last time she came around was for Mr. Blackburn's wedding, and you barely introduced her to anyone. You came in and went out like a ghost."

Nate felt a pressure he didn't know was there begin to lift from his chest. "Tell Asha you're on. I'm looking forward to tasting some of that seafood gumbo I've heard so much about."

Delphi then let out a loud laugh. "You'll have to wait in line, my friend. Every time Austin comes home, he and Alanna fight over which one of them will get to sample it first. By the time those stomachs have taste-tested the pot, there's hardly any left for the rest of us. But you're more than willing to try." He then took on a sobered expression. "I completely blame ABMS on your need to succeed in the past. I know it, and understand it all too well."

Paige gave a confused expression. "What is ABMS?"

"The Angry Black Man Syndrome." Delphi explained. He then chuckled lightly. "I have a slight case of it too, if you can't tell. That's why they had to peel me off Ramon's ass at one time so many years ago. However in Nate's case, it caused him to be painfully blind to everything and everyone. He could only see and work toward one thing: proving that he could surpass anyone's limited expectation of him."

Delphi then gave a wolfish grin as he nods toward Nate. "You won, man. You've proven your worth, and defeated the haters that wanted to see you fail. Now, claim your prize and live your life."

Chapter Twenty Five

Old school R&B music blared loudly in the afternoon air by the time Nate, Paige, and Rachelle pulled in front of Levi and Terri's estate. Nate felt a bit of remorse that his mother couldn't join the festivities, having dropped her off at the airport only a few hours earlier.

Belinda stayed in town for a few weeks after the shooting, until Nate was released from the hospital and was able to move around fine on his own. She'd given both he and Paige words of encouragement, along with her blessing, before heading back to Chicago. She'd promised to visit again soon.

The news of Gerry Spivey's arrest, his brother's death, the indictment of Mayor Penne, and the dismantling of the Hunter Group's US territory made large circuit news across the country. Word quickly spread regarding the Chicago connection involved and the Mayor's arrest. Nate watched the news with grim satisfaction during his recovery time. The story replay of FBI authorities escorting the indicted mayor from his North side home in handcuffs playing over and over on CNN was extremely satisfying. Jolsten was promoted to replace Harrison as chief of police, and in turn recruited Harmony to join him as his new deputy. Wanting to lay roots closer to her sister Holley, she happily accepted.

Now weeks later, after fully recovering and his club now in its final stages of reconstruction, Nate was escorting his now fiancé to a welcome party to formally introduce her to his family.

His brothers and sisters.

The people who had been his ride or die since 1990 at Natchez State University.

People who really cared about him.

People who gave a shit as to whether or not he was truly happy, and refused to accept anything less than the best for him.

He loved them. Every last one of them.

It was more than a man could hope for in three lifetimes.

Nate parked his Rover behind several cars already lined around Levi's circular drive. After escorting Paige and Rachelle from the vehicle, they walked up to Levi's grand entrance and rang the doorbell.

Levi opened the door, grinning widely at the party.

"It's about damn time you got here, Nate! I thought I was going to have to send my brother out to hunt you down."

"Ha, ha," Nate playfully rolled his eyes. "The party doesn't start until I get here anyway." He clapped his hand lightly across Levi's back. "It's good to see you, man."

Levi smirked. "It's good to see you too, *Houdini*. I'm glad you finally decided to stop disappearing and show your face around here."

Nate snorted. "Like I had a choice. Asha practically reamed me a new asshole when she called. She threatened that if I didn't show up with Paige and Rachelle, she would personally administer a dose of kick ass on me for the next year. And I am not trying to hear her mouth, nor your wife's for that matter."

Levi laughed. "Smart choice." He leaned over and gave Paige a quick kiss on the cheek. "It's good to see you again, Paige. You're looking well."

Paige beamed under his compliment, and Nate took a step back to observe her radiance. She'd been so nervous getting dressed to come to the party that she'd changed her outfit four times. Only after convincing her that his friends were down to earth people who would accept her even if she arrived in a brown paper bag, had she finally calmed down. However on the drive over, her anxiety had once again begun to rise. Maybe now she would finally accept and be comfortable around his family.

"Thank you very much, Levi." Paige replied. She then turned to her sister. "This is my sister Rachelle."

"And how are you this evening, Rachelle? You're just as welcome in my home as Paige or Nate. Feel free to make yourself at home here. You're family now." Levi advised as he opened the door wider for them to step inside.

Rachelle blinked at Levi for a moment, before finally finding her voice. In the short time they've spent together, Nate was starting to realize Rachelle held a serious negative view of men, stemming from the neglect of her father. Wanting to give her the knowledge that not all men were selfish pricks, he'd begun an effort to try and break down her walls by displaying what a loving, caring man will actually do for the woman he cares about.

Treating her with all the love he would show either Terri or Asha, Rachelle had gradually begun to feel at ease around him. He could tell she was slowly trying to embrace the idea that men could be caring human beings. She wouldn't say what happened while she was in captivity; however she did mention that being with Jayme during that short amount of time opened her heart in a way she never before believed possible. Nate hoped that whatever the influencer, Rachelle's attitude would continue to grow more positive the more time she spends with quality men.

"Thank you very much, Levi. It's nice to be here." Rachelle replied softly.

They then walked into the great room, where the party was alive and roaring.

^^^

"Nate! Get over here and give me a hug! I'm not moving from this spot, so you can damn well walk over here to greet me!" Paige turned around to find the voice that had called out her fiancé, before releasing a huge smile.

Terri Blackburn, round with her first child, currently occupied the leather chaise as she lounged on its backrest. Her shoes were removed, and her feet tucked securely underneath her while she absently rubbed her protruding stomach. It appeared she'd been speaking to a short, older man, along with a tall, lanky fellow appearing to be in his mid-twenties when she noticed their arrival.

"Hey yourself. You look like you're going to delivery at any moment." Nate smiled affectionately.

Terri rolled her eyes. "Not fast enough. I'm ready for little..." she quickly glanced over at Levi, who had moved beside her and raised a single eyebrow in her direction. "...little Zion to be born."

Levi smirked as Terri fought back her grin. Paige briefly wondered what that exchange was about, but didn't dwell on it long. She and Rachelle followed behind Nate as they walked over to greet her.

"Mr. Salzmann, Justin, I'd like for you to meet a good friend of ours, Nate Kerr. And this is his girlfriend Paige, and her sister Rachelle."

"It's lovely to meet you all." Mr. Salzmann boomed. His voice vibrated loudly in contrast to the small demeanor his stature portrayed. Justin Salzmann just stared openly at Rachelle, who'd noticed his observations, and hung her head shyly toward the floor.

Hmm, little sister's got an admirer, Paige thought amusingly. She then turned her attention back to Terri.

"Hi, Terri. You look beautiful tonight. Pregnancy really agrees with you." Paige observed.

The normally mischievous twinkle in Terri's eye had faded a bit, but Paige didn't bother to mention that fact. Nate had explained to her last night how Terri was still quietly struggling with the loss of her father. Paige couldn't imagine losing someone when there was still unfinished business to settle, and she wished Terri the best of luck in her healing.

In response to the compliment, Terri smiled in Paige's direction, before turning a narrowed glare in Nate's direction.

"See, I told you I always liked her. Make sure this one stays, Nate." Terri commented, pointing her finger in his direction.

Paige couldn't contain the happiness that filled her at those words. Nate's friends had discussed her, and seemed to approve! It was wonderful to have the respect and appreciation of the friends of the man that she loved, as opposed to being the object of pity and ridicule. The experience was titillating, to say the least.

Nate huffed as he grabbed Paige's hand, proudly displaying the four-carat ring he'd given her when he proposed.

"This one is definitely staying, smart ass." Nate replied cockily.

Terri clapped her hands in excitement, while Levi whistled to get the attention of everyone in the room. Mr. Salzmann murmured his congratulations, however his words were lost as Paige finally took a good look around the room.

She suddenly realized there were *a lot* of people here. Some she'd met briefly before, while others were completely foreign. She felt nervous, wondering if his friends really could accept her. *What if these people didn't approve of his proposal?*

"I'd like to call everyone's attention." Levi announced loudly, tapping his glass of Hennessy on the table. Panic began to settle within Paige, as all eyes turned expectedly toward them.

"Nate decided, in typical Nate fashion, to get engaged without letting anybody know. So instead of this being a celebration that the Hunter Group has officially been disbanded, it's now turned into an engagement party." Levi then turned back to them, raising his glass. "Congratulations to you two."

Choruses of *Congratulations* and *It's about damn time* filled the room. Wine glasses then began to clink all over, sounding like musical charms throughout the party.

"The clinking means that they want us to kiss, baby girl. Typically they're supposed to wait until our wedding reception, however..." Nate whispered seductively in her ear as he moved in front of her. He placed his hand gently on her waist as Paige felt herself being drawn possessively within his arms. He then pressed her breasts against his massive chest.

Before she could think, she felt Nate's lips press gently against hers. That was all she needed to ignite a full range power storm inside her. She needed more. She could never get enough of this man. Raising her arms around his neck, she allowed Nate to taste every inch of her mouth.

"Mommy, when you and Daddy get like that, you tell me it's big people's way of showing they love each other. Is that what they're doing too?" A small voice sounded behind them, reminding them that they were still in the middle of a celebration, not back at home in Nate's room.

Nate gently broke off their kiss, and then turned her around so that she cradled his front. She bit back a grin as she realized he was also trying to hide the obvious erection poking her in her back.

Paige heard a feminine voice chuckle behind her. "Yes honey, that's definitely what that means. And we're all very happy for him."

Rachelle smiled warmly as she walked over toward Jayme. She bent low so she was eye to eye with the little girl.

"Hello, darling. I'm so glad to see you again."

Jayme hesitated for a brief moment before launching herself in Rachelle's arms. Sounds of sighs rang through the room at the sobering reunion. Asha then walked over to the two, and then threw her arms around both of them, before placing a gentle kiss on Rachelle's head.

"Thank you for keeping my baby safe. You're family now. I hope you know that." Asha stated, as silent tears glistened in her eyes.

Rachelle just nodded, too filled with emotion to speak as she held Jayme in her arms. Her eyes quickly darted to Justin, who continued to watch her with undisguised interest.

Nate left Rachelle alone with Asha to continue their conversation as he guided Paige around the room to thank everyone for their well wishes. Paige found the sea of faces swimming one after another overwhelming, yet incredibly humbling. It was wonderful to have so many people wanting to wish them well.

They spoke with the majestic looking Captain Bernard, who Paige remembered being part of the SEALS team that helped to identify each kidnapped victim. As they turned to leave, the Captain leaned over to whisper something in an attractive, older black woman's ear. Nate explained that woman he was talking to was Asha's mother, Ms. Meredith St. Claire.

Paige was then introduced to an older, boisterous Latina woman and her husband. Paige vaguely remembered the woman's name being introduced as Kay. The couple had been engaged in a hearty conversation with another younger looking couple, which Paige immediately recognized from their television appearances. Chad Forrester, along with a singer she recognized as the winner of the new artist of the year Keva Westbrook, stood together holding hands.

Next, they thanked Laura and Myles Fontana, who Nate had explained were the parents of Harmony and Holley Rune. The couple had recently gotten married a couple of month's prior, and looked extremely happy together.

As they continued to move throughout the party, Paige recognized and greeted the couple whose wedding she attended a few years back. The tall, Indian-descent man had his arm wrapped possessively around the waist of his lovely silver-haired wife. Master Bryce Blackburn and his wife Evelyn couldn't contain their appreciation for the rescue and recovery of Jayme. They stood alongside Dr. Charlie Wilson, and his beautiful wife Rita.

Nate pointed out Delphi's parents, who were standing off to the side speaking with Delphi's oldest son Austin, and their other daughter Alanna. He also pointed out another couple that had gone to Natchez State with them, Jackie and Kennedy Saunders, along with their handsome teenage son, who stood shyly next to his father. They were speaking with Officer Ron Jolsten and his wife, along with Veronica Traylor, Tyson Bowman and Reid Cross.

Everyone seemed to be having a really good time.

A small commotion drew Paige's attention toward the front of the room. Lafayette, Lucas, and Killian strolled in, along with Harmony, Holley, and a stunning mahogany hued woman Paige wasn't quite sure of her name, but recognized her face. Lafayette was grinning from ear to ear as he held the stunning woman close to his side, before she broke off from his embrace to walk over to Dr. Wilson and his wife.

"Hello, Daddy," Paige heard her state. "I know we've got a lot to talk about. We'll talk after the party, ok?"

Dr. Wilson grabbed the woman in his embrace. "As long as you're happy, Peanut. That's all your mother and I ever wanted for you."

The woman nodded her head, smiling at her father's pet name for her as she gazed adoringly back at him. "I am. I definitely am."

Lucas was shaking his head as he followed close behind, a ghost of a smile shadowing across his face. He walked over to Levi and whispered something in his ear, causing Levi's expression to become pale with shock.

"Are you shitting me?" Levi asked, not at all concerned about making his voice discreet.

"Nope." Lucas said amusingly, obviously aware of the inside comment. He nodded toward Harmony. "Ask her."

Harmony just smiled. "I'll let Lafayette explain in the way that only he can."

"Oh, I'd be more than happy to," Lafayette smugly accepted, turning toward the now curious crowd. He cleared his throat exaggeratedly, and bent over for a mock bow. He then held up his hand.

"Hold your applause for the end, please."

Lucas rolled his eyes. "Will you just get on with it? Before the next century rolls around?"

The stunning woman walked over to Lafayette, and slipped her hand inside his.

"Go ahead, honey. It's time."

Lafayette looked down affectionately at the woman by his side. "But I love to draw out the drama."

She chuckled. "I know you do, but later. We can do other things that can be drawn out."

Lafayette's nostrils flared, before he gave a knowing leer. "You're right." He then turned to the crowd. "For those of you who weren't aware, I've been applying to become part of the FBI's behavioral analyst division since I moved here to Houston. The first part of my recruitment was finalized a little over a year ago."

He nodded toward Killian. "Which was why Lucas and I were so hungry in recruiting Killian to join our company. We knew that if I got selected, Lucas would need immediate help to handle the caseloads at Blackburn, LLC. Unfortunately, my application was also a point of contention with my baby Zaria here. She believed that if I were recruited, the FBI would send me into parts unknown, and any chance at a stable future with her would be lost forever."

Lafayette then turned a grateful smile toward Harmony. "When Harmony learned about my application, she pulled some strings to have me transferred permanently to her Houston unit. Part of my final recruiting was to become involved as a live field agent during an op."

He gave a quick wink toward Jayme, who smiled bashfully in return. "The op was the dismantlement of the Hunter Group."

Paige heard a gasp of astonishment from Jolsten. She still wasn't certain how HG figured into his recruitment.

"Are you telling me you were that field agent Harmony sent earlier to case the club, and to set up perimeters so we could see what was going on?" Jolsten asked, realization slowly dawning across his face.

Lafayette nodded his head. "Affirmative. That was part of the reason why I needed to leave the debrief you were holding. I had to go set things up."

He then smiled loving down at Zaria. "The other reason was that I needed to talk to this chocolate drop right here, before she walked out of my life for good. She'd told Holley earlier that she'd been considering accepting a consulting job in Arizona to get a fresh start, and I damn sure couldn't have that. I had to talk to her, and then go and set up those cameras around the backdoor of the club. Afterwards, after all the shit with HG finally got settled..." Lafayette held up Zaria right hand for the room to see the platinum wedding bands gracing their hands. "We caught a plane to Vegas and got married a few days ago."

When the cheers began to soar throughout the room, Lafayette held up his hand once more. "I asked that you hold the applause." Laughter soon followed his mock chastisement as he continued to speak.

"Since the Hunter Group has officially been disbanded here in the continental U.S., I've officially been accepted into the FBI agent program. And since Harmony is joining Jolsten's law enforcement team, that left a sweet opening within her unit...and I was just advised today that I will be filling that hole."

Paige joined the rest of the room in a thunderous applause and cheering calls toward the couple. It seemed like things were finally coming together for everyone, and she was thrilled that everyone could take a bite of happiness and mold it for their own.

She then turned to smile at Rachelle. Jayme must have disappeared among the crowd of adults, because Rachelle seemed intensely interested in whatever she and Justin were discussing. Waves of satisfaction rolled through her as she watched her sister's shy response to the seemingly entranced young man. Maybe Justin could help to finally soften the heart of her cynical sibling.

She hoped so.

^^^

"Oh my god! I'm balling like a baby!" Asha exclaimed, clapping her hands together. Paige caught her dabbing her eyes with a napkin, only to have her eyes leak tears once more. "Ok, everyone, I need to say something. Gather round." Asha demanded.

Paige felt herself shuffled among the herd, as she and Nate were pushed closer to where Asha stood near the winding staircase. Asha grabbed Harmony and Jolsten's hands, entwining them within her own as she looked over the crowd. Tears continued to flow down her cheeks while she gave a watery smile.

"First of all, I want to thank each and every one of you for helping me crash Terri and Levi's place." Light laughter sounded in the room as she threw a smirk toward Terri. "I wanted to make sure my girl was as comfortable as possible during her last few weeks of pregnancy, and I figured both she and Levi might as well get a head start on people invaded their space."

"Ha, ha brat. It just so happens that I like people invading my space." Levi called out.

Asha twisted her lips his way. "Yea, my bet's still out on that. That panic button is still raring to go, my friend." Asha turned back to the crowd, and Paige heard Levi mutter, *What is she* talking *about?* toward his wife.

"Nevertheless," Asha continued, "Thank you all for coming, and for helping us give recognition to our little circle of true heroes." She lightly shook Jolsten and Harmony's hands as she looked over the crowd. "If it weren't for their incredible insight and bravery, we may have never found my little girl. There aren't words to express how much your help has meant to us, will *continue* to mean to us, as we watch Jayme blossom and grow older. From the bottom of our hearts, Killian, Lucas, Capt. Bernard, *everyone*, Jaymes and I just want to say *Thank You.*"

Killian walked over to his sister, sweeping her into a huge hug as he embraced her within his arms.

"We're family, remember? You don't have to thank us. That's what we do."

"And speaking of which," Terri piped in. "Since it's obvious that Nate has now included two additional women to our little mix, I'd say that justifies the need to get two more tickets to our *Ladies Only* cruise."

Paige's ears perked up. "What cruise?"

"We're going to the Caribbean in July, sweetheart. Get ready for a week of relaxation, girl bonding, and shopping. Just the women, though." Zaria called, looking pointedly at Lafayette as he shook his head in amusement.

Exhilaration pinged through Paige at being considered part of their closely-knit circle. She grinned widely at Nate, before turning back to Zaria.

"Rachelle and I can't wait. We'd be happy to go!"

Childish laughter caught Paige's attention as she glanced over her shoulders. A beautiful dark haired young woman walked over to Asha, holding a giggling Jayme in her arms. A tall, muscular young man followed closely behind, rolling his eyes to the ceiling as he held his arms behind his back. He had the same hazel slanted eyes as his mother and uncle, and his face held a mixture of both amusement and exasperation.

"I can't say enough how *wonderful* it is to have all of these adopted aunts and uncles in our family!" Alanna announced as she placed Jayme on the floor. Jayme giggled as Alanna gave her a quick tickle, and then sprinted over to hide herself behind her brother Austin's tall legs. "Now seems like a wonderful time to introduce and solicit your support for the *Help-Alanna-Get-Her-New-Harley-Davidson-Sportster-Custom-Made-Motorcycle-So-She-Can-Bike-Ride-Across-The-Great-State-Of-Texas* fund. The pool of donations can be as vast as you'd like, and no contribution will be turned away. I, of course, am the foundation's chair and CEO, and will accept checks, money orders, wire transfers, and of course cash. Who would like to be the first to donate to this worthy cause?"

Asha quickly lost her cheerful grin as she narrowed her eyes at her daughter. "You are *not* getting a motorcycle," she stated firmly.

"But Momma! I've already done all the research, looked into the safety features, looked up some basic training classes..." Alanna protested.

"I've already told you no. Let me have to say it again, and there *will* be consequences and repercussions." Asha said softly. Her face broke no further argument that she meant exactly what she'd said.

Everyone burst out laughing, as if it seemed they were already well accustomed to Alanna's antics.

Paige chuckled softly to herself. Asha, it seemed, was just like her grandmother. It didn't matter that her daughter was in her early twenties, and that most people would consider her to be an adult old enough to make her own choices. Asha expected her word to be obeyed regardless.

Alanna groaned loudly, but gave no further rebuttal.

Austin just smirked knowingly at his sister. "I told you brat," he teased.

Chapter Twenty Six

The party finally wound down a few hours later. Everyone again gave their well wishes to Lafayette and Zaria, along with Nate and Paige, before leaving for the night. Paige, Rachelle, and Jayme decided to catch a ride with Holley and Killian to discuss details about the upcoming cruise. They promised to meet Nate back at his home later that evening.

Now, old friends Nate Kerr, Delphi and Asha Allen, and Terri and Levi Blackburn sat around the room, enjoying glasses of alcohol and light, carefree banter.

The original circle of friends from Natchez State University.

Friendships that had sustained time and heartbreak.

Relationships that had proven that love could overcome any heartache, and could in return give personal redemption.

Every one of them was better for the lesson.

Levi shook his head as he rubbed Terri's swollen feet. "Man, would you believe back in 1990 that we'd be here today?"

Asha laughed. "Hell, no. Not in a million years."

Delphi snorted. "I did. I could've told you that you'd be with me, had you just listened."

Asha smiled indulgently at her husband. "Maybe you're right."

Nate looked around thoughtfully. "Well, I for one never expected to be here. Work was all I knew. It was my coping mechanism. Now, here I am taking time out to enjoy my friends, I'm engaged to a sexy as hell woman, and owner of the former *Escapades* night club."

"*Former*? What do you mean?" Delphi asked.

"I've decided that I'm going to reopen the club under a new brand. I'm going to call it *Chances*."

Terri moaned loudly when Levi hit a particular sore spot on her ankle. He winked at her as he kept rubbing, before she turned her attention back to Nate.

"What does *Chances* mean?" Terri asked once she'd regained her senses.

Nate shrugged unapologetically. "I'm a classic man. I believe in reciprocating respect when it's shown to me. I want what every man in America wants: the chance to be prosperous, the chance to take care of his family without fear of retribution, the chance to earn the love of his woman, or man if that's the side of the fence he's swinging on, and the chance to grow wiser with each passing day. And I don't want my chances of obtaining my life's goals cut short by someone else's personal agenda."

"Here, here," Delphi agreed, raising his Hennessy glass.

"You know Nate, in all the years we've been here, I've never really gotten an opportunity to swing by your club. With my tour dates, it never really seemed like a good time. However I would love to come by your place when it opens again. Maybe do some promotional sets to help launch the opening? You got an area where I could perform?"

"Of course I do! That would be fabulous, Asha. Man, that would really define the class of clientele I'm hoping to attract. Thank you so much."

Asha waved him off. "Don't mention it. It's the least I can do. I feel like the debts I owe to you guys for bringing Jayme home will never be fulfilled."

"Speaking of Jayme, was she ok going home with Holley and Paige?" Levi asked.

Delphi smiled. "She was fine. I think Rachelle is her new best friend now. It'll be awhile before she's comfortable being at home again. However, letting her convert one of the other guestrooms in the house into her new bedroom, and then installing steel bars over the windows has helped some."

"We'll be with her every step of the way in helping her heal." Terri vowed.

"Yes we will," Nate promised. His heart warmed at the beloved faces staring back at him.

His friends. His family.

Raising his glass, Delphi decided to make a toast. "'To my friends, my brothers," he nods at Terri, "...my sister, and my wife. I love you guys, more than you could possibly know. Who knew that God had a greater plan for our lives?"

He chuckled softly as he twirled the contents of his glass, and then shook his head in amazement. "He found a way to intertwine our lives together so tightly, nothing can break our bond. We've seen a lot of things over the past few decades, and He knew we would need each other for support, through good and bad times. Our bonds will last through the test of time. They will never be undone, and they will never falter."

"Here, here." The chorus chimed.

^^^

"Paige! Rachelle! I'm home! Where are you guys?" Nate sounded as he walked through his front door. The drive back to his home had been full of contented quietness. It gave him more time to think and to appreciate everything in his life that he'd been blessed with.

"I'm upstairs in Soldier Field." Paige called.

Nate chuckled to himself. He'd started referencing his football themed rooms by the stadiums in which the teams played a few years ago. He thought it was cute that she'd picked up his habit.

Strolling casually up the stairs, he wondered what she was doing.

And had his question answered as soon as he walked into his bedroom.

Holy shit.

His heart stopped as he gripped the top of the doorframe. He found himself gasping for air, as his eyes stayed glued to his bed.

Paige was laid out across his orange satin sheets, like the hottest wet dream his dick could ever imagine. She was decked from shoulder to calf in the sexiest see-through Chicago Honey Bear cheerleading costume he'd ever seen. The Honey Bears were the official NFL cheerleading team for Chicago, until they disbanded in 1986. However Nate still remembered how fucking sexy they were whenever they strolled across Soldier Field's turf.

The see-through orange, white, and blue halter Paige wore gripped tightly across her straining breasts. Her hardened, chocolate nipples poked seductively through the mesh of the fabric. Her two-inch micro-mini skirt, with its matching insignia belt, barely covered the curve of her delectable ass. As Nate's dick stretched painfully within his slacks, he noticed one other feature that nearly had him passing out.

His sweet golden bear had decided to smear herself with thick, golden honey all over her neck, stomach and thighs. He groaned loudly as he began to remove his suit jacket and tie.

"To what do I owe this wonderful, delectable treat, my love?" He rasped.

Paige grinned coyly back at him. "You've been wonderful toward me and my sister these past few weeks. We hadn't experienced this much kindness, love, and dedication since our grandmother passed."

She glanced down at her outfit, a small smile hinting at the corner of her mouth. "I just wanted to give you something in return. I asked Rachelle if she wouldn't mind spending some time at Holley's tonight. She and Jayme decided to make it a girl's sleepover." She shrugged. "I wanted you to enjoy your treat undisturbed."

She then moved seductively over his sheets, spreading her honey dipped thighs wider. He could see a hint of her swollen labia underneath her skirt smiling seductively back at him.

"And I want you to feel free to scream as loud as you want, without fear that someone will hear you." She smiled saucily.

He almost came right then and there. He cleared his throat as he hungrily ate up the vision in front of him. He slowly began to move toward the bed, wetting his lips as he stroked his goatee in a thoughtful gesture.

"And what makes you so sure that it will be *me* that will wind up screaming?" He cocked at eyebrow at her.

Paige then took her hands and cupped her breasts together, presenting the soft treats up to him as a gift. She rotated her hips seductively on the bed, legs stretched wide and inviting. She then ran her hands over her taunt stomach to lubricate her fingers with the sticky, sweet liquid, before letting her fingers trail further south toward her glistening pussy. Taking her thumb, she rubbed her hardened clit slowly clockwise, gasping as she clearly enjoyed her manipulations, before slipping two fingers inside her wetness. She then took those same fingers and began sucking both her arousal and the honey from their tips.

Nate felt as if he would literally pass out.

Paige grinned at him as she slowly slid from the bed. She walked over to where he had stopped to ogle her. Taking his hand, she led him back toward his bed, gently pushing him down to sit on the edge.

"Sit back and enjoy, baby. I got you, just like you got me."

She then reached over and grabbed her cell phone, scrolling through its contents to select a song track from a saved playlist.

Nate stiffened as his favorite genre began playing through the speakers: Chicago House Music. He rarely played the music in his club, as he found a lot of southern partiers didn't really appreciate the unique blend, often dismissing it as another techno fad. However, true Chicago *househeads* were known to not only love the acid house sound, but also preferred house played over any other type of genre. Since Paige was from Detroit, she was well aware of the lure the music held.

Paige slowly leaned over to run her tongue along Nate's lips, trailed her tongue to wet his beard with her saliva, before rolling away from him in time to the music.

She then lowered herself down in a resting squat.

And began to twerk.

Oh. My. God. His dick jumped in his pants as he watched Paige gyrate to the rhythmic sounds of Mike Dunn's *Phreaky Motherfucker*. Suddenly, his shirt felt too confining. He quickly tore it off and threw it on the floor. Or the bed.

It went somewhere, dammit.

As his lustful eyes watched her ass cheeks move up and down, and her small waist roll back and forth to the bass rhythm, simulating exactly how she would look riding his stiff dick, his pants became too restricting as well. So he chucked those off, and threw them on the floor. Or the bed.

They went somewhere, dammit.

Now he sat in his boxer briefs, watching the most erotic, seductive, cheer/twerk routine he'd ever seen in his life.

Tossing her wild, golden streaked brown hair over her shoulder, Paige looked at him seductively once more, running her tongue over her bottom lip as the song came to a close. Nate sat immobile, too filled with lust to speak intelligently. Lifting his hand, he crooked his index finger in an indication for her to approach him. Standing directly in front of his open legs, she leaned over so that he could practically taste the sweetness rolling across her skin.

"Mine," he groaned as he twisted his fingers in her locks. He pulled her mouth roughly against his. The sweet flavor of honey, mixed with the flavor of Paige's golden brown skin immediately assaulted his taste buds. Groaning with an urgent need for more, he pulled her on top of his lap so that her legs straddled the outside of his thighs, never releasing the hold he had on her mouth.

He felt Paige's body beautifully surrender under his manipulations. He got even harder as her body grew softer under his touch. Tearing his mouth away from hers, he ran his tongue across her jawline, down her throat, and over her shoulder, sucking and tasting the honey across her skin. With one hand, he easily removed the halter-top and pulled it from her chest. Her succulent breasts bounced free of their confinement, and he groaned again as he stared at their perkiness.

"Your breasts are so fucking beautiful. So juicy. So fucking mouthwatering..." He ran his tongue across her skin as Paige gasped from his touch. She ground her pelvis seductively against his erection, and he tilted his hips upward in an effort to relieve some of the pressure boiling within his balls. He took a hardened nipple in his mouth, sucking greedily before moving to the other side to give equal attention. When he had her gyrating so hard against his dick that he feared he might burst, he pulled her upright to her feet.

"If you don't stop, I'll come right now in my briefs. And you'll get none of Daddy's dick. Now, you want Daddy's dick, don't you?" He smiled wryly and he shoved his briefs to his ankles, taking his stiffened erection in his hand to alleviate some of the pressure. He rubbed his hand down the quivering muscles of her stomach, catching some of the honey smeared over her skin. He then used his thumb to capture some of the moisture sprouting from the crown of his dick, combining it with the honey to lubricate down his shaft.

Paige's eyes never wavered as she lustfully watching him stroke himself.

"Yes, I want Daddy's dick. I want to feel Daddy's dick inside me, pounding me, thrusting into me." She licked her lips, before raising her eyes to stare passionately at him.

"I want it all."

Hooking her thumbs in the side straps of her micro-mini, she shimmied out of her skirt, and let it drop to the floor. She then cupped her breasts and massaged them, before giving a hard twist on her nipples.

"Then come here and take a ride." Nate challenged.

She moved to once again straddle his lap, doing a small, rhythmic bounce on top of his thighs before slowly dragging her wetness across the skin of his straining cock.

"Don't fucking play with it, girl. Take what you want while I'm still giving you an opportunity. Otherwise I'm going to claim you without an apology," he growled.

She smiled from underneath her lashes. "I think I may like a little claiming. But until then..." she reached between her legs and grabbed his dick firmly in her hands. Positioning her core above him, she merciless slid down his aching cock.

Nate hissed with every inch she consumed. It was like hot fire gripping his dick. He gritted his teeth as he watched his dick disappear inside her.

"That's so sexy," he rasped.

"*You're* sexy." She then began bouncing hard on his lap, stealing each breath from his chest. "Your muscled thighs are sexy. Your goatee is sexy. Those fucking suits you wear are sexy. Your confidence is sexy. And that fucking bowlegged stroll you have gets my juices flowing every time." Her breath hitched as she ground her hips against his thighs, pushing his dick further inside her channel. "Can you feel my juices running down your balls?"

"Hell yea," Nate managed. He wound his arms around her waist to steady her movements, helping her thrust harder against him as his eyes started crossing blindly at the sight. "I feel *everything*."

"Do you feel how much I love you, Nathaniel Kerr?" She asked, taking his jaw in her delicate hand and forcing his gaze to stare into her eyes.

His heart swelled with the intensity of the moment. There was no one else in the world that could captivate his every attention like this woman. Absolutely no one.

"Yes," he choked, tears burning hotly in the back of his eyes as he struggled to maintain his control. "Yes, I do. I feel it. I feel *you*. My baby. My heart. My *Theia.*"

With that, his control shattered. He gripped her waist so hard he was sure she'd have bruises in the morning. He didn't care. The only thing he cared about was marking her. Claiming her.

Loving her.

He took control of her riding, forcing her down on his lap harder and harder with each passing thrust. The beast was loose, and he intended to show her exactly how untamed K.O.W. actually was.

His dick screamed in pleasure as his hard thrusts caused a quivering inside her cunt that couldn't be mistaken for anything other than pure ecstasy. Paige threw her head back and screamed his name, jerking wildly on his dick as she came.

That was the call he needed to free the hot lava boiling in the base of his tight balls. The heat worked its way through his dick, causing him to scream out as well. He pulled her to his mouth, latching on to the skin right above her breast. He then bit down hard, sucking the honey into his mouth as his dick shot his seed wildly inside her core.

Groaning with the intensity of the moment, he felt his dick twitch uncontrollably as it fought to release the last remaining drops of semen inside her. Releasing the skin he'd just tortured, he ran his tongue across the swelling passion mark quickly blossoming across her chest.

Letting out a contented sigh, he hugged her closer in his embrace as he felt her arms circling his shoulders. Laying his head against her chest, the comforting sounds of her slowing heartbeat was the most beautiful melody he'd ever heard in his life.

"Mine. I love you too, Paige," he whispered.

Epilogue

"Are you sure you have everything you need?" Nate asked, looking at the rows of luggage lined against the front door of Terri's home.

Paige bit her lip to keep from laughing at his comical, overwhelmed expression. He'd complained that the sheer number of bags each *Lady* had decided to bring looked as if they'd packed all of Neiman Marcus to take a 7-day cruise. Terri had overheard his earlier berating, and quickly put him in his place before running upstairs to her bedroom when the sounds of little Celine crying filtered through the baby monitor.

Despite Terri's scolding, Nate still looked overwhelmed.

"Yes, baby, don't worry. We have everything. And if we don't, I'm sure there are shops at one of the ports of call where Rachelle and I can purchase what we need. In addition, there are the onboard shops we can use as well," Paige insisted. She smiled affectionately back at him, then gave him a quick kiss on his lips. Nate smiled at the gesture, but still looked dubiously at the bags, shaking his head.

"If you think so," he conceded.

"Hey man! Help me bring these bags outside. Make yourself useful, instead of standing there pawing your fiancé." Delphi called from outside the open door.

Paige glanced over Nate's shoulder to see that the limo they'd ordered had finally arrived to drive them to Galveston. From there they would meet with Tyson and Reid and board their cruise. She leaned up to give him another quick peck on the cheek.

"Don't worry," she repeated. "Nothing will happen to us. Reid and Tyson are meeting us in Galveston, and will be on the cruise making sure everything is ok. A select number of staff have already been notified that the *Painted Lady* is coming on board with her girlfriends, so

210

they'll have additional security hands helping them out as well, just as a precaution," she reassured, sensing what Nate's true issue was.

He grabbed her gently by her waist, before closing his eyes to place his forehead against hers.

"I just worry about you, that's all. I have to make sure you're taken care of. It's my job. I have to make sure you're all right," he admitted softly.

Paige melted at the sincerity and vulnerability of his confession, his words stroking something deep within her. She reached up to stroke his goatee, love pouring from every touch.

"As long as you love me, I'm safe."

Nate pulled away to search her face. Finding comfort in whatever he saw, he gave her a soft smile before turning to grab a couple of the larger trunks.

"Damn. This is ridiculous," he muttered, as he dragged the luggage out of the front door.

"I am so happy for you guys," a feminine voice spoke softly behind her. Paige turned to see her sister smiling wistfully in her direction. "I never thought I'd see the day where I didn't think men couldn't be trusted." She nodded her head toward the door Nate disappeared through. "But Nate, Justin, and Delphi have shown me that there are some men that are more than capable of loving a woman the right way, as long as her heart is open to receive it."

In an unexpected move, Rachelle moved to pull Paige in a sisterly embrace before giving her a quick wink, shocking Paige with her open display of affection. "I'll see you outside. I am so excited! I've never been on a cruise before!" She then quickly sprinted out of the door after Nate.

Paige shook her head in amazement. Rachelle rarely hugged or showed any type of affection prior to her kidnapping. Now, it seemed like hugging had become second nature to her. In addition, the numerous times she'd spent at the Allen's home babysitting Jayme had been therapeutic as well. Witnessing a strong, loving family like Asha, Delphi, and their children had probably done more good for Rachelle than a million psychologists ever could.

"Your sister is something special, I hope you know that." Asha said softly as she walked into the foyer, with Jayme holding on tightly to her thighs. She patted her daughter's head affectionately. "Honey, why don't you go help Daddy figure out how to load our luggage in the limo? I'm sure he'll love your input before Mommy leaves on her trip."

Jayme's face beamed as she jumped up and down clapping her hands. "Yea! I can be the luggage boss! I'll tell Daddy you said it was ok!" With that, she sprinted out of the door after Rachelle.

Paige snorted. "He is *so* not going to appreciate that extra help."

Asha laughed. "I know. He's still grumpy that he lost the bet regarding Levi losing his shit once Terri had the baby. Levi's been beside himself with self-inflicted angst, and driving everyone crazy. You'd think he was the first man in history to have a baby! Though the icing on the cake was when Terri had a girl! I am so loving life right about now!"

She grinned playfully. "I'm also glad I decided to fly back here and ride with you guys to the port, instead of flying back to Galveston with Reid and Tyson after the Essence Festival. We'll have to Face Time Levi from the limo to make sure he's coping until Momma gets here."

Paige joined in the laughter as they both walked outside toward the circular drive. "I'm still getting to know him, but he does seem a little bit unhinged," she admitted.

"Completely psychotic are the words I'd use to describe him." Harmony commented as she strolled up the walkway. "Since I'm starting at the station with Jolsten in a couple of days, I was initially sorry I couldn't go with you guys. However now in hindsight, I think it's for the best. It'll help me get a head start to ward off any false alarms he may raise from 911 calls. His control is completely shot, and he's not handling it well at all. Do you know he had the nerve to ask me while babysitting one day to make sure Celine takes her nap at exactly 3:00p.m. on the dot? Not 3:01, not 3:02, but exactly 3:00p.m. And if she slept longer than 30 minutes, he wanted me to wake her up." Harmony rolled her chocolate brown eyes. "I mean really, the kid is a baby! I can't demand that she'll go to sleep and wake up on command. The poor kid should be able to sleep whenever she wants to."

"That's because he's trying to get Celine on a sleeping schedule," Holly chuckled, her bright red hair flowingly freely down her back. She walked up to her twin sister to throw her arms casually around her shoulders. "It's not working though. Celine still sleeps all day, and parties all night. Levi is walking around here looking like one of those zombies from *The Walking Dead.*" She laughed as she shook her head in amusement. "I say hats off to him, regardless of how frantic it must be making him right now. I know I'm *so* not prepared to entertain that chapter in my life anytime soon. Just finishing my degree was stressful enough."

Harmony gave her sister a quick squeeze. "And I am so proud of you! I knew you could do anything that you set your mind to. Graduating with that Summa Cum Laude tag underneath your name on that graduation certificate is nothing to balk at."

Holley beamed at her sister's compliment.

Paige pursed her lips in thought, as she pondered her and Nate's future possibilities.

I wonder how Nate would handle being a new Dad?

After a moment, she ultimately shook her head. *No use in going down that line of thought,* she chided herself. They had plenty of time for kids. Right now, they just wanted to enjoy each other, and were looking forward to the wedding they were planning next fall.

"Well, I for one feel sorry for my brother-in-law," Zaria commented as she walked out of the house carrying a large duffel bag. She smiled as Lafayette walked silently up to her, kissed her cheek, and then took the bag from her hands. She then threw her arms around Holley. "I've never seen Levi look so out of sorts."

"Mama and Evelyn are flying in tonight to help him out, so he'll only be alone with Celine for a few hours. I'm sure he can handle that. Besides, it's nice to see that little bundle of joy wrap her tiny fingers around her father." Asha stated.

The object of their discussion chose that moment to walk out of his front door. His long dark hair, usually managed and controlled, was scattered wildly around his head. His typically pressed dress shirt and slacks displayed deep wrinkles and disarray. If it weren't for the smile etched across his face, Paige would have sworn someone had hit the usually all-together man with a gigantic ball full of chaos.

"I know you guys are talking about me," Levi said knowingly as he walked over to them holding his daughter. Little Celine was wrapped in a light pink jumper, matching frilled socks, and a cute pink and white-laced headband wrapped around her forehead. She gurgled happily as she tugged on one of her father's long strands of hair. Her dark eyes, light dusting of curly dark hair across her head, and olive skin tone showcased the features she'd picked up from her mother. However the strong will and quick show of frustration she demonstrated whenever Terri didn't breast feed quick enough was true form from her Dominant father.

"I certainly am, my friend," Asha taunted as she smirked back at him. "You're my boy and I love you like a brother, but I knew you'd find yourself over your head with her." She then walked over to take Celine from his arms, cooing at the infant as Celine gave her a wide, toothless smile.

"Hey sweet-sweet." Asha murmured, cradling the baby in her arms. She hummed a soft tune as she rocked Celine gently back and forth.

"You're holding her like you want another one," Terri said jokingly, walking up beside her husband. Levi smiled lovingly at his wife as he wound his arm around her waist.

Asha blanched. "Hell no. My three are more than enough. Besides," she turned a knowing gaze toward Holley, Zaria, and Paige. "Those three will be making our family bigger in the next coming months, I'm sure."

It was Paige's time to blanch, along with Holley. Zaria, however, seemed to consider the prophesy with interest.

"I already told you that I'm not barking up that tree anytime soon." Holley stated, but looked expectantly toward Zaria.

Zaria merely shrugged her delicate shoulders peeking out from her red-stripped maxi dress. "Maybe not today, but you never know," was all that she would comment.

"Levi, get your ass in here and help with all of these bags!" Killian called from the doorway.

Levi grinned and shrugged lightly. "I'm coming!" He yelled, before sprinting back to the open door of his foyer to grab more baggage.

^^^

As I looked around my circle of friends, my heart felt as if it would burst with the amount of love I felt for each woman standing around me. Each one of my girls had come full circle with their past and present, and had hopefully grown wiser to embrace a brighter future. They'd experienced a lot over the years, and each woman, each **Lady,** especially myself, had survived, overcome, and triumphed over whatever hell life wanted to bring her way. Our hearts had been broken and healed in a way that would forever define us, as women of strength, endurance, and most of all, love.

I was proud of myself, of *all* of us.

Hot tears burned the back of my eyes as my emotions threatened to give away my thoughts. I quickly blinked them away before anyone could see.

"Ok, the *Ladies Only* adventure cruise is about to get started." I announced. "Before we go, I want everyone to think about the obstacles they've had to overcome in life. Think about how much you've endured, how much hurt was thrown your way to try and break you."

I took a moment to take a deep, cleansing breath as I rocked Celine gently in my arms. "Next, think about how you were able to turn that hurt around. Think about that hidden strength you didn't realize you had, and how it shielded you in times when you needed it most."

Each woman stood around in a semi circle, unshed tears dwelling in their eyes as they reflected on their past. I could see when the realization of all that they'd experienced resonated in their thoughts as they stood a little taller, a little prouder.

"Now, maintain that feeling of strength, and transfer that strength into a personal theme song you want to play in your mind whenever you walk into a room. Now burn that song into your memory. The next time you ever feel insecure, scared, or intimidated by *anyone*, just remember that song. Have it play in the recesses of your mind to give you strength, to give you courage. For instance..." I waved the hand that wasn't cradling my goddaughter high in the air in a celebratory pose, and then gave my friends a cocky grin.

"My personal theme song is from that *Game of Thrones* series on *HBO*. Whenever *Daenerys Targaryen* commands her dragons to kill someone, there's this score that plays that gets me riled up each and every time." I lifted my chin confidently as I smirked back at the group. "When I think about that song, I can't help but to be confident, just like her."

And it also makes me want to kick a little ass, and tell a bitch to bow down...

Holley nodded excitedly at the thought. "I love that, Asha! And I know exactly what my song will be! It's from the last *300* movie, when *Leonadis'* wife raises her sword at the end, right before they kill all the Persians." She sighed wistfully as she looked at her twin sister. "I love that movie."

Terri smiled. "I like that, but I need to think about what my song will be. I want it to be just as strong." She shrugged, sheepishly biting her bottom lip. "It doesn't really sound intimidating having that theme song from *Frozen* playing over and over in my head."

Zaria laughed loudly. "I think you're the only adult on the planet who isn't sick of *Let it Go*." She visibly gagged. "If I hear that song one more time, I'm going to scream."

Everyone joined in the laughter, relishing in the sisterhood we'd found.

And I relished the family that would forever be stamped in my heart. As I began to hum Mariah Carey's *Anytime You Need a Friend* song softly to myself, I felt Terri quietly slide her arms around me in a show of support and love.

I knew that I would never feel alone and helpless again.

216

About the Author

Amanda (Mandy) has always had a love affair with the written word, especially when it's used to showcase love. Like many authors, her love sparked a desire to place her own imaginative thoughts into context.

Mandy currently resides in the south suburbs of Chicago, but considers Jackson, Mississippi her second home. Her favorite pastimes are traveling and meeting new people, and reading steamy novels from one of her favorite authors.

More Books By This Author

Missing the history involving a Natchez State University graduate? Go back to the beginning and catch up!

The Painted Lady (The NSU Beginning) Book One (Asha's Story)
The Swan Lady Book Two (Terri's Story)
The Diamond Lady Book Three (Holley's Story)
The Hidden Lady Book Four (Paige's Story)

Excerpt From The Painted Lady

Delphi gave me a lopsided grin. "I didn't cook, but I do have some food for you. I know how you detest eating in the Café; and I know you didn't eat before the coronation tonight. All you were thinking about was trying to look good in that dress-which you do by the way. You look absolutely perfect, if that was even possible. I hope you know that." He turned and walked into the kitchen.

"Thank you," I blushed. "And yes, I'm starving. I'm not even going to ask how you knew that." I leaned over to peep into the kitchen to see what he was doing. "Did you want me to help you?"

"No, I got it. Let me serve you this time. It pleases me."

"Oh, ok." Why were my cheeks heating?

I heard plates and glassware moving around as Delphi continued to ponder around. Finally, he walked over to me and sat two plates on the table along with a bottle of grape juice, my favorite.

"Oh yeah!" I exclaimed excitedly, doing a fist pump in the air as I took in the plate's content. "Jeannie's! Right on time!" Jeannie's Restaurant was the local diner all students went to when they wanted a good, semi-home cooked meal. Well, if one considered a greasy pork chop sandwich, ribs slathered in hickory barbeque sauce, or thick wedge cut home fries. Jeannie's food was the highest quality a student could expect out here, beating out both the Café and the SUB hands down. It was also much closer than driving to Port Gibson. It sat about two miles off campus, so it was a rare treat when a person without a car was finally be able to indulge.

Delphi laughed. "Yes, I knew you'd appreciate it. You're so easy to read. I hope you like it." He'd bought us both shrimp baskets with fries and soda bread. I felt my mouth water as I took my first bite. Heaven!

We sat in silence as we savored our meal. Delphi finished before me and leaned back in his chair to wait for me to finish. "I have one final treat for you, little one."

I looked up at him, a question suddenly burning in my gut at hearing his endearment. "You know there's something I've always wanted to ask you."

"You can ask me anything. I want you to ask me. What's up?" Delphi asked curiously.

"Why didn't you ever give me a nickname?" I asked. "I know people labeled you with 'Delphi' a long time ago because you're from Philly; but you told me at one point that you would give me a nickname. What ever happened to that?" I asked.

Delphi let a sly look come upon his face. "Well, let's just say I decided a while ago that the name I will call you will be uniquely for you. No one else will have the privilege or the honor to call you that. For now, calling you Asha is fine for me. I haven't earned the right to call you anything else." He paused and glanced at my lips. "But I have every confidence that I will."

That threw me. "OK... everybody, including me, calls you Delphi all the time. So are you saying it bothers you when you hear it?" I asked bewildered.

He shook his head. "No, not at all. Most people on campus call me Delphi like we're the greatest of friends; but they really don't know me. It's the only alternative they have to feel a connection to me. They then try and link that connection to something they can relate to, like my hometown. I've found that very few people try to make a real honest effort to get to truly know a person, inside and out. Most prefer the superficial association rather than the deeper connection. They believe there's less risk of having to make themselves just as open and vulnerable."

His face turned serious. "I don't need to attach a label or try to link you to Chicago because I'm too weak not to have taken the time to get closer to you. I think I've earned the right to call you Asha for now. Like I said, soon I'll earn the right to call you something else— specifically for me."

220

I let his words sink in. "Okay, then. Well, when I've earned it, what will I call you?" It seemed he had taken a lot of time to ponder this issue, more than I would have previously thought. Now I was even more intrigued about what his response would be.

"Sir Jaymes," he said simply, staring directly into my eyes.

Confused, I stared back for a beat. "Isn't that your name already? And what's with the sir?"

"Yes, but no one calls me that, not even my parents. My friends at home call me Jimmy and my parents still call me Junior because I'm named after my father, even though I passed his height during junior high school." He leaned forward in his chair, reached out and let his finger slide down my cheek. "The SIR is a significant detail, but we won't go into that right now. We'll discuss it more when you've earned it."

"Oh." And for some reason, I was okay with that answer. His finger brushed against my cheek once more before moving away from my face. That I wasn't okay with.

"Okay." Delphi smiled at me and leaned back, steering the conversation to a lighter topic. "Ready for your last surprise?"

"Yes."

Delphi stood and walked over to the refrigerator. He pulled out a maroon box and walked back to the table. He placed the box down, grinning knowingly in my direction.

"Oh my God!" I squealed, clasping my hands together. Inside the box with the Baker's Square logo sat my favorite pie in the whole world, a French apple cream cheese cake. I looked at Delphi. "Thank you so much," I said, feeling the tears welling up.

"Don't thank me. You're well worth the trip to Jackson to buy this. I wanted your special night to end with a special sweet treat," he said indulgently.

Suddenly I had an impulse. "Wait. Close your eyes for a minute," I said as I scrambled to the kitchen to grab a fork.

Delphi did as requested as I walked back over to the table. I opened the box and took out the cheesecake. "Open your mouth," I murmured near his ear. He opened his mouth slightly, still keeping his eyes closed. "Wider." I coached. He opened it just a fraction more.

"Wider." He finally opened his mouth fully, waiting for my next command. I took my fork and dipped it into the cheesecake. Once I had a large scoop, I placed the fork in his mouth.

"Now close your mouth," I whispered. Delphi closed his mouth over the cheesecake and moaned a little at the flavor. I leaned even closer so that my mouth was right next to his ear. "Now you know exactly what I taste like," I whispered seductively.

Connect with Amanda Moncrefe

I really appreciate you reading my book! Want to tell others about the series you've just read? Feel free to leave a review or rating on my Author Page on Goodreads (www.Goodreads.com) or Amazon. You can also connect with me through my social media coordinates:

Visit my Webpage:
http://www.amandamoncrefe.com

Like me on Facebook:
http://www.facebook.com/amandamoncrefe

Follow me on Twitter:
http://www.twitter.com/amandamoncrefe

I'd love to hear from you!

Mandy